ROOSTER'S BLUES HOUSE
MYSTERY

MISSISSIPPI KILLER BLUES

A Novel By

SCOTT MICHAEL

MISSISSIPPI KILLER BLUES
Rooster's Blues House Mystery
Copyright © 2017 Scott Michael

Book design by:
Arbor Services
www.arborservices.co

Printed in the United States of America

MISSISSIPPI KILLER BLUES
Rooster's Blues House Mystery
Scott Michael

1. Title 2. Author 3. Fiction

Library of Congress Control Number: 2016918023
ISBN 13: 978-0-692-80231-1

Dedicated to my wonderful and loving wife Barbara, as well as Max, my son and Megan Scott, my daughter. They mean the world to me.

I would also like to give a huge thank you to Stephen Solomita for all of his hard work

Some of the proceeds from the sales of this book will be going to Ovarian Cancer Research Fund Alliance.

PROLOGUE: 1986

"Rosie Bell, I do believe you are the most stubborn woman ever to walk on God's green earth." The black man sitting behind the wheel of his 1978 Chevrolet Impala winks at the small boy in the backseat. "Ain't that the truth, Rooster?"

Robert T. Feathers, called Rooster by one and all, runs his hands through his red hair and looks at the woman sitting next to him. According to his mom, he's the stubborn one, not Rosie. Maybe that's the reason his mom is dead, the reason he's been launched into the unknown. Maybe he's just too stubborn. Because there has to be a reason or else the world doesn't make sense. There has to be.

"I practically begged you," Marcus Montgomery tells Rosie, "not to drive into Oxford, Mississippi, on game day." He shakes his head by way of emphasis. "No, sir. When Ole Miss takes the field, it's time for anybody with the sense God gave a chicken to stay at home in Clarksdale. We could have done this yesterday without all this craziness."

Rooster had once asked Rosie why Marcus put God into every other sentence he spoke. Rosie's answer had puzzled him all the more. "If it's God's thinkin'," she'd explained, "you can't deny

1

the truth of a thing. Cousin Marcus, he doesn't care to have his judgments questioned."

But Rooster's too preoccupied at the moment to pay attention to Marcus Montgomery. For the first six years of his life—until his mother died in a fire from which he somehow escaped—home was Clarksdale, sixty miles to the west. The populations of both towns, Oxford and Clarksdale, are roughly the same, a bit under twenty thousand residents. The difference is that the University of Mississippi (along with its eighteen thousand students, rabid football fans, one and all) is located in Oxford. On game day, especially when Ole Miss plays a hated rival like Louisiana State, another fifty thousand fans roll into town, flooding every downtown street, sidewalk, and alley. The inevitable result, postgame, is chaos.

"You know, Marcus, if we'd left earlier—like I asked and you promised—we'd have arrived at halftime, and not an hour after the end of the game. These folk you see 'round us playin' the fool? They would have been somewhere inside, watchin'."

Rosie's tone is measured, as always, but she's still managed to put a period at the end of the sentence. If they'd come into Oxford before the game ended, they'd only have to dodge the pickups and cars parked in every available space, including the middle of the road. Now, with tens of thousands of fans pouring out of the stadium and into the streets, it's impossible to get through. They've been circling Courthouse Square for the past forty minutes without getting any closer than a quarter mile. That would be near enough on most days—there's nothing wrong with Rosie's or Rooster's legs—but not with two suitcases and a pile of boxes to carry.

Rooster continues to stare out the window. He's old enough to know his mother's not coming back, old enough to know she's in heaven with Hog, the bloodhound they buried in the backyard last spring. He'll never see her again, except in his dreams where she makes an appearance almost every night, often accompanied by the roar of an uncontrolled house fire. Rooster's mom was his rock before the fire, his anchor. And if Rosie minded him during the day, she went to her own home at night. That's changed, though he isn't sure exactly how. What he does recognize, the knowledge coming into sharper focus almost by the hour, is that he'll divide his life into two parts from here on. Before the fire and after the fire. Oxford, Mississippi, especially on game day, is definitely after the fire.

"Only one thing to do, Marcus," Rosie says. "We'll carry the suitcases, but you'll have to come back tomorrow afternoon with those boxes. There's just nothin' else to be done."

"Rosie, if you weren't my wife's cousin, I believe I'd say somethin' rude about now. I might even use profanity, and with the Lord's forgiveness."

When Rosie fails to reply, Marcus reconsiders. Tomorrow being Sunday, he and his wife and his four children will spend the morning in church. Marcus is a God-fearing man and known for his religious devotion, but what with the prayers he offers on a daily basis, he figures those three hours on Sunday morning to be duty enough. The after-lunch prayer service is more like a burden because Reverend Stewart tends to review every sin found in the Bible, every sin and every punishment. Marcus hadn't realized there were so many varieties of hellfire until Reverend Stewart took over the pulpit at Spirit Church of God.

"I s'pose I could come along tomorrow afternoon, Rosie, but you'll have to call Bethany and make it right. She won't be happy about me skippin' out on prayer service. No, ma'am, when it comes to your cousin? Lord knows, the woman has a fierce temper."

Rosie smiles. "Now, Marcus, I don't think it becomes a man to fear his wife. Didn't the Lord intend a woman to be a man's helper?"

"Rosie, I never did learn exactly what a helpmeet is. No, sir, I believe that word is subject to various definitions. But I am sure that if you don't promise to call Bethany, you'll have to come to Clarksdale and fetch them boxes your own self."

Rooster watches a long line of men and women snake through the crowd, joined hands to hips. They're singing the Ole Miss fight song as they go. *Take that ball and hit your stride.* Ahead, five men, their voices raised, surround a tow truck with a car on the hook. As a siren wails in the distance, two policemen run toward the tow truck, their whistles adding to the din.

"Time to move, Rooster."

Rosie opens the door and slides out. She reaches back for Rooster's hand and draws him to her. The boy's eyes are as round as coins and his mouth hangs open. Marcus stands behind the

Chevy's open trunk, a pair of suitcases in hand. Rosie takes the larger one for herself and hands the smaller to Rooster. She wants to comfort the child, but there's no point. Rooster caught a pair of bad breaks and they can't be undone. His indifferent father, first, then his mother's passing. Overcome by smoke, Farah died trying to reach her child when he was already safe. Well, last Rosie heard, nobody said life was supposed to be fair. You took the blows and moved on; you lifted your head and avoided self-pity at all costs. And the challenge in this particular case won't go away just because Rooster's too young to recognize it.

The afternoon is hot, despite it being early October, hot and humid enough to lift Rooster's red hair into a coxcomb. His hair draws the attention of a few revelers, doubly energized by the Rebels' victory and the close score, 21–19. They glance at Rosie, too. A black woman charged with the care of a white child isn't especially unusual, but this particular black woman, despite the sheen of perspiration, is a little too well dressed, a little too young, and a little too attractive. She wears a turquoise blouse over a white skirt, not a wrinkle in either. A sunburst brooch over her left breast glitters, even in the flat light cast by a low, glowering sun. Her upright carriage also appears out of place, as does her confident, measured stride and the jut of her firm chin.

Rooster's too busy watching a brawl on the other side of the street to notice the inquisitive glances tossed his way. A small group of LSU students, stupid enough to venture out on the street after the game, are exchanging punches with a much larger knot of Ole Miss students. This is about honor, something Rooster will come to understand well. Now as he watches the cops near the tow truck draw their batons, he tightens his grip on Rosie's hand. This woman is all he has. Later in life, he'll come to know that the arrangements for his care were made before the fire. Farah Feathers had no close relatives, and her husband disappeared a month into her pregnancy. She knew that if something happened to her, Rooster would be left to face the prospect of a Mississippi Children's Home or the foster care system, both crapshoots played with loaded dice. By granting custody to Rosie Bell in the event of her death, Farah had opted out of the game.

Ten minutes later, Rosie and Rooster stand in front of a three-story building on the edge of Courthouse Square. On the other side of the street, set well away from the sidewalk, the white courthouse and its high clock tower seem enormous to Rooster, enormous and somehow threatening. Closer to him, a mustached Confederate soldier stands atop a high marble column, his expression grim.

Rooster wants to ask about the courthouse—what it is, what it's for—but Rosie leads him into the building behind them. She guides him up two flights of stairs to a sparsely furnished apartment on the third floor. The door is open and Rosie steps inside without knocking. On the other side of the room, a middle-aged man wearing gray slacks and a blue tie over a buttoned-down white shirt sits on a chair by the window. A professional smile pulls at his ample jowls as he rises.

"How do, Miz Bell. Name's Rob Rhea. I'm an attorney, repre-senting the seller in this case. Welcome to Oxford." Rhea holds a plastic cup half filled with amber fluid in his left hand. "Hope you don't mind my celebratin'. It's not every day we're treated to a victory like this one."

Rosie lays her suitcase to the floor. "No, Mr. Rhea, I do not object and I won't hold you up any longer than necessary."

"I thank you kindly for that. Did you bring an attorney?"

"I didn't, Mr. Rhea. I believe I can handle this myself."

The attorney's smile widens. "Then why don't we get right to business. I've taken the liberty of spreading the paperwork out on the table. The seller has already signed, so all we need is your signature."

Despite Rosie's promise not to hold up the lawyer's celebration, she reads every document, including the fine print, before she signs. Only then does she hand over three certified checks stowed in a voluminous handbag.

"I believe these are correct," she says.

Bob Rhea examines the checks and nods as he slides them into a hand-tooled briefcase. As he latches the briefcase, he looks from Rosie to Rooster and back again. Rooster's standing by the window, staring down at the crowd below. The boy appears small and lost, in sharp contrast to Rosie Bell. Bell's gaze is frank enough to be disconcerting, as is her confidence. Both contrast sharply with her youth.

"I hear tell you plan to turn this place into a nightclub, Ms. Bell."

"A blues bar, Mr. Rhea. Rooster's House of Blues, to be exact."

Bob Rhea gets to his feet and places a business card on the table. He's skeptical. It shows in his eyes, though he says nothing. "Well, ma'am, I wish you the best of luck. And if you should need a local attorney sometime in what I hope is a long and prosperous future, I'd take it kindly if you call me first."

Rosie closes the door behind the lawyer and turns to face the boy. Rooster is still by the window, still looking out. Wrapped in his own misery, he's too young even to seek the company, or the comfort, of others. But Rosie's pain is also ongoing. Odd as the pairing might have seemed to others, Rosie felt, and still feels, that Farah Feathers was the sister she never had. They shared every hope, every fear; they shared every holiday. Now Rosie's pain is ongoing, an empty place in her heart she'll carry into her own grave. Though she marry, though she give birth to a dozen children, Farah's place will never be taken.

How much worse it must be for Rooster. Rosie can't imagine what's going on in the boy's mind, in his heart. For all her personal pain, she's still in charge of her life. But Rooster? Rooster must feel like he's in outer space, orbiting an alien planet.

"Rooster?"

"Yes?"

"We're home, boy. Let's take a look at your room."

CHAPTER ONE

PRESENT DAY

A long plume of dust trailed behind the pickup as it glided along a dirt road in Lafayette County, ten miles from Oxford, Mississippi. In the silvery light cast by a nearly full moon, the plume reminded Ellerbee of the day, many years ago, when he peeped through the window of an isolated farmhouse at a woman taking a shower behind a translucent shower curtain. How old was he? Fourteen? Fifteen? He can't remember exactly, but he's sure about his first impulse, to come through a side door, trap the bitch in the shower, and give her what she really wanted. And he could have done it, too. The farmer and his two boys were shopping for equipment in town. He'd watched them as they drove away. All he had to do was . . .

But he was still too young, still too afraid, so he'd snuck away, through a patch of woods to where he'd stowed his bicycle. Then he pedaled off, taking the image with him, wondering what got him hotter, the woman's helplessness or her body.

Ellerbee laughed to himself. He was a sneak all right, a sneak now and a sneak back then. In fact, Sneak was his nickname, his street name, originally bestowed by schoolmates who despised him, then reaffirmed by his fellow inmates at Parchman Farm, Mississippi's largest prison. A true farm, Parchman encompassed

seventeen thousand acres, and Sneak had somehow crossed half
of them to drive a shank into the back of a hated enemy. The COs
found out, probably from one of their snitches, but they couldn't
put a case on him, and they eventually settled for beating him into
the hospital. No big deal, really. Two broken ribs, a fractured nose,
a torn ear, no lost teeth.

Sneak tapped the steering wheel as he reminded himself to focus
his attention on the job at hand, a job assigned to him for the third
consecutive time, which wasn't fair. Originally, Monroe had taken
his turn, but not now. Now Monroe had assumed the role of su-
preme leader, directing Sneak to do this or do that. Sneak Ellerbee
was a small man, five seven and barely 140 pounds. Monroe stood
two inches above six feet and weighed in at more than two hundred
pounds. Plus, the man was dead game in a fight and had elevated
cruelty into an art form. Sneak was going along. For now.

But there was a larger question here, a question Sneak was
reluctant to acknowledge. With relatives in Texas and Southern
California, relatives willing to take him in, he could pack up and
move on at any time. And he had good reason to get his ass out
of Dodge. Monroe was crazy by nature, and getting crazier by
the day. He probably thought he was invulnerable, an evil genius,
so much smarter than the cops that he couldn't be caught. To
Sneak's way of thinking, that kind of attitude was the kiss of death.
Criminal geniuses were a dime a dozen in Parchman.

So, why? Why didn't he move on? The answer, which Sneak
didn't want to admit, was Alma-Beth Patterson, Monroe's sister

and Sneak's . . . Sneak wanted to use the word lover, but Al-ma-Beth didn't love anyone. Love was outside her capacities. But she definitely had her hooks into him, and the mere thought of leaving her behind filled him with something close to panic.

A few minutes later, as he considered these questions, Sneak turned onto a gravel road that circled a large farm. The cotton fields on both sides of the road were nearing harvest, and the erect plants stood a bit over four feet high. Lit only by a mist-filtered moon, the rows passed into the distance like the soft white clouds Sneak once associated with heaven. That was before he realized that no degree of pious behavior would prevent his drunken stepfather's kicking his ass while mommy watched, too drunk to intervene. Or even want to intervene.

Sneak glanced into the rearview mirror at a trailer hitched to the back of the pickup. The unit was tracking nicely, and the ATV in the trailer's bed hadn't shifted. Satisfied, he turned back to the road after cresting a rise only to find something in his path, a shadow within the shadow cast by a towering hickory. His mind whirled for a moment, but then he slammed on the brakes.

The trailer jumped as the pickup skidded to a stop, its wheels spinning in the air. For a moment, Sneak thought it might flip, a disaster beyond measure. He breathed a sigh of relief when it finally settled on its fat tires, then turned back to stare through the windshield at the biggest wild hog he'd ever seen. The boar had to weigh seven hundred pounds. Its bottom tusks were as long as knives.

As he wiped his forehead, Sneak grinned. The .357 revolver stashed under the seat wouldn't be near enough gun for the animal. He'd need something bigger, maybe a rocket-propelled grenade or a helicopter gunship. Not that he was tempted to hunt the beast. Sneak had more pressing obligations on this particular night. Meanwhile, he wasn't going anywhere until the hog moved on, not unless he turned around, which he couldn't do on the narrow road unless he got out and unhitched the trailer. Wild hogs mostly ran off when you confronted them. Mostly.

The hog stared at him for what seemed like minutes, then finally emitted a single grunt. Properly signaled, three sows trailed by a bevy of squealing piglets crossed the road behind him. The boar held his ground for several seconds after they disappeared into the woods, staring directly into Sneak's eyes. Sneak stared back until he realized, with a start, that the animal's dead, blank eyes reminded him of Monroe's. The effect was so profound that he left his foot on the brake even after the hog trotted away, listening to the chatter of the cicadas as they sought one last chance to mate before the first frost killed them all.

The yip of a coyote jolted Sneak out of his small trance. He put the truck in gear and continued on his way, another six miles before he pulled to a stop. In and out, quick and clean. Sneak pulled to a stop and shut the engine down. He jammed the .357 into his waistband, walked to the back of the trailer, and lowered the tailgate to form a ramp. The chocks and cables holding the ATV in place came next. He released them within seconds, every motion practiced as he lined them up against the trailer's side rails. The stakes here were as high as stakes get. There was no room for error.

The four-wheeler, a HuntVe, electric powered and nearly silent, started with the press of a button. Sneak backed it down the ramp, hurrying now. He would have to cross several fields, following a track used by farm equipment, his path taking him within a hundred yards of a farmhouse. The family would probably be asleep, sunrise being several hours off, but he couldn't be sure. Nor could he be sure that once he reached Highway 7, a state road, some deputy sheriff wouldn't come up on him fast.

Sneak didn't hesitate, despite the danger. He drove with the four-wheeler's lights off and ducked into the shadows whenever possible. As he approached Highway 7, he scanned the road in both directions. The terrain here, as in the rest of the county, was either gently rolling or dead flat, and headlights could be seen from a long way off. But Sneak's eyes found only the cotton fields and a small lake that reflected a pale, swollen moon.

Reassured, Sneak guided the ATV to the edge of the road, got off, and walked to the back of the vehicle. He inserted a key into a padlock securing the top of a large metal box to its face, raising the top as he let the face drop down.

The female body inside the box was trussed in ropes that bound the woman's knees, ankles, and head to her chest. The job had been easy enough when she was still flexible, but rigor mortis had now set in and her cold flesh was too hard to dent. She was wedged in pretty good, too, and Sneak had to yank with all his strength before she slid free and dropped to the ground with a thud loud enough to make him shudder. He stared down at the woman for a moment, trying to recall her real name. But it was no good. If the girl ever told him her name, he'd forgotten.

"Dumb-ass," he muttered as he kicked her body into a ditch. "Dumb-ass bitch." That's the name Monroe gave her and the name she'd answered to, the name she called herself.

"Dumb-ass bitch wants water. Dumb-ass bitch wants food."

By the time Monroe got through with her, Dumb-ass Bitch was begging for her own death.

"Please, please, please, please, please."

CHAPTER TWO

My first two guests arrived an hour before kickoff. I heard them lumber up the stairs, past the restaurant on the first floor, the blues club on the second, to my apartment on the third. Or, rather, one of them lumbered, Alderman Parrish Odem IV. Parrish weighed close to three hundred pounds and stood five feet seven inches tall, standing up or lying down. His wife, Samantha, on the other hand, was a will-o'-the-wisp who spent most of her days in the gym. She more or less floated up the stairs.

"Is that my colleague, Alderman Odem?" Rosie Bell asked me.

"The one and only."

"You think he'll make it to the top?"

I glanced at the two picnic tables at the back of the room. They held a simple buffet: sliders, wings, shrimp, and two bowls of potato salad, one with bacon and one without. Galvanized tubs packed with beer and a decent chardonnay rested on the floor at either end of the tables. Good to go.

"Parrish is a man," I observed. "Who knows what he wants."

"Amen to that, Rooster."

Rosie Bell and I were as close as mother and son. No surprise, because she'd raised me after my mother passed. I was six at the time, with no father and no close relatives. She was a black

15

woman, still young and blessed with high aspirations, and I've come to believe I must have been somewhat of a burden to Rosie Bell. Not that she ever said so or even demonstrated the slightest regret, but I was expected to govern myself, and to rise, as she'd risen. To achieve.

The end result, Robert T. Feathers, was a mixed bag. I did have my achieving side, but I had a much rougher side, too, and the halves were often at war. My closets and drawers contained two styles of dress: T-shirts and jeans on the one hand; hand-tailored suits, fitted shirts, and silk ties on the other.

Rosie had made a better job of her personal ambitions. At age twenty-six, thirty years ago, she'd purchased a broken-down, three-story building on Courthouse Square. She put a sit-down restaurant on the first floor and a nightclub, Rooster's Blues House, on the second. An apartment took up the third floor, the apartment where I grew up. Before the deed was signed, Rosie had already enrolled at the University of Mississippi, part time at first, then full time until she earned an accounting degree. Now she represented Ward 4 on the city council and operated Bell Accounting Services, which she owned. I don't mean to imply that her journey came cheap or easy. Fact is, if I had Rosie Bell's determination, I'd most likely be president, despite hailing from the greatly maligned state of Mississippi. It took Rosie seven years to get a master's degree, and another ten to grow Bell Accounting from a storefront operation doing cut-rate tax returns to a profitable, twenty-employee firm closely tied to the university.

"Hi, Rooster, are we early?" Samantha asked over her husband's wheezing.

"Never too early for me, darling. Hope you arrived hungry." I delivered the lines deadpan—Alderman Odem was already approaching the buffet table—and Samantha rewarded me with a grin. Perpetually rumored to be on the verge of divorce (the rumors generally included a personal trainer, a pool boy, or both), Samantha refused to defend her reputation, a failure that infuriated her husband's political rivals.

Samantha turned to greet Rosie as my next guests arrived, three childhood friends, Perry Poe, Chuck Jackson, and Don Smith. My parties are by invitation only. I throw them whenever the Ole Miss football team plays an away game, as they would today, a late game starting at eight o'clock. The cost? Thirty hungry people fueled by game-day adrenaline and free alcohol can eat enough wings to keep Purdue Chicken in the black for a month.

Despite the expense, I loved the parties, just like I love to party. After all, a blues club is a natural party, and I deliberately sought out bands that inspired patrons to get up and dance. But I was definitely mixing business with pleasure here. My restaurant and nightclub were located on Courthouse Square in the center of town. The Square might not rival Fifth Avenue or Rodeo Drive for opulence, but it's about as upscale as Mississippi gets. That's not how it started out thirty years ago when Rosie carried me from Clarksdale to Oxford, but times had changed, and there were those, including one or two politicians on the city council, who felt that Rooster's Blues House attracted an undesirable element. The owner, you see, rides a Harley-Davidson. Worse yet, he wears the colors of a motorcycle club he once headed: Velvet Hammer, MC. Worst of all, it's not unusual to find a dozen customized motorcycles parked out front on any given night.

Thus, my parties were all about public relations. I had a seventy-inch curved-screen TV hanging on the wall of a living room that dominated the apartment, along with a Bose sound system to back it up. The food was good, if simple, and the wine and beer free. At first, I'd targeted Oxford movers and shakers, men and women of influence, only to find that I couldn't turn away old friends. A mix had evolved, a mix of folk who would almost never mingle under other circumstances: black and white, jocks and nerds, bankers and deputy sheriffs, college professors and terminal one-percenters who quit school in the fourth grade. One and all, odd as they were, every partier shared a single trait. They were fanatic Ole Miss fans.

I happened to be in New York a couple of months earlier and a friend took me to a Yankees game. I enjoyed the game very much. The Yankee's pitcher, Masahiro Tanaka, threw a split-finger fastball that was almost unhittable. But as I sat there, enjoying a beer and a hotdog that had the consistency of oatmeal, I couldn't help but compare New York sports to Mississippi's. New York had two of everything: two professional baseball teams, two football teams, two basketball teams, two hockey teams, even two soccer teams. With exactly zero professional teams, Mississippians (except for those few misguided souls who cheered for Mississippi

State further to the south) were loyal only to the Rebels of Ole Miss. This alliance was greatly magnified in Oxford, what with its twenty-one-thousand students, and I knew that if I looked through the window at the Square below, I'd find it bustling. As I knew that an hour from now, when the game began, every bar and restaurant would be packed and the Square sure to be deserted.

I spent the hour before kickoff mixing with my guests. I made introductions, exchanged small talk, inquired after wives and husbands, children and grandchildren. Rosie also worked the room, as did the other politicians in attendance. One of the restaurant's busboys brought up food and carried down the trash, a mix of chicken bones, shrimp shells, and plastic plates. Fueled by alcohol, the chatter grew more intense as game time grew near. Still, there was something missing, an insistent drumbeat that played just below the melody. Over the past several months, five local women had gone missing. Four had turned up several days later. The fifth, Marie Blocker, gone for two days, had yet to be found, dead or alive.

Marie Blocker was one of mine, and if that sounds overly paternal, so be it. A student at Ole Miss, she was on her way home after a shift at the club when she vanished, leaving her car on a back road, the engine running.

Marie had a smile so warm and genuine it could stop you in your tracks. That didn't matter, not to me. I would have felt exactly the same if she'd been the dishwasher in the restaurant downstairs, a grizzled ex-biker who might have passed for Marie's grandfather.

You can call me old-fashioned if you want, but I thought of my workers as family. And just maybe, as I'd never married or had children, they were as close to family as I'd ever get.

There was no way to pretty up the murders, not after the funerals, several of which I attended. Thad Carson had to be aware of that because he'd attended the funerals as well. Thad was Oxford's police chief and therefore responsible, even though four of the killings had taken place outside the city limits. I'd half expected him to decline when I invited him, but he'd shown up, along with Susan, his wife.

As far as I could tell, my guests were on their best behavior. The afternoon had to be about football, and they naturally gravitated to our one celebrity. Bo Wallace had quarterbacked Ole Miss to a home victory over Alabama only a year before, and everybody wanted to shake his hand. Both games, today's and the prior season's, were against a hated enemy, an enemy ranked number one in the country. It was too important to ruin with the nightmare that had settled over Lafayette County.

There are exceptions to every rule, and I discovered one, a woman named Ivy Ashton, by a window overlooking the Square. I couldn't say what she was looking at. We were twenty minutes from game time and the Square was emptying fast, as if the mayor had just called for an emergency evacuation and folks were running for their lives.

"How's business?" I foolishly asked.

Despite the given name, Ivy was a thirtyish woman and stylish to a fault. As the proprietor of Miss Behavin', an upscale boutique, she had to be. Oxford's growth over the past twenty years had been explosive, with the population doubling since 1990. Minimansion developments broke ground every year, which was another thing about Oxford. The city had become a mecca for retiring Mississippi millionaires, investors who managed their holdings from the comfort of a home office, executives from Memphis, only fifty miles away, and students who maxed out daddy's credit card every month. On weekends, the Square reeked of money, and there were enough high-end SUVs running around to replace the lost herds of buffalo.

"Business was good today, Rooster. Nothing slows down Oxford on game day."

But not yesterday, or tomorrow. Except for record sales at the gun shop, business was drastically off on the Square. Students were holed up in their sorority houses, their dormitories, or their homes, especially at night. I couldn't blame them.

"I swear, Rooster," Ivy continued, "if this goes on much longer, I'll have to eat my fall collection. Your chef downstairs wouldn't have a good recipe for silk chemise, would he?" She shook her head. "I can't believe this is happening here. Not in Oxford."

That particular sentiment was shared by almost every resident interviewed on the local news. Not in Oxford, Mississippi. It couldn't happen here. But it was definitely happening here, and if the Oxford Police or the sheriff was close to making an arrest, he was keeping the information to himself. Earlier, I'd spoken to Deputy Sheriff Annie-Fay Keefer.

"I'm working patrol, Rooster," she'd explained. "I'm not part of the investigation."

"I'll settle for a rumor."

"The rumor is that Sheriff Price Sibley hates Oxford Police Chief Thad Carson. Fears him, too."

"And why is that?"

"Because Thad's young, ambitious, and the only path up for him is the elected positon currently held by Sibley."

"That's not a rumor, Annie-Fay. That's a fact."

"Maybe so, but it's all I've got."

CHAPTER THREE

The small talk ended abruptly when the teams lined up for the opening kickoff. Bodies revolved to face the TV screen, heads turned, eyes widened, mouths opened. The powers that be, the almighty pundits, had ranked Alabama number two in the nation. Ole Miss had opened the season at fifteenth, but moved up to twelfth after two wins against much weaker competition. I'm not that big on rankings, but I still had to wonder if the team was up to the challenge. I believe that most of my guests felt the same way because the hush, as our kicker approached the ball, was thick enough to be molded.

The good news began to flow within seconds. The Alabama return man took the ball on the goal line and advanced it fifteen yards before crashing into an Alabama blocker who'd somehow lost his sense of direction. The ball popped out and fell to the turf, whereupon an Ole Miss defensive back named C. J. Moore fell on it. We were now first and ten on the Alabama eighteen yard line.

Four plays later, Nathan Noble kicked a field goal and we were up 3–0.

One thing about college football, the clock stops on every other play, allowing plenty of time for commercials and plenty of time for talk. Was the fumble good news? Yes, but . . . But we could have moved the ball across the goal line and scored a touchdown, so maybe Alabama's holding us to a field goal was a taste of things to come. Bama's defense was legendary, and we were going with an untried quarterback named Chad Kelly. More to the point, Alabama was at home and we hadn't beaten them in Tuscaloosa since 1988.

The ball moved back and forth for most of the quarter. Alabama had a 240-pound running back, Derrick Henry. Once Henry got up a head of steam he was hard to bring down. Tacklers tended to bounce off or be knocked over. But Alabama proved unable to sustain a drive, although Henry broke off several long runs. Unfortunately, Ole Miss shared the same fate. Backed up close to our goal line much of the time, we played a defensive game.

My guests cheered or groaned after each play, their hopes and fears rising and falling like children on a see-saw. At one point, a man named Larry `The Barber' Tadford came up beside me, as he usually did when I invited him to the party.

"Damn, Rooster," he said, "I bet the farm on Ole Miss. If they lose, I can't go home."

The Barber didn't have a farm. He operated a motorcycle repair shop on the edge of town. But I completely understood the sentiment. I'd stopped gambling a few years before, and not because I was a winner.

"What'd you take?"

"Eight points."

"I thought the line was seven and a half."

"I made my play early in the week, but the way it's goin' . . ."

When things go bad on a football field, they tend to go bad in a hurry. Toward the end of the quarter, Alabama began to roll. Derrick Henry pounded us for short gains until a third-down pass brought the ball to the Ole Miss thirty-five yard line. A facemask penalty left the ball on our sixteen. Another third-down pass left Alabama with a first and goal on our three.

"You think we can beat these jerks, Rooster? Can we really beat the number two team in the country with a quarterback who's been feasting on junior college competition?"

The voice belonged to Barbara Michael, owner and manager of Oxford Workouts, a fully equipped gym frequented by power lifters, including myself. Barbara personally managed the half of the gym devoted to cardiovascular fitness, teaching four or five classes every day. Toned didn't begin to describe her body.

On their first play from the three, Alabama tested the middle of the line, a run that went nowhere. Their quarterback, Cooper Bateman, faked to the center of the line on second down, then handed off to his wide receiver coming across the backfield. At 188 pounds, Calvin Ridley was fast and elusive, but not fast enough to escape Robert Nkemdiche. The son of Nigerian immigrants, Nkemdiche, at three hundred pounds, had the grace of a ballerina and the speed of a wolf on the hunt. He broke through Alabama's defensive line to level Ridley in the backfield for a loss of eight.

Two plays later, Alabama settled for a field goal. The score was now tied.

"I don't like it," Ted complained. Then he repeated himself: "I don't like it."

He didn't like it any better after we went three and out following the kickoff. Broadcasters call it the momentum, as in Alabama definitely had the momentum after their last drive. But what I felt in that room was more like Alabama had the juice, the mojo, the magic that great teams carry into every game. They were number two, after all, and we were number twelve. Nobody would blame us for losing, and if the game was close, we might even pick up a notch or two in the rankings.

Oh ye of little faith. My half-empty glass filled to overflowing two plays later. Justin Bateman dropped back and tossed a pass about thirty yards out that floated into the hands of an Ole Miss defensive back named Trae Elston. I can't say which one of his teammates Bateman expected to make the catch because there were no Alabama receivers within ten yards of the ball. Elston used that open space to advance the football to the Alabama twenty-six.

So much for mojo. So much for momentum. The room exploded, a screaming, joyous din punctuated with rebel yells that filled every square inch of the space. And not only from my guests, but from the club downstairs, and the restaurant on the first floor, and every bar and every restaurant in Oxford, and from the many thousands of students in the Grove, a wooded park inside the university.

A pass to Jordan Wilkins put the ball on the six. A second pass, to Quincy Adeboyejo, carried us inside the one. Second down and less than three feet to go. Next to me, I heard The Barber implore his Creator: "Please, Lord. Just this one time. Help me out just this one time."

It appeared, at first, that Larry's prayer had fallen on deaf ears. We ran the ball into the center of the Alabama line twice but were outmuscled each time. The Alabama defense was just too quick and too powerful.

"We're playing to their goddamned strength," Larry moaned, his piety of a moment before somehow forgotten. "Now what? A field goal? Three fucking points? How many chances are we gonna get, Rooster?"

Our head coach, Hugh Freeze, answered Larry's questions within a few seconds. Freeze wasn't about to settle for three points. His creds were also on the line, and I watched him pace as Kelly approached the ball. We needed to advance the ball eighteen inches to score a touchdown, about the length of my forearm. How could we fail? How?

It's said that the shortest distance between two points, say the tip of a football and the end zone, is a straight line. I don't dispute the wisdom of that observation, but when Kelly handed the ball to Jordan Wilkins coming across the backfield, when Alabama's defense stayed home to protect that straight line, when Wilkins skipped into the end zone untouched, we couldn't contain ourselves. High-fives, fist bumps, hugs, and kisses. Even Rosie, usually so reserved, was yelling at the top of her lungs.

The celebration didn't stop (though half the party paused long enough to refill their glasses) until Nathan Noble kicked off.

Kenyan Drake fielded the ball on the lip of the end zone and ran it out to the twenty where he was met by C. J. Moore, who'd already recovered a fumble. Moore didn't really bother with a tackle. He wanted the ball, which he promptly ripped out of Drake's hand. It dropped to the turf and was still moving when a Mississippi defensive back, Carlos Davis, came up with it. We were now first and ten on the Alabama twenty.

The cheering became more or less constant as Ole Miss lined up. Kelly took the snap, faked a handoff, and tossed the ball into the end zone. The pass went incomplete, but the refs flagged the Alabama defender for obvious pass interference and placed the ball on the four yard line. First and goal.

Now the entreaties became nearly universal. Please, please, please. C'mon, c'mon, c'mon. From behind me, Chuck Jackson, one of the ex-jocks I'd invited, shouted, "For God's sake, you asshole, don't run it into the middle."

Unfortunately, that's exactly what Ole Miss did, run the ball into the middle of the line for no gain. A second-down pass was batted down by an Alabama lineman, and suddenly it was third down. Suddenly it was either cross the goal line or settle for a field goal. We were on the four yard line, not the one-half yard line. If we didn't move the ball into the end zone, Coach Freeze would take the three points and the ten-point lead that came with them. Smart football, for sure, but three points wouldn't satisfy anybody in that room.

The tension was bouncing off the wall, little ricochets of energy that had me shifting my weight from foot to foot. If I'd squeezed that beer bottle any harder, it would have shattered. A few feet away, Professor Harry Ozier was hopping up and down like a demented kangaroo. Next to him, Nita Ozier stood as if frozen, mouth and eyes open, both hands beside her ears, fingers crossed.

Kelly took the snap, faked a handoff to a wide receiver coming across, then started up the middle, looking for a hole in the Alabama line, a hole that wasn't there, a hole that hadn't been there for the entire game. I can't say what went through Kelly's mind, but he hesitated for what seemed like forever, then bounced to the outside, found a path to the corner of the end zone, and plunged forward. Two of Alabama's defenders, a linebacker and a safety, came across to meet him. All concerned knew exactly where the goal line was and exactly what was at stake. At the three yard line, as the safety came in low, Kelly went airborne, a last desperate plunge. He passed over the safety but took a tremendous hit from Shaun Hamilton, a linebacker who outweighed him by twenty pounds. Somehow, Kelly's momentum carried him into the end zone, somehow the ball crossed the line.

Ole Miss 17, Alabama 3.

The collective response, joyous for sure, didn't last all that long. With 6:43 left in the half, Alabama's kickoff return man, Cyrus Jones, bobbled the ball in the end zone, then took a knee. It was Alabama's ball, eighty yards from our goal line, and I think most of us were already counting our chickens. If we held Bama here, we'd go into halftime up a pair of touchdowns.

Jake Coker, Alabama's new quarterback, had other ideas. He completed passes on third and eleven, and on third and five. Derrick Henry ran the ball for nine yards in the next series, and took a pass in the flat on the series after that. First and ten on the Ole Miss twenty-four yard line.

An Ole Miss lineman blocked a pass on the first play from scrimmage. Coker passed again on second down but threw behind the receiver. On third down, Coker again tried to pass but couldn't find an open man. For just a moment, I thought we had him trapped in the backfield, but he somehow wriggled free and scrambled up the field for another first down.

Two plays later, the ball was inside our end zone. Two minutes later, when the ref's whistle announced the end of the first half, our lead was down to seven points. You could feel the anxiety in the room. It'd been twenty-seven long and bitter years since we beat Alabama at home. If we blew this one, it might be another twenty-seven. Fortunately, I'd provided a perfect antidote to the onset of a panic attack. Bottles were opening, corks were popping, the buffet table was now under siege. The best news was that there wasn't a single person in that room I couldn't go to for a favor.

CHAPTER FOUR

My apartment above the club was divided roughly in half, with the half closest to the stairway entrance devoted to entertainment of one kind or another. The party tonight was free, of course, and I'd write it off as a business expense. But I also occasionally rented the space to small groups. A curved sectional couch of red-brown leather, fifteen feet from arm to arm, faced the television, and there were another half-dozen armchairs with small tables between them scattered about. If pushed, I'd have to admit that the furnishings lacked character. Comfortable, yes, but nothing a decorator would admit to creating.

The walls told another story. Fifteen years before, I'd stumbled into the private security business, my start so far down the ladder I was below ground. Five years later, Velvet Hammer was a serious business with five hundred employees. One arm of the company handled overall security for offices, factories, and warehouses. Here I competed with dozens of corporations, including a few of the big boys up north. The second arm provided security for events, mostly concerts by traveling bands in Mississippi and nearby states. The venues were sometimes fairly small but also included sites as large as Tiger Stadium, home of Louisiana State University.

Tiger Stadium seated over one hundred thousand fans on game day, and a lot more when you covered the field with plastic chairs.

At Velvet Hammer, we offered peace-of-mind service. The promoter needn't worry about a thing; the artists either. From the attendant who handed fans a ticket in the parking lot, to the behemoths who guarded the stage, to the bodyguards who remained with the performers, Velvet Hammer provided each and every service. All the musicians needed to do was show up and play.

Event security, though lucrative, presented enormous problems with staffing. With few exceptions, I was forced to lay off my employees at the end of each concert. My workers understood the facts of life and they didn't complain. There simple wasn't any work for them to do until the next job came along. For me, on the other hand, recruiting and training personnel when that next job came online was a constant challenge. Part-time workers aren't known for their reliability, and some came to me in poor condition, to say the least. Of course, when I had enough applicants, I carefully screened each and every one, eliminating the bad apples before they spoiled the proverbial barrel. That rarely happened.

I could go on for a week about the headaches involved in staffing a concert for the Rolling Stones, but my business problems aren't really the point here. No, Velvet Hammer had provided security for the Stones, U2, B. B. King, AC/DC, Willie Nelson, Guns N' Roses, Motörhead, and many more. Whenever possible, I'd prevailed on the band members to sign a concert poster. More than a dozen of these framed posters now graced my walls, and I'd yet to throw a game-day party where my guests didn't gravitate to those posters during halftime. That particular night was no exception.

I found Barbara Michael standing before a particularly lurid Guns N' Roses poster of a scantily clad woman with a long-barreled revolver jammed beneath the waistband of her black thong. As I approached, Barbara gestured to the poster.

"Those are some serious glutes." When I didn't challenge the observation, she quickly added, "There's something about the relationship between gravity, time, and the elasticity of human skin that turns my stomach."

Barbara and I had indulged in a brief affair several years before. I don't know exactly why the affair ended, but that's the story of my love life, beginning, middle, and end. I was thirty-six years old and had never been married, or even close to marriage. Now, according to Rosie, I was an excellent catch. I was seriously fit, reasonably attractive, and successful enough to have purchased the building, the club, and the restaurant from Rosie when I sold my security business. Yet somehow the women in my life kept slipping away, not after a fight or even a civil disagreement. One day, sometimes without prior warning, the magic up and disappeared, a sad truth immediately recognized by the relevant parties.

My latest, Vera Califano, now resided in Madison, Wisconsin. Vera had come to Oxford after graduating New York University with a degree in broadcast journalism. She called her job with the local ABC affiliate WLOX "paying my dues." The goal was New York, LA, or Chicago. Oxford was the twenty yard line, Madison a first and ten at midfield.

Handwriting on the wall. Handwriting I'd deciphered many times in the past. Vera was looking north, east, and west. Anywhere but south.

"Ya know, Barbara," I said, assuming that her dry observation was intended to draw a compliment, "if you were any more toned, you'd bounce when you walk."

Barbara's smile was quick and a bit crafty. Her eyes narrowed as her mouth expanded, prompting the appearance of shadowy laugh lines that would deepen over the years. She wore a pink blouse, probably silk, and black slacks that clung to her hips without being tight. An onyx pendant with a small ruby at its center fell to the top of her cleavage. As good an excuse as any for staring.

I didn't ask Barbara about Oxford Workouts. I spent enough hours in Barbara's gym to know that the women's end of the health club was suffering, with maybe half as many ongoing classes as there were before the killings. Instead, we fell into a conversation about our horses, currently stabled at a local horse farm, one of the few farms in Lafayette County not devoted to cotton. We were both morning riders, often starting out before dawn, and although we rarely rode together, we sometimes passed each other on mist-shrouded trails. Barbara usually galloped her mare, a retired thoroughbred named Scarlet who could outrun my Tennessee Walker, Little Harry, going backward. I'd hear Scarlet first, often at quite a distance, so that when she finally came out of the fog with the steam rising from her body, her eyes wide, her nostrils flaring, her ears turned to face Little Harry, horse and rider seemed to be emerging from a dream.

The conversation wandered on for a few minutes, but if Barbara was sending a signal, I couldn't read it. Barbara knew about Vera because I'd been stupid enough to throw Vera a going-away party, back when we still spoke about continuing our relationship. In any event, I had other guests and I was about to move on when I saw Annie-Fay Keefer reach into her handbag. She came out with a cell phone, spoke into it for a few seconds, and finally returned it to her purse.

"Give me a minute, Barbara."

I didn't have to explain myself as I started toward Annie-Fay, a Lafayette County Deputy Sheriff. Barbara's eyes registered her alarm. The football game was an escape—and a brief one at that—from the carnage. Somebody was out there murdering women, and not for gain of any kind, but only because he liked to kill. It flew in the face of everything Southerners, especially country people, wanted to believe about themselves.

Annie-Fay and her husband met me halfway across the room. I remember her composed expression, the mask of a professional. Annie-Fay had delivered bad news often enough to contain her feelings.

"I've been called in." She might have left it there, but I was blocking her path and I wasn't moving. "A body, Rooster, on Highway 7."

"Is it Marie?"

Annie-Fay shook her head. "I don't even know if it's a man or a woman. We're gonna run a detour while our investigators, such as they are, process the scene."

"But you'll let me know, right?"

Annie-Fay visited the club a couple of times a month. Now she was eating my food and drinking my wine. I saw her expression slip so that when she did speak, she was clearly annoyed.

"Fine, Rooster, I'll let you know."

CHAPTER FIVE

The second half proved as exciting and unpredictable as the first. Alabama's kickoff nailed us on the ten yard line, but we made a first down that brought the ball to our own twenty-four. Then, on third and inches, a bad snap from center left Chad Kelly trapped in the backfield. Kelly heaved the ball in the air a split second before he took a tremendous hit. Fifteen yards downfield, surrounded by a pair of defenders, Laquon Treadwell leaped high only to have the ball trickle through his fingers, bounce off the helmet of a defender, and land in the arms of a second Ole Miss wide receiver, Quincy Adeboyejo. Already behind the defense, Quincy ran the ball into the Alabama end zone. We were now up 24–10.

The room erupted and I dutifully cheered, but I couldn't stop thinking about Marie, of her ambitions, of her dedication, of the life she hoped to live. Marie's parents were lifelong county residents who could trace their heritage back to the Revolution. They were salt-of-the-earth types, pious and hardworking, but they were too poor to provide for their daughter's education at the university. Marie handled that herself, working four nights a week at the club, returning to her home late at night to study, and never to my knowledge complaining. Marie was quick with a joke and always smiling, even as she fended off the offensive remarks of some drunken asshole. She radiated optimism, a quality I appreciated.

Ole Miss kicked a field goal the next time it had the ball, and scored a touchdown on the series after that, to go up 30–10. Game over, right? But there was no quit in the Alabama offense. They scored a pair of touchdowns to bring the score to 30–24 early in the fourth quarter.

We countered on the next series when Chad Kelly rolled out on an option play designed to draw Alabama's pass defense toward the line of scrimmage. The ploy worked perfectly, and he tossed the football over their outstretched hands to a wide-open Cody Core. Cody took the ball into the end zone without being touched. Ole Miss 36, Alabama 24.

On the next series, with Alabama on their own twenty-five, we intercepted another bad pass from Jake Coker. A few plays later, Laquon Treadwell carried a Chad Kelly pass across the goal line. The score was now 42–24 with ten minutes left to play.

Credit where credit is due, Alabama didn't give up. A pair of touchdowns, one the result off an onside kick, brought the score to 43–37 with four and a half minutes left as Alabama kicked off.

Kelly managed a first down, but then went four-and-out. Our punt left Alabama on their own five yard line with three minutes to play. Plenty of time, especially under college rules. If they moved the ball past our goal line, they'd win.

I think, by then, only The Barber was confident of the outcome. He'd taken Ole Miss plus eight points and couldn't lose. The man was already counting his money. The rest of us held our collective breaths until a desperate Jake Coker finally tossed a pass intercepted by Tony Bridges. Game over.

Rosie approached me fifteen minutes later as the first of my ecstatic guests wandered off. Outside, the Square was now one big celebration. The experts on ESPN, the talking heads, had pretty much written us off, what with our untried quarterback, but we'd beaten Alabama at home for the first time in twenty-seven years. From the club below, I heard Eric Gales launch into "Voodoo Child." The after-game party was on.

"You get some bad news?" Rosie asked.

"It's that obvious?"

"Rooster, I believe I taught you not to answer a question with a question."

I shrugged. "Another body, not yet identified, but . . ."

"In the county? Or here in Oxford?"

"In the county."

Beneath the perfect makeup, the pale lavender pants suit, the Akoya pearls, and the gold pin in her lapel, I sensed that Rosie was exhausted. Politics had seemed like a lot more fun before she was elected.

"We're nowhere," she said.

"Are you talking about the investigation?"

"Yes, the Oxford police are no closer to finding Terri Crawford's killer than on the day they found her body." She looked up at me and said, "Price Sibley is a damn fool."

Price Sibley was the elected sheriff of Lafayette County. He and Thad Carson, Oxford's Chief of Police, were barely on speaking terms. Sibley, approaching seventy, believed the forty-something Carson would challenge him next time out, though Carson continued to tell reporters that he loved his job. As a direct result, the two departments weren't cooperating on the murders, or anything else. Carson's department was investigating the single body found inside the city of Oxford. That would be Terri Crawford's. The other three bodies, and now a fourth, had been recovered in the county, a domain that Price Sibley had ruled for the past thirty years.

In the movies, the FBI rides to the rescue at this point, but murder was a state crime, and the Feds lacked jurisdiction. If asked, they'd assign agents as consultants, test evidence in their labs, and supply a profiler to evaluate the evidence. But they hadn't been asked.

"What about MBI?" I said. The Mississippi Bureau of Investigation, a unit of the Department of Public Safety, had dozens of trained detectives. Unlike the FBI, they didn't have to wait until asked. They had jurisdiction throughout the state.

Rosie pursed her mouth, an expression reserved for matters so distasteful they shouldn't be spoken of in decent company. "Do you mean Commissioner Bobby Stapp?"

"That's the man."

"Rooster, Bobby Stapp plans to run for attorney general. He wants a serial killer investigation that's going nowhere about as much as he wants a case of shingles. And then we have your friend,

Thad Carson, our beloved chief of police. If Thad's heart was on fire, he wouldn't ask Stapp for a glass of water. That's how much he hates the man."

I went down to the club a short time later. It was packed, even the balcony which ran the length of the building. Up front, Eric Gales was laying down a solo that had the crowd on its feet. Gales played his guitar upside down, with the E-bass string on the bottom, but he wasn't left handed. He was taught by his left-handed older brother, who also learned to play upside down because no left-handed guitar was available. Eric played traditional blues, but with more than a touch of Jimi Hendrix. Tall and slim, he had a wispy goatee and tied his hair to the top of his head so it projected upward like the tip of a helmet. Eric used the whole guitar, every fret, and there were times when he carried the blues to places I never knew the blues could go. This from a man who was reared one flight above a blues club.

Most nights, a good band, ringing cash registers (which, in fact, were digital and didn't even buzz), and a little Jack Daniels eased whatever troubles I carried into the club. That night was the exception. I couldn't watch our servers as they moved through the crowd, or H-Man, our bartender, as he mixed drinks or lined up beer mugs or bullshitted with the regulars, and not think of Marie. Marie grew up among country folk and could turn a single syllable into a paragraph. She was church going and attended service every Sunday. I think, on some level, she didn't approve of Rooster's Blues House, especially when the occasional short-skirted coed, driven by one-too-many cosmopolitans, danced across the bar. If so, Marie kept her disapproval to herself. She knew what she wanted and that was a degree from the University of Mississippi. Marie wanted to be the first member of her very-extended family to graduate from college.

That, of course, would never happen.

I spent a few minutes consulting with Aaron and Zach Cloninger, better known as the Frog Brothers. Aaron and Zach were the managers, respectively, of the club and the restaurant on the first floor. Neither had learned of the body discovered out in the county, though both asked if I had any news of Marie. I didn't lie to them, but I didn't mention the unidentified body either. The ongoing party was a one-night-only celebration. The bad news could wait until morning.

Somewhere along the line, I told myself that it didn't have to be Marie, that other explanations were equally reasonable. A hit-and-run accident, a suicide, a sudden heart attack, or somebody else murdered. The last had the biggest pull. There were meth labs in the county, and a ready market inside the university. More than likely, some of the revelers who now cheered Eric Gales had indulged, either before they arrived or in one of the bathroom stalls.

So, why not someone else? Some other poor fool gone to the grave, and for the usual reasons, greed or jealousy or even what passed for love in the mind of a rejected husband or suitor. Why not?

Barbara Michael wasn't buying. My earlier conversation with Annie-Fay, followed by Annie-Fay's sudden departure, had set off Barbara's alarm bells, as they had Rosie's. I didn't lie to Barbara when she confronted me on my little perch at the end of the bar. I made the same argument I'd been making to myself.

"Even if you're right," she said, "it won't really make any difference."

"Why's that?"

"Because I live alone, Rooster, in a little house with a line of hedges between me and the house next door."

I knew that Barbara kept a gun in her house, a .38 revolver with a pearl handle. And while she wasn't Annie Oakley, she definitely shot well enough to hit somebody in the same room.

"I know what you're thinkin'." She laid a hand on my shoulder, her touch gentle. "I've got a gun I know how to use, and my doors and windows are locked at all times. But some of those women were taken from their homes. Right through the front door with no sign of a break-in. That's what I'm hearing on the news, and the way I understand things, I'd be a damn fool not to be scared."

Behind us, the crowd was already starting to thin, but no woman left without an escort. I watched for a moment, then called H-Man over and did something I should have done while Marie Blocker was still alive. I told H-Man to make sure the women who worked for us got to-and-from home safely.

"I don't care if you have to rent a van. Just make sure it gets done."

Barbara waited until H-Man walked to the other end of the bar. Then she said, "I don't think our police department, Thad Carson included, has a clue. And as for Sibley, I doubt the man is even looking. Next time out, I think we'll beat him."

The charge against Carson was unfair, even if technically true. The Oxford cops had only one case to work with, the murder of Terri Crawford. The rest had occurred in the county, domain of Sheriff Price Sibley, the official Barbara hoped to defeat in the next election. But that's how things stood in Oxford, Mississippi, that fall. People were scared and looking for someone to blame. Political careers were on the line, some a decade in the making, and the politicians knew it.

Barbara was long gone by the time Annie-Fay called at midnight. When I read her name on the caller-ID screen, I found myself paralyzed for a moment. I'm an optimist by nature, but I had to steady myself before I answered.

"It's her." Annie-Fay's tone was matter-of-fact. She was a cop, after all. "It's Marie."

A short time later, I went down to the street, straddled my Harley, and kick-started the engine. The vibrations running through the frame were somehow comforting. The hog had always been about escape, about rallies with a hundred riders sporting the Velvet Hammer colors gliding into a town, about freeing myself, at least temporarily, from the endless, business-related headaches. But I couldn't outrun my troubles on that night, though I brought the Harley close to the edge on every turn, though I ripped down the straightaways, the rushing wind in my ears reminding me of an all-consuming fire. The bullet was in the air and I was moving toward it.

I stopped at the peak of one of the few real hills in the county, got off the bike, and walked to the edge of a cotton field. The field ran for hundreds of yards, an arrowhead of soft creamy bolls illuminated by the moonlight pouring over my shoulder. In the far distance, the arrow's tip pierced a pine plantation that appeared blacker than the dark sky at the horizon. I'd been to this spot many times, mesmerized by the play of light and shadow, but most of all by the Milky Way. The stars seemed to pour through the tops of the pines as if they were being created anew, moment by moment.

As I watched, an owl cut across the field closest to me, the slow, powerful beat of its wings as silent as the rush of stars above me. The bird clutched a small mammal in its talons, probably a mouse. The creature was still moving as the owl settled onto the branch of a dead hickory and began to feed.

CHAPTER SIX

I began my Sunday morning as I almost always did, at Rosie's, arriving before she dressed for church. Rosie lived in a modest brick ranch house in the 4th Ward, the ward she represented on the city council. I think she could have afforded better, though I knew little of her finances. But Rosie was, if anything, a realist, and she fully believed that a black man or woman living in the South needed to maintain a low profile. Thus, her jewelry and her wardrobe were expensive but understated, as was the car she drove, a Toyota Avalon with every conceivable accessory. Rosie also had a gold ring that she wore every day. The ring had a ruby at the center, a ruby she told me was from Burma, home of the finest rubies ever mined. Yet the ruby was quite small and she'd chosen white gold for the mount, which was commonly mistaken for silver.

Rosie had come of age during the Civil Rights movement of the 60s and 70s, a violent time that most Mississippians hoped was over. Our police department and the sheriff's office were fully integrated now, right down to the promotional videos on their websites, and nobody thought twice about the presence of black students at the university. Progress, yes, but as Rosie had pointed out more than once, Mississippi is tradition-bound, and there were still places, maybe whole counties, where black people were not welcome.

I learned, early in life, not to argue with Rosie. But her efforts to instill middle-class values in her dependent had failed miserably. Instead, she'd nurtured a chameleon equally at home in a business suit or a leather vest, a man who could present a business plan to a banker or stand off three opponents in an all-out bar brawl. And I never apologized, either, not even to Rosie, who I loved as much as I loved any human being on this planet.

Rosie was in the kitchen when I arrived, along with Marci Hanson, an orphan she took in a few years after I left home. Marci was what Mississippians call "slow." She wasn't retarded, and what she absorbed she took to heart, but with a single exception, acquiring knowledge was a hard slog for Marci. The girl—she was almost sixteen now—cooked like an angel.

Marci was busy at the stove, frying chicken to go with the waffles already toasting. I watched the oil bubble around the chicken for a moment, tasting breakfast with my nose. A cruet filled with Rosie's homemade raspberry syrup rested in the middle of the table, along with a small bowl of softening butter.

Cholesterol-sodden breakfasts, not to mention lunches and dinners, are also part of our heritage.

"Morning, Rooster," Marci called without turning.

"How'd you know it was me?"

"Because you walk like a horse."

Rosie greeted me with a kiss on the cheek and a sharp look devoid of humor. I knew that cold look, knew I wouldn't get out of the house without a lecture, knew I'd follow my own conscience no matter how sharp her argument. Still, I was pleased that she waited until after breakfast so as not to ruin my appetite, only my digestion. We'd retired to the back porch, carrying mugs of coffee. It was still early, the weather cool, and Rosie had donned a tan sweater. I watched her pull the sleeves over her fingers.

"You goin' off half-cocked again, Rooster?"

"Marie was one of mine."

"That's not an answer, but I'll let it go. You're like the boy who jumps into the lake from a ledge. Is the water ten feet deep? Or two feet deep and lined with jagged rocks? The boy doesn't know and doesn't care."

Rosie had a good point. In the past she'd accused me of being obsessive-compulsive. According to Rosie, I'd become obsessed with some activity, pursue it as if my life depended on the outcome, then suddenly switch horses in midrapids. My football life illustrated the point too accurately to be comfortable. I began to play Pee-Wee League football in fourth grade, and continued to play through high school. For all that time, I was the fastest, strongest kid on the field, so strong and fast that recruiters began to scout me in my sophomore year. My dream, from beginning to end, was Ole Miss, the dream of every high school football player in the state.

Unfortunately, when graduation finally rolled around, my dismal academics failed to meet current NCAA standards, and by a wide margin. Ole Miss was not in my immediate future. Or my distant future, if I didn't get my act together.

This was a failing I'd brought on myself, but with Rosie encouraging me (when she wasn't berating me), I didn't give up. Instead, I opted for Northwest Community College where Coach Bobby Franklin ran a combination football-rehab program for talented misfits. This was hardass, smash-mouth football with the emphasis on the smash. Brutal practice followed brutal practice, and more than a few of Coach Franklin's rebellious recruits, unable to discipline themselves, dropped out of the program. Give me everything you have, then give me some more. That was Franklin's single demand.

I accepted the punishment and made it through the program. My reward, an Ole Miss walk-on scholarship to play the game of football, was a dream come true. Right?

I entered the university that fall expecting to begin team workouts in the spring. Then, purely by accident, I stumbled onto the private security business, working for a number of the fraternities and sororities that dominated the campus. For the first time in my life, I began to make serious money and to imagine a lot more in my future.

A dream come true became a dream forgotten. I never donned an Ole Miss uniform, but I stayed long enough to receive a degree in criminal justice, even as I built the security business I described earlier. I'll say, in my defense, that I knew I'd never make the pros. Big and fast as I was, as much as I'd stood out on a junior college field, I'd never be big enough or fast enough for the NFL. So, again, a smart move?

Velvet Hammer made money from the day I started to the day I sold it to a much larger company back east. I had five hundred employees on my payroll in the commercial division, and more than two hundred trucks on the road. Another man, a true entrepreneur, would have gone national. He would have expanded into the eastern and western cities while he dreamed of villas in Spain and ski lodges in Jackson Hole and a blockbuster initial public offering. Instead, this particular entrepreneur sold the company and purchased a blues bar in Oxford, Mississippi.

"There's no yardstick that can measure the depth of this lake," I told Rosie.

"What's that supposed to mean?"

"It means I don't know what to do. I don't know what I can do, but I need to do something. No, correct that. I have to do something."

Rosie tossed me that sour look she used when my grammar deviated from the acceptable. I ignored her.

"What I fear you're about to do, boy, is stick your nose into other people's business until somebody chops your damn head off."

If anyone but Rosie had subjected me to this kind of lecture, I would have ended the conversation, and not politely, long before it reached this point. The way it happened, I said nothing, hoping Rosie had exhausted her stock of reprimands. The silence extended for several minutes as we watched a pair of gray squirrels chase each other through the branches of an acorn-laden oak, until I began to hope that I could take my leave without further grief. Then Rosie laid a hand on my arm and said, her tone deceptively gentle, "What's happening with Vera? Have you heard from her?"

CHAPTER SEVEN

I drove across town, from Rosie's house to the small brick building where an old friend, Donald Tisdale, rented a three-room apartment on the second floor. Tisdale and I first met on the campus at Ole Miss. We arrived with identical walk-on scholarships, both intending to become Rebel superstars. Skid, as he was universally known, made it to the playing field, unlike yours truly. A third-string running back mostly used on special teams, he broke into a late-season game against LSU after a couple of minor injuries to the men ahead of him. Ole Miss was down three points, with six minutes to play.

This was Donald Tisdale's big chance, which he fully understood when his number was called on the first play. A few seconds later, he caught a pass out in the flat, slipped the first tackle, and advanced the ball twenty yards downfield. Then, with one defender between him and the goal line, he faked right and cut left, a move that left the defender frozen in space and would have resulted in a sure touchdown if Skid's feet hadn't gone out from under him, throwing up a huge divot. As it was, he landed on his helmet and lost control of the ball, which then described a neat arc before dropping into the arms of an LSU safety who carried it all the way to our nineteen yard line.

A year later, after two operations, Skid Tisdale learned to walk without a limp. But he never again trotted onto a football field, settling, instead, for a degree in criminal justice and a career with the Oxford Police Department. Recently promoted to detective, one of two on the force, Skid and his partner, Barry Brown, had investigated Terri Crawford's murder. I'd questioned Skid about the results, only to find him unusually close mouthed. The chief wanted to keep the probe confidential. So sorry, Rooster.

I knocked on Skid's door, softly at first, then harder, then harder still. When a haggard Skid Tisdale finally opened up, his physical condition did not come as a surprise. The man loved to party but was subject to the sort of hangovers that leave you whimpering like a scared puppy. And that's when you're not bent over the john.

Women had pretty much flocked to Skid all his life. Even at thirty-six and hungover, he was extremely handsome. Handsome on the verge of pretty. Skid had the kind of face, what with the soft mouth and big blue eyes, that stimulated the nurturing element of the female personality. This was an illusion because the man was anything but soft. A hard-ass on the football field, he'd become a hard-ass cop. Skid was dead game.

I pushed my way past Skid, plucked a tiny T-shirt from a chair cushion, then took a seat. As I waited for Skid to follow, I smelled coffee brewing in the kitchen behind me and heard the patter of small feet making tracks for the bedroom.

"What happened, Skid? You forget?"

Skid pressed the heel of his right hand to his temple and pushed hard. "Forget what?"

"That what goes up must come down?"

"Rooster, that I deserve my present condition is not in dispute. Now, if you'll be so kind as to fetch me a large mug of black coffee with three teaspoons of sugar, I believe I'll find the energy to discuss whatever it is you came here to discuss."

I dutifully fetched, adding a mug for myself, then waited until Skid took a first sip.

"Marie's body was discovered last night," I said.

"Whereabouts?"

"In the county, near Abbeville."

Skid looked directly into my eyes for a moment. The look was pure cop, an evaluation of my present state. Skid was a regular at the club and knew Marie well. He'd been one of the first of the would-be seducers she rejected.

"Shit," was all he said.

I glanced at a trophy-lined shelf on the wall across from where I sat. "This business, Skid, it has to stop."

"I'll wave a magic wand. First thing, buddy, as soon as I uncover its whereabouts."

"I wasn't thinkin' of you. You're a cop. You have rules."

Skid brought the mug to his lips and drained it. He was wearing an Under Armour T-shirt with B. B. King's likeness on the front, and purple boxers that matched the color of the ropy scars on his left knee.

"What exactly is it you think you can do that I can't do?" he asked, pointing a finger at me. "Or haven't already done?"

"I can talk to people who'd never talk to a cop."

"Does that mean you're so delusional as to believe the identity of Marie's killer is common knowledge? Seek and ye shall find?"

"I don't know what it means, but I can't stop thinking about Marie. I feel like I have to do something, even if I don't know what that something is."

From inside the bedroom, I heard the opening notes of a rock tune I couldn't identify. Skid paused for a moment, then returned to me. "Rooster, you have the hardest head in the county, so I'm not gonna waste my breath talkin' you out of this foolishness. Just tell me how I fit into your scheme. Or how I'm supposed to fit in."

Not only had Skid attended many of my game-day parties, but I'd once provided front-row seats at a Kid Rock concert for Skid and a girl he'd fallen in love with, one of many. Now, I'd never be so crass as to demand that Skid repay the debt. I wouldn't have to because Skid knew I was holding his marker. If I remembered right, Skid and Grace spent the weekend after the concert at a hotel in Memphis.

"I'll keep it simple. I want to see the file, the autopsy report, the crime scene photos, the lab results . . . whatever's in there. I also want you to talk to me about any suspects. Remember, I'm a trained investigator myself."

Velvet Hammer was at its peak when I acquired a private investigator's license. At the time, I contemplated opening an investigations division. I never got to it, but I'd been renewing the license ever since.

"Man, you're askin' for the moon. My job is all I've got." Skid paused, but I didn't challenge his claim. I couldn't. Finally, he said, "We have to keep this between us, Rooster."

"I'm ready to stand up to any torture short of electrodes to the gonads."

"If Thad Carson finds out, it won't be your gonads subject to electrocution. But I'll let that go for now." Skid opened a drawer, removed a bottle of ibuprofen, and dry-swallowed two. "I believe you'll be disappointed, by the way. If I was close to an arrest—or even if I had a major suspect—I wouldn't let you within a hundred yards of those files. But you know the worst part?"

"I haven't got a clue."

"I believe there's a solution in the case files, in all of them together. The victims must have something in common, a point where their lives intersected. The attacks couldn't have been random, not when some of the women were snatched from their own homes with no sign of forced entry. I feel it in my gut."

The sudden appearance of a young lady, a perky brunette wearing one of Skid's T-shirts, brought the conversation to a halt.

"Hi, Rooster," she said.

I didn't recognize her, but I returned the greeting. "How you doin' this mornin'?"

"Just fine." She favored me with a fleeting smile as she turned to Skid. "I'm goin' in the shower, Skid. Bein' as I have to be out of here in an hour. Just in case."

I didn't ask Skid what "just in case" referred to because I didn't want to know. "You still haven't told me about the worst part," I said.

"What happened to those women after they were taken is horrible, Rooster, and there ain't no way to diminish it. But no competent investigator would allow that to distract him. If there's an answer, it's in the days and weeks before they were kidnapped. Maybe they all visited the same hairdresser, or shopped at the same boutique, or volunteered at a food pantry. That worst part I mentioned? I think I could put the pieces together if I had access to all the case files, but the way it is, Sibley's holdin' most of the puzzle parts, and he ain't likely to share 'em anytime soon. That's the worst part."

Skid's anger was obvious enough, his frustration as well, and I held my piece until he calmed a bit. Then I said, "So, do I get to see the paperwork?"

"Yeah, you do. You do because you're right. You can talk to people who won't talk to me. Look, it's Sunday and the station goes pretty quiet late in the afternoon. Come by about six, to the back door. I'll be waiting outside."

CHAPTER EIGHT

I made my way back to the club after wrapping it up with Skid. It was early afternoon, and although our doors wouldn't open for another couple of hours, prep work was under way and most of my staff was in the house. I didn't have to make any sort of announcement—the news had been made public earlier that morning—but I called the troops together. Oddly enough, my faith in God is stronger than most, a lot stronger than my faith in religion. I think I generally mistrust people who claim to know the Lord's thinking, but I was baptized at age eleven, in part to please Rosie, and the habit of prayer remains with me, though it's eased off to the occasional.

I spoke for a few minutes about Marie and how much I admired her, then told my workers that I intended to donate the night's profits to a burial fund. I also put a hat on the bar, a nice roomy Stetson, in case anybody else wished to contribute.

The practicalities completed, I called on Aaron Cloninger to offer up a prayer. Aaron wasn't particularly religious, but he'd grown up the son of a Baptist preacher and knew how to string the right words together. Not that there was anything of real comfort to be said. Marie's death seemed entirely wrong, a gross violation of even the most elementary justice, and no appeal to the Lord's inscrutable ways could change that. We stumbled through anyway, as humans have been stumbling through since Cain killed Abel. Tears abounded. Even H-Man, with his eighteen-inch biceps and twelve-pack abs, had to wipe his eyes.

The tears, the grief didn't reach me because I couldn't shake my anger. I wanted revenge, simple as that. And I wasn't just kidding when I told Skid there were people out in the county who'd talk to me, but not to him, one percenters who prided themselves on lives lived outside the law. I knew them because I hosted one-percenters in my club almost every night. We had an unspoken agreement. Leave your ongoing feuds in the Square with your bikes. The club is neutral territory.

Once Aaron finished, I went upstairs, to my living quarters behind the front room used for parties. Two rooms and a full bath were all I needed, and all I had. The first room, right off the entrance, was a combination bedroom and living room, with a kitchen area just big enough to make coffee and reheat leftovers. The second room served as my office. A computer and two monitors, one for general use and one for the security cameras in the club and restaurant, sat on a large oak desk. As I generally backed up my business files with hard copies, four-drawer file cabinets rested on either side of the desks. A small bookcase against one wall held supplies. To its left, a fireproof safe protected cash and important documents, including my deed, mortgages, and loan agreements.

Kneeling, I opened the safe, counted out two thousand dollars, and stuffed the bills into an envelope. Then I shaved before I changed my clothes, swapping blue jeans and T-shirt for a pair of black slacks and a blue polo shirt. Finally, I ran a brush over my hair, which refused to flatten. This was a battle I'd been fighting all my life, and the outcome was a foregone conclusion.

I left the club at two o'clock, heading for the single-wide trailer belonging to Harold and Janette Blocker, Marie's parents. I'd met them twice after driving Marie home when her ancient Chevy broke down, and now I felt the need to pay my respects. The ride took me south on Highway 7 in my pickup, then onto a paved road, finally onto a poorly maintained gravel road that dead-ended against a stretch of unbroken forest.

The grass in the little yard surrounding the Blockers' trailer was neatly trimmed. Toward the front, a pear tree loaded with ripe fruit threw off a sharp, sweet fragrance that pulled at me as I stepped out of the pickup. Flowerbeds lined the front of the trailer, yellow and white chrysanthemums for the most part. Off to my right, a small vegetable garden was as carefully tended as the lawn.

This was more or less what I expected, having been here before. But I didn't expect to find a pair of Sheriff's Department cruisers parked in front and Deputy Keefer standing guard outside.

"Uh-uh, Rooster," Annie-Fay said when I approached the door. "Boss man's conductin' a personal investigation and does not wish to be disturbed."

Sheriff Price Sibley had been in office for more than three decades, and his general approach to his craft hadn't changed in all that time. Aggressive policing is the nicest way to put it. Sibley encouraged a shit-kicker attitude in his deputies. Subtlety was a trait unknown to him.

"I've been hearin' rumors, Annie-Fay."

"Like what?"

"Like Sibley's the problem, not the solution. Back in town, the cops only have the one body to work with. Price has five now, and he's still makin' noises like the murders are unrelated. Somethin' else, too. Word is that your department is lookin' at one of the Mexicans working on that development north of town."

"He's not lookin' at one Mexican, Rooster. He's looking at all of them." Annie-Fay's tone was slightly amused.

"And why would that be? Is he guessing?"

Annie-Fay shook her head. "Boss-man's got a theory. You curious about where his theory begins?"

"I am at that."

"It can't happen here, not in Lafayette County. That's where his theory starts."

"And it ends with the only outsiders he can lay his hands on?"

"Rooster, you didn't hear it from me."

Sheriff Price Sibley took that moment to walk through the door into the sunlight beating down on the yard. Sergeant Tyler Hardin, his bodyguard-driver, preceded him. Hardin looked the part. He stood a few inches above six feet and had the kind of steroid-driven body that commonly appeared on the covers of fitness magazines.

Sibley stopped when he saw me, then rose to his full height, expanding his chest along the way. At six six and close to 250 pounds, Sibley was imposing enough to intimidate most of the law breakers he encountered. But to me, at that moment, he looked a bit like a freak. His thick torso was perched on a pair of short, skinny, and very bowed legs, while most of his bulk—an extra thirty pounds at least—rested on the top end. The man had the jowls of a hippopotamus.

"What are you doin' here, Rooster?"

Sibley's tone was confrontational, and I knew why. A couple of years before, I'd eighty-sixed his asshole of a son from the club. The kid was drunk, stupid, and somehow convinced that his daddy's exalted position would protect him. A single blow to the chest convinced him otherwise and he went on his way. Later, I heard that the sheriff wanted an investigation, but Thad Carson talked him out of it. My security system included cameras that covered every inch of the club except the bathrooms. The kid tried to punch me four times before I lost my temper, and I could prove it. Still, I had regrets. In a just world I would have thrown the asshole off the balcony.

"I'm here to pay my respects, Sheriff. Marie Blocker worked for me."

"Doing what?" Tyler Hardin asked.

Hardin's sneer just about screamed for a violent response, one my entire body ached to deliver. His gun didn't stop me, or even scare me. Hardin was protected by his badge and the authority of the state, and by Annie-Fay's presence. If I got into it with Tyler Hardin, she'd have to take a side, and it wouldn't be mine.

"Like I said, I'm here to pay my respects. As for any questions you may have . . . call my lawyer."

Sergeant Hardin glared at me as he held the door for his boss. He'd been Sibley's favorite boy going back to the day Hardin killed a combative meth dealer with his nightstick. Two blows were delivered, one to the hip and one to the head. The second proved fatal before the first ambulance arrived. Justified, of course.

The window opened as Hardin started the Ford. Sibley's head popped out. "I'm hopin' I don't have to repeat myself at some later date." He spit into the dust. "But you need to stay in town, tendin' to your own business."

I turned to Annie-Fay as Sibley's cruiser sped off. "I don't know how you can work with that man, Annie-Fay."

"Which one?"

"Either."

Annie-Fay looked at me for a moment, her expression serious, then said, "The bodies were tied, Rooster. All of them. And in the same way. When we cut the bonds, they were in full rigor mortis and hard as a block of ice." She hesitated, then said, "Any claim that the murders are unrelated is pure bullshit."

"Tell me something I don't already know. Hell, something the whole county doesn't already know."

"How about this. The Lafayette County Sheriff's Department has exactly one trained investigator. That would be Deputy Harris, who's been on sick leave for the past two months."

CHAPTER NINE

In the great state of Mississippi, we have an overabundance of two things: cotton and poor folk. In fact, you generally find Mississippi at the bottom of any list when it comes to the number of people living in poverty. That's nothing to brag about, I suppose, but it does have one benefit. In Mississippi, it wasn't a crime to be poor. No, in Mississippi, your character was determined by what you made of a fate common to many, black or white. The goal was respectability, especially for country folk. You made do with what you had. You asked nothing of your neighbors, yet knew that in time of trouble, your neighbors would offer aid. The respectable ones, anyway. There were plenty of the other kind as well.

Harold and Janette Blocker were respectable, but their determined quest to find that niche hadn't protected them. Their world had collapsed and there was no putting it back together. I knew their grief would be a physical thing, that I would smell it and breathe it, that I'd take it in through the pores of my skin.

My knock on the door was answered by a woman who appeared to be in her late twenties. She had tattoos, bright-colored, running from her wrists to the sleeves of her blouse, and a hummingbird, its wings nearly iridescent, on the left side of her neck. A green stud in her left nostril twinkled when she took a deep breath at the sight of me.

"What are you, the undertaker?"

"My name's Robert Feathers," I said. "Marie worked for me. I've come to show my respects."

"Well, you might as well come in. The whole congregation at First Baptist's planning to show up later this afternoon. You know anyone who needs fifteen casseroles? My name's Samantha. I'm Marie's sister."

Samantha stared at me throughout this little speech, her green eyes defiantly confrontational. The woman had put anger in the space reserved for grief, and I could read the strain in her gaze and in her hunched shoulders.

I stepped directly into a small, crowded living room dominated by a couch and two chairs, both overstuffed. An open Bible, an enormous, large-print edition, rested alongside a photo album on a scarred coffee table. Family photographs covered one wall, including a yellowed photo of a bearded man in a Confederate uniform who reminded me of the soldier on the monument in front of the courthouse.

The Blockers were seated on the couch, looking small and bewildered. Anne-Marie held a lace handkerchief in one hand. The other rested on her husband's knee. Harold was leaning forward, as though he was about to rise but couldn't remember what for.

The Blockers stared at me for a moment. Then Janette said, "Afternoon, Rooster. It's kind of you to come." She turned to her daughter. "Samantha, would you fetch a glass of tea and a slice of that red velvet cake for Rooster. He was Marie's employer."

Harold motioned me to one of the chairs and I quickly sat down. I hadn't the slightest idea of what I needed to say, but I stumbled forward with my condolences, hoping against hope that I wouldn't trigger Janette's tears. Harold merely nodded. He was a roofer by trade, and his seamed face reflected decades crouched beneath a burning Mississippi sun.

I pulled the envelope from my pocket and held it out to Harold. "We took up a collection at the club, to help with funeral expenses. Everybody contributed."

This wasn't exactly the case, but Harold accepted the envelope and said, "I thank you for your kindness, Rooster." He put the envelope on the coffee table next to the Bible as his wife spoke up.

"Do you know how long it'll be until Marie's body comes home to us?" A single, broken sob burst from her throat, and she leaned against her husband. "She was our baby, Rooster. She was our baby and she's gone. I don't understand why this happened. I don't understand why the Lord sends monsters to walk among us. Here, look at this."

Janette picked up the photo album with trembling fingers, fumbled through it for moment, then finally thrust it in my direction. I didn't want to look, but I had no choice whatsoever.

A record of Marie Blocker's basketball career, in middle school and high school, covered both pages, along with a yellowed clipping from the *Oxford Eagle*. I stared down at the photos and saw Marie grow from a child into an adolescent, from an adolescent into a young woman, all in the space of five years. She carried the ball in each of the photos, and the color of her uniform varied from red to white. In some she'd been caught in the act of shooting; in others she was dribbling or passing off. But her expression hardly varied. Her lips were pinched, her eyes narrowed, her chin tightened into a little ball. I'd noted that same expression on her face many times. It told me there was no giving up for Marie Blocker. She would get where she was going, no matter how many obstacles she found in her way. The attitude had served her well over the years, but it hadn't saved her.

I laid the book on the coffee table as I fumbled through my brain, looking for something to say. But if an appropriate response to the photos existed, it was beyond my reach, and I took the easy way out by answering her initial question.

"There'll be an autopsy down in Jackson, probably within a few days. From there, it's up to the medical examiner. Maybe in a week, or even two."

Samantha walked into the living room at that point. She handed me a glass of tea and a plate. The slice of cake on the plate was thin, most likely because the Blockers expected a crowd and needed to conserve. Never mind the simple fact that most of these folk would come bearing food of one kind or another, cakes included. It wouldn't have surprised me to learn that the Blockers had been up all night baking.

I shoveled a small piece of cake into my mouth and declared it to be delicious, which it was. Then I said, "Did the sheriff mention any suspects? Did he tell you he was close to making an arrest?"

"That son-of-bitch interrogated my parents." Samantha ignored the sharp glances flashed by those same parents. This sort of language wasn't to be used around company. "He wanted to know how many men friends she had. Get it, Rooster? He said men, as in more than one. And he also wanted to know how many days a week she stayed out. Sibley didn't ask if she stayed out. He just figured she was a slut and . . ."

This time, Samantha couldn't ignore the look on her mother's face. "All right," she said, "I'm sorry. But the sheriff actually wanted to know if Marie had any Mexican friends. And he also told us that you had prostitutes workin' at your club. He didn't actually say that Marie was one of 'em. He didn't have to."

Sibley's basic claim, that I was some sort of a pimp, was based on a single incident. A few years earlier, one of my servers, a bartender-coed named Kathryn began hooking on the side. She was caught, sentenced to thirty days, and left town within a few hours of her release. No big deal? Not according to Price Sibley who used this single incident to demean the Blockers, which was completely in character. Our sheriff wanted to be feared by the people he was supposed to serve. He wanted to rule them.

I left twenty minutes later, after again extending my condolences. Samantha followed me into the yard. The afternoon was cool by

Mississippi standards with the temperature in the mid-eighties and the humidity near a hundred percent.

"Where you livin' these days?" I asked.

"Dallas." She brushed the hair off her forehead, displaying her tattoos along the way. There was one of a snake with a fanged skull instead of a head. I didn't inquire into its significance. "But it looks like I'll be home for a while."

I nodded. "Look, Marie had a lot of friends at the club, and I know they'd like to meet you, so if you have a chance . . ."

"Thanks, Rooster, that's good of you. Marie said you were a sweetheart and it looks like she was right. I'm tied up now, but down the line you can expect me to make an appearance. I may have been raised in the country, but I am definitely not a country girl." She hesitated for a minute before continuing. "The sheriff, it doesn't look to me as if he's gonna find the man who killed Marie. Don't look like he's even tryin'."

"I won't argue that point."

"Well, if the sheriff won't get this bastard, who will?"

I went with the logical response. Sooner or later, the state police would have to take charge. The clamor for a solution, an arrest, an end to the fear was already building. It could not be ignored forever. But there was something I left out, another possibility. Suppose the sheriff made an arrest. Guilt or innocence wouldn't matter. Not only would an arrest temper the outcry, it would afford Bobby Stapp a perfect excuse to remain on the sidelines. At least until the next killing.

CHAPTER TEN

On my way back to Oxford, I stopped for a moment on Highway 207, a bit north of the city limits. Across the road, a squadron of bulldozers and backhoes had ripped apart several hundred acres of farmland. Eventually, a hundred upscale homes would rise—from earth that for centuries had known only cotton—to form a housing development called Heritage Gardens. Heritage Gardens wasn't the first development to go up in Oxford, and it wouldn't be the last. Lafayette County's population had doubled over the past twenty years and was still growing.

The construction didn't really interest me. My focus was on the edge of the clearing where ten double-wide trailers were arranged in two long rows. Three sheriff's cruisers and a transport bus had formed a semicircle around the first row. As I watched, a small posse of deputy sheriffs hustled a column of perhaps ten protesting men onto the bus. Price Sibley, thirty years the sheriff of Lafayette County, would undoubtedly deem this part of a thorough investigation when he next spoke to the press. After all, he'd rounded up the usual suspects. As for me, I'd tuned the truck's radio to the *Howard Stern Show.* Stern was a favorite of mine, but on that particular afternoon, as the men vanished into the bus's interior, a competition between Stern's producer, Gary, and his engineer,

Scott, over who was the best father seemed almost surreal, as though my ears and eyes were tuned to a pair of vastly different planets.

I continued on to the club a few minutes later. I checked with my managers first, to make sure preparations for the evening were moving along. Then I greeted the members of a band playing the club for the first time, the Haggard Collins Trio. I wanted to make sure they weren't complete stoners, a problem I'd encountered more than once in the past. I found them young, sober, and grateful.

From my office, I placed a call to Alcohol Beverage Control. I needed a liquor license for a new restaurant I planned to open in a month, and I'd placed my application to sell alcohol a full six months earlier. Meanwhile, ABC was jerking me around. The application is under review, they told me again and again, and there's no timetable for a final decision.

"I'm very sorry, Mr. Feathers, but I really have no say in the review. I'm not a participant."

"Can you connect me to someone who is?"

"Well, let me see."

Six minutes later, he came back on the phone. "I'm so sorry, Mr. Feathers, but the man you need to speak with is out of his office at the moment. If you leave your number, I'm sure he'll call you this afternoon."

"That's what you told me last time I called."

"I'm sorry, sir, but you're mistaken. This is the first time we've spoken."

Southern politeness, legendary as it may be, is a double-edged sword. All those "sirs" and "sorrys," wielded as they were by this pompous jerk, aroused the most primitive elements of my personality. I wanted to reach through the phone line and tear his head off his shoulders. Instead, I thanked him for his time and hung up.

Once I calmed down, I turned to an ongoing problem. Our profit margin at the restaurant was down about 15 percent and I needed to know why. My initial thought, that we were messing up on portion control, went nowhere. I was now looking to our vendors' packing lists and invoices.

The first thing I noticed was a lack of checkmarks on the packing lists. Deliveries were supposed to be checked in, item by item. Nothing, not even salt, was to be placed on a shelf or in the refrigerator until it was checked against the packing slip. I intended to take that demand a step further. I called down to Zach Cloninger and asked him to come up to my office. Zach managed the restaurant on the first floor. All deliveries came through his kitchen.

An awesome cook, Zach was as tranquil as his brother was spirited. He showed no emotion when I handed him the packing slips in question and told him that I not only wanted every shipment carefully checked, but all meat, chicken, and shrimp weighed out. Nor did he dispute the evidence or blame someone else, although I knew he'd assigned check-in duties to one of the other cooks.

"I'll get on it," he said before heading back downstairs.

As I watched him leave, I found myself wishing all my employees were like him. The club's manager, Zach's brother Aaron, refused to accept a single word of direction without lobbying for its direct opposite.

I arrived at police headquarters on time and found Skid waiting for me out back, as promised. He didn't look all that happy to see me, but at the moment I really didn't give a damn. I wasn't asking for copies of the documents, only for a look at them.

"This afternoon," I told him, "I paid a condolence call on Marie's parents. The sheriff was there when I arrived. He asked the family how many Mexican men Marie went out with. He also told them I was a pimp and implied that Marie was one of my whores."

"What could I say, Rooster? Most of his deputies are just waiting for the day he retires. The one that ain't related, anyway." Skid smiled that mischievous, little-boy grin that regularly drew women into his orbit. "Unfortunately, rumor has it that Sibley's put a coffin in his office and that's how he plans to leave."

Skid led me through a deserted squad room to a tiny room in the back, the kind you don't want to enter if you're suspected of a crime. Inside the room, on a small table, I found the documents I'd requested. I took a seat as Skid closed the door but left the paperwork untouched for a few minutes, afraid of what I might find. When I finally dredged up the courage to open the autopsy report, the reality was even worse than I imagined.

The forensic pathologist in Jackson who performed the autopsy, Dr. Gerald Moore, had taken several dozen photos of Terri

Crawford's body, many of them close-ups of the 152 shallow knife cuts that covered every inch of her body, from her scalp to the soles of her feet. There were bite marks as well, to her breasts, buttocks, and thighs, irregular tears in her flesh too ragged to be matched to a suspect. Her flesh was also scarred by ligature marks, deemed to be postmortem.

Though she'd lost a great deal of blood, the knife wounds hadn't killed Terri. According to Dr. Moore, the cause of death was manual strangulation. I wanted to stop my thoughts right there. I told myself that speculation, at this point, was a pure waste of time. But I couldn't stop the questions that whipped through my brain because I knew that Marie Blocker had suffered an identical fate, Marie and all of the other women.

Had Terri's killer grown tired of her? Had she begun to bore him? Or had she grown so weak that she was unable to respond and unlikely to recover? Or was she fully conscious when he wrapped his fingers around her throat? Did she thrash beneath him as he stared into her eyes? Did she fight for her life?

However it went down, he wasn't finished with Terri Crawford. Despite obvious trauma to the victim's throat, vagina, and anus, no foreign DNA was recovered during the autopsy because the victim's body was obviously sanitized. Minute traces of freshwater algae in her hair made it likely that her body was carefully washed in one of the many ponds and lakes in the region.

I took another moment to review the lab reports. Terri's blood and tissue had been tested for various chemicals, from heroin to arsenic. The result in every instance was negative: no alcohol, no dope, no poison or sedatives. I grabbed the case file next, skimming some of the material. The Oxford Police Department doesn't have a crime scene unit, and Skid had worked the scene by himself. His efforts uncovered exactly nothing.

The victim's family and friends came next. Skid had investigated Terri's boyfriend, her associates, and various relatives out to her second cousins. He'd also tracked her movements in the forty-eight hours before she was kidnapped and interviewed every sex offender residing in Lafayette County. Most had alibis, while the few who didn't lacked a motive.

Like Dr. Moore at the autopsy, Skid had taken a number of photographs, most of Terri Crawford's body as it was recovered from a ditch. I had to lean close to make out the details because Skid wasn't much of a photographer. What I saw chilled me. Terri's body was tied down, her head to her knees and her knees to her chest, while her arms were tucked between her thighs and her chest. Nice and neat, a package ready for transport.

CHAPTER ELEVEN

I wanted to talk to Skid about the investigation, but when I came out of the interview room, he was standing by the door, keys in hand.

"Caught a job," he told me. "A burglary in the Wellsgate development. I'll catch up with you later at the club."

I waited until he'd gone, then returned to the case file where I gathered a handful of crime scene and autopsy photos. I don't know what I would have said if a cop wandered into the squad room while I copied them. None did.

I returned to my pickup, shoved the key into the ignition, but then leaned back without starting the engine. On impulse, I placed a call to Dr. Ralph Kowalchek, chairman of the Criminal Justice Department at the university. A transplanted Yankee, Kowalchek's creds were impeccable. He'd spent fifteen years with the FBI's Criminal Behavior Unit at Quantico, earned a doctorate at Penn State, and written a pair of textbooks popular with colleges throughout the country.

Kowalchek was a jazz fan, but as there were no jazz clubs in Oxford, he settled for an occasional infusion of Delta blues. I'd also taken his course as a student. While I found the class interesting, Kowalchek had a sharp tongue that he freely exercised. I usually avoid college professors with big mouths because you're not allowed to smack them. Right now, however, I had no obvious line of investigation and I needed guidance.

I had Kowalchek's phone number in my contact list because I'd long intended to invite him to one or another of my parties. The professor had worked on a number of famous cases, including serial killer investigations, and he liked to talk about them. The cases were interesting, and his descriptions, after a few drinks, were just gruesome enough to fascinate without offending.

"Ah, the famous Robert Feathers, aka Rooster."

"I hope I'm not interrupting."

"Actually, I was in the middle of writing the only decently constructed sentence of my literary career. Sadly, it has now fled my consciousness. What can I do for you?"

"First thing, I want to invite you to the away-game party on Saturday."

"Before I thank you formally, I'd like to hear the second thing."

Once a cop, always a cop. I told him that I'd seen the case file on Terri Crawford and I wanted to discuss it with him. To his credit, he didn't quiz me on what I planned to do with the information.

"Rooster, did you not take my course? Do you not remember the section on profiling?"

I did remember. The profilers at Quantico demanded every scrap of information before they conducted an analysis, including autopsy reports, crime scene photos, toxicology results, test results on trace evidence, the victim's background, police interviews, and a lot more. I had only a secondhand description to offer, so I didn't waste time. I played my hole card.

"Actually, I was hoping someone, the chief or the sheriff, had already consulted you. Being as you're the only expert we have."

"They did not."

I managed not to laugh at Kowalchek's offended tone. "That surprises me, professor, and if I had the case file, I'd share it with you in a heartbeat. I don't. So, if a carefully prepared account of the information I reviewed isn't enough, I'll leave you in peace."

Kowalchek sighed into the phone. "As a student, Rooster, you were always too quick to draw conclusions in the absence of data. Impetuosity is the mother of dead-end investigations. As I explained to you at the time."

I started the truck and headed for the club. Along the way, I described the material I'd reviewed and recounted the gossip that had come to me by way of Skid and Deputy Keefer. Kowalchek stopped me from time to time, and I assumed he was taking notes. He asked no questions, though, merely waiting until I finished. Then he promised to call me later and hung up.

***

I passed through the club on the way to my office. Clovis Haggard was blowing the place up with a hard-rock approach to classic tunes like "Matchbox Blues" and "Hellhound on My Trail." They deserved better than a meager audience, much better. Unfortunately, the news about Marie had done its work. There wasn't a single coed in my club. No coeds, no horny frat boys seeking their favors.

Up in my office, I accessed the security footage for the night Marie disappeared. I knew the sheriff would demand the data at some point, and I wanted to review it first. Tomorrow, I'd have my office manager and resident geek, Lee Henderson, copy the data to a thumb drive.

I set a full bottle of Jack Daniels next to the keyboard and went through nearly half as I reviewed the footage over the next few hours, occasionally fast forwarding, occasionally rewinding. I was able to follow Marie almost from moment to moment by switching back and forth between the three cameras in the club. My search was for anything out of the ordinary, maybe someone hitting on Marie a little too aggressively or watching her a little too closely.

Marie's initial appearance, alive and vibrant, flashing that easy smile, nearly blew me out of the chair. I was seized by an emotion that mixed rage and grief and righteousness into a stew without a name. She just couldn't be gone. I recalled Janette Blocker's question. How could the Lord allow monsters like the man who murdered her daughter to walk the earth? Most likely, the question was too much for her, and that's why she turned to the photo album. Memories were all she had now, and while they were currently a source of pain, I knew they'd become sustenance in the long run.

I don't remember how old I was on the day Rosie took a photo album from a closet shelf and carried it to the living room couch where I sat.

"This album belonged to your momma," she explained. "I believe you're old enough to deal with what's inside. If you feel you're not, I'll put it back on the shelf."

I read that album the way the pious read the Bible. As if there were treasures concealed in every photo. I still take it out from time to time, but now I understand my mother's life in simpler terms. She suffered the early loss of her parents first, three years apart, then a husband, but she kept on going. I, of course, knew that my father was probably still alive, even though I couldn't have been more than nine or ten at the time. Why hadn't he sought me out? And why did he walk out of his family? Was it me? Did I somehow drive him away? Before I was even born?

"Had nothin' to do with you," Rosie explained. "See, your daddy wasn't a bad man, just weak and quick to give up."

I can't know my mother's feelings when Patrick left, whether of rage or despair or even relief. But she'd kept photos of her husband, including photos taken at their wedding, and I spent many hours examining them. I could see myself in his broad features, in the shape of his forehead, and I couldn't help but conclude that the only real difference between me and him was that I never made any commitments I couldn't keep. I knew my limitations.

I spent hours reviewing the video of Marie's last day at work. I wouldn't say that I wasted my time, but I was no closer to unraveling the mystery when I finally paused the video than when I started watching. In the first place, the club attracted customers as diverse as college professors and outlaw bikers who'd spent most of their lives in prison. It was almost impossible to stand out, no matter how weird your appearance. In the second place, a number of patrons—and not all of them male—hit on our servers every night. The girls either learned to deflect unwanted come-ons or they found another job. There was a line, of course, and my bouncers were quick to intervene when some asshole crossed it. But that didn't happen to Marie on the night she disappeared. Her shift, on that quiet Wednesday night, was uneventful. She put in her hours, served up drinks and food, and finally headed home.

At some point, random or carefully planned, her path crossed the path of a semihuman figure that drew its substance from the pain of others. I'd never been much for horror movies because I didn't believe in vampires or zombies. But I did believe in serial killers. Now I'd seen what they could do. A number of Terri Crawford's autopsy photos had been shot from a few inches away, the better to capture the edges of her wounds.

CHAPTER TWELVE

Ralph Kowalchek phoned around eleven. Though I'd been drinking pretty hard, I was far from drunk. I was a high-capacity drinker anyway, but the video, still running, had pushed enough adrenaline into my system to keep me sharp. I grabbed a pen and a pad when I recognized Kowalchek's voice, expecting to take notes, but never wrote a single word. Kowalchek's message was too simple. I wouldn't forget.

"Allow me to begin with a disclaimer," he said. "What I'm going to tell you is little more than a series of educated guesses. This is not a profile."

"I see."

"Do you?"

"C'mon, professor, give me a break. I'm looking for somewhere to start."

"And that's another thing. What leads you to assume you're qualified to conduct an investigation?"

"I'm a licensed private investigator. I passed an exam."

Kowalchek's laugh was genuine, if not actually mocking, but he let the question drop. As I'd hoped.

"I'll start with the one item that might actually help you. Given the scattered disposal sites, some in obscure locations, your man is either native to Lafayette County or has been living in the county for many years. In my opinion, you can pretty much eliminate newcomers."

"Like Mexican construction workers?"

"Exactly."

I glanced at the monitor to my right. Marie was standing by the bar, looking a bit weary at the end of her shift. She was stacking drinks on a tray and studying a check. The red light from a neon Budweiser sign glinted from a small gold cross at her throat.

"So, what else, professor?"

"I believe the subject to be a white male in his early thirties to midforties. Local, as I said. He's intelligent, though not well educated, and his preparations for the targeting and abduction, for the enactment of his central fantasy, and for the disposal of the bodies were carefully rehearsed before the initial abduction. He's been formulating this strategy for a very long time, and I wouldn't be surprised to learn that he reads books about serial killer investigations. Sanitizing the victims' bodies was no easy task, but the only physical evidence recovered thus far is algae, and only traces at that."

"What about jail?"

"Jail?"

I refilled my glass and took a small sip. "You said he's been preparing for a long time. I've known more than my share of ex-cons, and there's a whole lot of 'em who see prison as a place where you go to perfect your skills. One example, if dealing is your thing, you hang around with other dealers, exchange smuggling techniques, swap contacts, arrange meets when you're discharged."

"That's insightful, Rooster. Because I don't believe that our subject began with Terri Crawford, although she might have been the first woman he actually killed. These men are driven by an obsessive fantasy they've been nurturing for a long time."

"How long?"

"Sexually motivated homicides are commonly committed by men who exhibited sexual aggressiveness in childhood." Kowalchek paused to draw a breath. "Let me put it this way. The terms psychopath and sociopath are rarely used these days to describe serial killers. Now we call them malignant narcissists. And it seems likely that they were born, not made. This man believes himself superior to every human being on the planet. He tells himself that he's so much smarter than the cops that he can't be caught. And his courage? He proves his manhood by taking risks that he doesn't have to take."

"Do you mean the disposal of the bodies?"

"I do."

Why was the killer leaving bodies where they were sure to be recovered? It didn't make sense. Lafayette County is a mix of farms and forests, and there are dozens of remote ponds, many with surrounding swamps, including the pond he used to sanitize the victims. The bodies could have been easily concealed and might never have been found. Instead, they were transported over patrolled roads and left in the open. The risk? In Mississippi, every jury's a hanging jury. Marie's killer didn't care." Kowalchek coughed softly, then abruptly changed the subject. "What time," he asked, "should I arrive on Saturday?"

"The game starts at four. Come over at three, you and your wife. But I have one more question. The cliché is that these men can't stop killing. Is that true?"

"It most definitely is *not* true, the Green River Killer being a prime example. Also, the BTK Killer. He stopped for years. In addition, there are numerous cases in which a string of homicides connected to an individual are uncovered. They end suddenly, for reasons that can only be guessed at."

"Tell me the guesses?"

"That the killer became incapacitated, perhaps by illness, or even death. That he was convicted of an unrelated crime and sent to prison. That he moved to another location, the better to pursue his fantasies. That he simply stopped."

I was still on the phone with Kowalchek when Skid knocked on my door. He glanced at the monitor on my desk and flinched. I motioned him to a chair, said my good-byes, and hung up.

"You find anything?" Skid asked, motioning to the screen where Marie, frozen in time, smiled at some offhand remark.

I poured him a drink and filled my own glass. "Not a fucking thing, Skid. Just another night. Good music, good eating, good drinking, and happy customers. "

Skid and I finished our drinks and headed downstairs. I was in the mood for a little music, but the midnight hour was fast approaching and the band was through for the night. I had to settle for a CD that H-Man plucked from our large collection. Dead since 1972, Reverend Gary Davis was a blind street musician discovered on the streets of Harlem. His finger-picking style remains the envy of acoustic guitarists who came up after him. Though he played blues and ragtime, the reverend was better known for his gospel, and his version of "Motherless Children" never failed to touch emotions that I preferred to avoid.

I led Skid onto our balcony, which ran the length of the building. The Square was almost deserted, as was the club. We stared out for a moment, until Skid finally spoke.

"So, you learn anything tonight, anything I don't know?"

I described Kowalchek's theory. A white man, local, in his midthirties to midforties, with a history of sexual assaults. Skid only laughed.

"You know why cops don't like profilers?" He answered his own question. "Because they try to make the obvious profound. Listen and understand, children. Does he think I'm looking for grampa? Or men from goddamned Cincinnati? Do you think I haven't spoken to every registered sex offender in the county?"

I caught the eye of one of our servers, a college boy named Dan Smith. "Bring us a couple of shots. Pronto. Skid's having a meltdown."

Skid laughed. "You're so full of shit, Rooster. You go nuts when somebody talks down to you."

I thought of my recent conversation with the clerk at Alcohol Beveridge Control. I'd shown remarkable restraint, all things considered, which would not have been true ten years ago.

"Talk to me about the sex offenders, the ones you interviewed."

"First thing, the list is mostly bullshit. Sex offenders are added when they register but never taken off. Eight of the men on the list turned out to be dead. Another ten moved away years ago."

"That's eighteen. What about the other twenty-two?"

Skid took a second to organize his thoughts, then counted off the items on his fingers. Five, he told me, had rock solid alibis. Seven were too old or too sick or both. Four were convicted of statutory rape when they, themselves, were juveniles, and two eventually married the woman they supposedly raped. That left six, all of them convicted of a violent sexual assault.

Dan turned up with our drinks, and we paused to look out on a sky dominated by smoky-black clouds. The clouds were tattered at the edges, with isolated stars showing through in places, but they were closing fast. I didn't have to wet a finger to know a wind blowing out of the south would bring rain. I could smell the waters of the Gulf in the breeze.

"Tell me about the six," I said. "You say you spoke to all of them?"

"I did, Rooster, and guess what? They all claim innocence." He shook his head. "If we had the manpower, we'd set up surveillance on one or two. We don't, simple as that. And we don't have the manpower to interview the sex offenders in neighboring counties.

But most of all, we lack physical evidence. Even if I develop a suspect, and even if I get him in the box without him asking for a lawyer, I have no leverage. Meanwhile, that burglary in Wellsgate? It was the third this month, and my beloved leader's makin' it priority number one. What with five bodies recovered in the county, he figures the killings to be Sibley's problem."

From inside, I heard H-Man shout, "Last call." A rush to the bar generally followed when times were good. Mississippi nightlife closes down at midnight, still early for serious partiers.

"What you said about talkin' to people who won't talk to me?" Skid said. "I don't deny the truth of it. But you need to consider this. The man who killed those women? If you get close, he'll kill you and have lunch afterward. Wouldn't mean no more to him than steppin' on a cockroach."

"That applies to you, too."

"But I get paid. And I can call in reinforcements at a moment's notice." When I didn't respond, he simply continued. "One thing you could do for me if you're so determined. I need to get a line on a sex offender named Gilmore Ellerbee. They let him out of Parchman six months ago. At the time, he was supposedly headed for a house out in the county, but he never showed up."

"If he's a parole violator, why isn't the state involved?"

"The boy's not on parole, Rooster. I called Parchman right after Ellerbee's name came up, spoke to a Deputy Warden name of Collins. Seems they suspected Ellerbee of shankin' another prisoner, but they couldn't prove it. So they punished him by denying parole until his time ran out."

"Are you tellin' me he was released without supervision?"

Skid wagged a finger at me and shook his head. "Up in Parchman, they don't worry all that much about the effect their decision makin' has on the general public. But Ellerbee failed to register, which he had to do, parole or no parole. If I get my hands on him, I can detain him long enough to sweat his ass."

I started to speak but paused as the opening notes of "I'll Fly Away," one of my favorite gospel tunes, floated out. The reverend's interpretation was relatively straightforward, yet his intricate, finger-picking style produced a rhythm that infected me. I began to keep time with my right foot even as I asked the only pertinent question.

"What makes you think he's in the county? Or even in the state?"

"Gilmore's a local boy, Rooster, born and bred in Lafayette County, with a long criminal history and a tenth-grade education. Deviant behavior and the county are all the man knows. We're talkin' here about an apple that didn't fall far from the tree. His only living relatives, a pair of cousins, are both doing time."

Our conversation ended abruptly when a dispute broke out inside the club. A disgruntled patron challenging his bar bill. I headed inside but didn't interfere with my bouncers, Grudge Metcalfe and his brother, Simon. Grudge and Simon were large men, and they moved to either side of an angry frat boy half their size.

"You need to slow down, partner," Grudge said.

The boy looked up into Grudge's face, his focus no doubt on a raised scar that ran across Grudge's forehead. I watched his Adam's apple bob as his shoulders dropped. "He's chargin' me for drinks I didn't get. He's cheatin' me."

"See, I don't mean to disrespect you, son, but me and H-Man have been workin' together for a long time and I know him to be honorable. Now if a mistake was made? That's somethin' you need to work out. Quietly."

I looked at Skid and nodded. He nodded back. Grudge and Simon could have torn the kid's arms halfway out of their sockets as they dragged him through the door. That's not the way I wanted it and not the way I'd trained them. Velvet first, then the hammer. Talk 'em down. Defuse and de-escalate. Good advice, but not a policy I was likely to pursue if I caught up with the man who harmed Marie Blocker. Should that happen, doubtful as it seemed to me at the time, restraint was unlikely to play a role in the outcome.

CHAPTER THIRTEEN

Sneak Ellerbee snorted a thin line of crystal meth, then headed out to the long porch fronting Alma-Beth Patterson's modest home. Instead of the beer he craved, he toted a can of Dr. Pepper. The meth pretty much guaranteed that he'd stay focused until he finished his task, but the last thing he needed was a trace of alcohol on his breath. Any trace.

Behind him, in the house, Alma-Beth and her brother, Monroe, replayed an ongoing argument about household funds. Before him, a soft, covering rain spattered on the leaves of the oaks and hickories bordering a lawn that was more dirt than grass. Alma-Beth wanted a new couch. Monroe wanted to put the money away. The back-and-forth disgusted Sneak because he knew it was about who was boss. They'd been goin' at it since they were kids, Alma-Beth three years older, Monroe nasty as a weasel in a nest of baby mice.

"It don't give me no pleasure to say this," Alma-Beth had told Sneak one night, "but I've come to believe that me and Monroe will take our differences to the grave. After all I've done to keep this family together, I feel like it ain't right."

And what would be right? Monroe doing her bidding, just like Sneak Ellerbee.

The unmistakable rumble of an approaching motorcycle brought Sneak to attention. Behind him, Monroe and Alma-Beth stepped onto the porch. The bike appeared a moment later, followed by a white pickup. The pickup stopped in front of the house, but the bike described a wide circle that took it onto the lawn before it came to a stop facing the road.

The man who got out of the pickup was in his forties, bearded, with a substantial gut. He wore the colors of the Hill Country Henchmen MC on a leather jacket.

"Hi, Alma-Beth," he called. "How you doin' tonight?"

Although it was three o'clock in the morning, and not night, Alma-Beth flashed a bright smile and said, "Doin' just fine, thank you."

The man nodded once. "Well, bein' that it's rainin' and I got a long way to go, I'll take my leave." His farewells made, he double-timed along the driveway before hopping onto the back of the chopper.

Sneak was off less than a minute later. His projected route would take him northwest, from Sardis Lake to the outskirts of Memphis, Tennessee, a journey of about ninety miles. If he jumped on I-55, he could probably cover the ground in ninety minutes. As it was, traveling over the back roads, through Tate and Desoto Counties, past the Coldwater River and Arkabutla Lake, he'd make delivery in a bit more than two hours. Sneak was a mule, he and Monroe, and no mistake about it. Ink had never come out and actually put words to the nature of the shipments, but Sneak knew he was transporting a load of crystal meth because there wasn't anything else in the county worth smuggling. He didn't know exactly where the meth was hidden, but he was aware of the price to be paid if he was caught with it. Given his record, he'd spend the rest of his life in a Mississippi prison.

Nevertheless, Sneak felt more or less at ease. He'd been riding the back roads of northern Mississippi since he was eight years old, fleeing his stepfather's routine beatings. Ethan Vann had rules for everything. You violated any one of them, off came the belt. After a while, Sneak decided that he could only protect himself by not being handy when the asshole felt like hurting someone. Better his mom, who'd been stupid enough to marry him.

Sneak had owned a scruffy bicycle when he made this decision, a miracle gift from a neighbor about to throw it out. He'd taken to the road as often as possible from then on. At times, when the weather was hot enough, he disappeared for days on end. And he didn't stop his incessant traveling after his stepfather took off and his mom settled into a lonely middle age. Once Sneak got his hands on a car, it was like he'd found himself, like he just uncovered the person he was meant to be. His memory, for one example. In school, he'd had trouble remembering the name of the first president. Now he only had to drive along a road once or twice before it attached itself, like the strand of a spider's web, to the map in his brain.

Sneak flipped on the radio and tuned it 98.1, a high-wattage station out of Memphis. Reception was good for a change, and he listened to Drake and Zeke introduce one of his favorites, Godsmack doing "Good Day to Die." Ahead and behind, the road was deserted, and he quickly settled into his first-time fantasy, one he'd revisited many, many times.

Sneak was barely eighteen, driving in Panola County, not all that far from the interstate he was now avoiding. He'd been thinkin' about nothin' he can remember when he came around that curve to find a blonde standing next to a car, the car with the hood up. The blonde had smiled as she raised her left hand, asking for help.

Seized for the second and last time with a sense of ultimate purpose, Sneak had slammed on the brakes. It was like she'd been out there for a hundred years, waiting for him, as he'd been waiting for her. Disliked by his classmates, the girls in school had not only rejected Gilmore Ellerbee, they'd avoided him, moving away whenever he came near. But not this one. This one had nowhere to go.

Once he left his car, Sneak hadn't hesitated. The knife opened and he read the fear in her eyes as she focused on the honed edge of the blade. "Please don't hurt me." He'd drawn immense satisfaction from her fear, though he never intended to hurt her, not if she complied, which she did. Thirty minutes later, he left her, at least in his own mind, no worse for wear.

Now he relived the encounter, adding details, embellishing, replaying certain moments over and over again. Remembering and rehearsing was how he spent much of his life. In prison, his memories were all he had. They'd sustained him.

A pair of oncoming headlights, still far off, drew Sneak's complete attention. Fantasy time was over. Not that he anticipated
any real danger, but it was better to be prepared. His truck was
registered to a woman in Memphis. He was the woman's brother,
on the way home. The phony ID in his wallet had passed scrutiny
before, but if it didn't this time, he had a .357 tucked under the seat.

The oncoming headlights, as it turned out, belonged to a Honda
Civic. Plus, it was raining so hard that Sneak couldn't tell if the
driver was a man or a woman. He was driving in Tate County,
population twenty-eight thousand. At most, two deputies patrolled
its four hundred square miles at this time of night. If those deputies
weren't sleeping, they were sure to be stationed near I-55, writing
tickets. They'd only ride these back roads if they were assigned a
job by their dispatcher.

Sneak listened for a moment to the music pouring through the
pickup's tinny speakers, Ozzie wailing on "Paranoid." Then his
thoughts turned, as they'd been turning more and more often, to
Monroe. He and Monroe had bunked together for a couple of
years at Parchman, often talking long into the night after they
did up whatever drug was currently available. Their conversations
generally took the same course. One or another would describe a
particular sexual assault, the details more fanciful than accurate.
An analysis would follow as they discussed the mechanics. Not of
the assault, but of the approach and the getaway.

According to Monroe, they had a mistake in common. Their
assaults were quick affairs, due mostly to the fear of getting caught

in the act. They were ultimately unsatisfying, too, for that very reason. Think how much pleasure might be taken, he urged, if you squirreled them away. Think about using them for several days, or even a week. And remember, the initial approach carries the most risk because it's unpredictable. The bitch might scream, or she might be armed, or about to meet someone. Fewer approaches meant fewer risks.

"I know you love the risk. I know that because I like risk, too. But if you take too many risks over too short a time?" Monroe had spread his hands to indicate the cell they occupied. "Look around, brother. Look at them iron bars and these concrete walls. Take too many risks and you're bound to be caught. Yes, sir."

It had sounded good at the time. It had sounded better than good. Monroe's descriptions had Sneak's mouth watering and his dick hard. Days of pleasure, of ecstasy, of lust fulfilled? There was nothing not to like. Or there wouldn't be if Monroe hadn't left out the part about the pain, about the killing, and most of all about leavin' bodies where they'd be found.

Talk about risk. Monroe took risks when he didn't have to, and that scared the piss out of Sneak. But Sneak had a game plan, too. Right now, Monroe was holding the money that Ink paid them for muling the drugs. That was because they'd need money to make their escape. One thing sure, they couldn't stay in Lafayette County much longer, not least because finding victims was getting harder and harder. They had to start over.

For the past two weeks, Monroe had been talking up the Florida panhandle near the Alabama border. He had friends there and enough money to get them started. They'd have to live quiet for a time, of course, until they stopped being newcomers, until Sneak learned the back roads, until they worked out the details. Caution was the watchword, after which the fun would begin again.

Sneak had no particular loyalty to Lafayette County, and he actually hated the stuck-up assholes in Oxford. If Monroe wasn't leaving Alma-Beth behind, Sneak would go along willingly. But Monroe was determined.

A memory jumped into Sneak's mind, full-blown. On a hot July night, with Monroe away, Alma-Beth, out of nowhere, had come up behind him and whispered in his ear. She'd leaned in so close, Sneak could feel her breath, moist and warm, on the back of his neck.

"I want you go around back and peek between the slats on the blinds in my bedroom window."

It was as if Alma-Beth Patterson had reached down into his brain, into the part called desire, and wrung the fucker out. And what followed did not disappoint. It still didn't.

As Sneak skirted the suburbs extending south from Memphis, his thoughts turned to his own vulnerability. If Alma-Beth didn't mean no more to her brother than the beat-up Lincoln he drove, neither did Sneak Ellerbee. That was the bottom line. They were both disposable.

The solution was obvious enough. Just steer this pickup to the interstate and head west, through Louisiana and Texas to the Rio Grande. First thing, Sneak had a sister in Laredo who'd put him up, even if he arrived without notice. Second thing, assuming he dealt the meth in small batches, he could live off the drug for years without attracting attention. So, why not? Why not get out?

Sneak shut off the radio as he approached his destination. He knew the answer, of course, and it wasn't a good answer because he was drawn to Alma-Beth for the worst fucking reasons. The woman could play him like a fiddle.

After retrieving his cell phone, Sneak dialed a number from memory. He let the phone on the other end ring twice, then hung up. Five minutes later he pulled to a stop on a gravel road flanked by dense forest. A second pickup, almost identical to the first, faced him, its headlights off. As always, there was nobody about.

Sneak cut his own lights, slid the tranny into park, and stuck the .357 behind his belt. His legs a bit wobbly after the drive, he ambled through the rain to the second truck. A moment later, he was on his way back to Lafayette County, pushing it a little now that his only fear was a speeding ticket. Ink would be waiting. Monroe would be waiting. Alma-Beth would be waiting.

As Sneak flipped on the radio, he smiled to himself. Of the three, Ink was by far the least treacherous.

CHAPTER FOURTEEN

By six the next morning, I was dressed and at my computer. I checked my email first, hoping for a message from the contactor working on my new restaurant. The man was almost impossible to reach, and I'd been considering a personal visit and a short, pointed conversation. My tolerance for bullshit has always been extremely low. But I had other things on my mind now, and I quickly accessed the archives of the *Oxford Eagle*, the *Daily Mississippian*, and the three local networks, turning to the many stories on the murders until I'd accumulated lists of names, ages, occupations, and locations where the bodies were found.

Initially, I was stuck by the differences. The women ranged in age from nineteen to forty-five. The youngest was a student at Ole Miss, the oldest operated a cotton farm, along with her two sons. Three were taken from their homes, three from their vehicles. Four were white, one Hispanic, and one black. Three were found at the very edge of the county. Two were found on the outskirts of Oxford. One was discovered inside the city limits.

I didn't know what to make of the information and I didn't dwell on it long. But the ego part was obvious. The man wanted the world to know about his exploits, but probably hadn't realized that the more graphic details would be withheld. Descriptions of the victims' injuries or the way they'd been trussed had yet to appear in the media. The cops had saved that information in case they developed a suspect.

At eight o'clock, I headed out to Rosie's, the results of my research filed away. The info might come in handy later, or it might not, but the work centered me. I was committed now and ready to go forward.

There was nothing special about my seeking Rosie's counsel. Keeping me grounded was her job, after all. But when I came through the door, I found her mind focused on other things. A subcommittee she chaired was scheduled to hold a hearing later that morning. Another developer had filed another application for another development. Oxford was not only growing larger but wealthier, and the expanded tax base meant better schools and better roads. New businesses were opening every day, many of them upscale, and Baptist Memorial was building a six-hundred-thousand-square-foot hospital out on Belk Boulevard.

Was there anything not to like?

Don't ask the fifty families living in a pair of trailer parks on the property in question. Renters all, if the application went through, it was good luck and good-bye.

"The price of housing has gone through the roof," Rosie explained. "There's just nothing available at the prices they're able to pay."

I helped myself to coffee, adding two sugars. "Who owns the trailers?"

"Clyde Drees."

"And the developer?"

"That would be National Builders. They're headquartered in Tallahassee."

"Well, you can forget about Clyde. The man's greedier than Midas. He'd evict his own family to fatten his bottom line."

Rosie laughed. "I believe you've captured the man's essence, Rooster. But I'm not fool enough to waste my time with Drees. After the hearing's completed, I've scheduled a private meeting with one of National's executive vice presidents. I'm going to tell her that compensating the families is in National's interest, otherwise they're likely to resist. Not that I support any violation of the law, but folks in Mississippi are mostly armed, so it could get ugly. Better to avoid the bad publicity by a display of generosity that will add little to National's overall costs, yet earn the support of all those liberal college professors at the university. You know, the ones you hope will buy your houses."

Rosie's play wouldn't truly compensate the families, but it was better than nothing and all they were likely to get. I announced my agreement, then switched the conversation to the killings.

"I have a plan, Rosie, believe it or not. I've been up most of the night thinking about it."

"I'm all ears," she said.

"My plan is for the board, or as many members as you can round up, to petition our beloved mayor, Big Bill Rowan, to pressure the governor. I want Rowan to demand that Governor Reed turn the case over to the Department of Public Safety." I leaned forward, more sure of myself now that I had Rosie's full attention. "The victims have to be connected in some way. Three were taken from their own homes with no sign of forced entry. Three were taken from their vehicles. In each of those cases, the cars were found with the engines running."

"How do you know all this?"

"I got a look at a case file and I researched online."

"Researched?" Rosie's grin ran from ear to ear. "Tell me you're not becoming a geek."

I stopped long enough to consider what I might do if I got my hands on the man who killed Marie. As far as I could tell, there wasn't a hint of geekishness in my plans.

"Look, Rosie, nobody walks up to a house, hoping to kidnap a woman they plan to hold for days, without knowing exactly who's inside. The victims were not chosen at random."

"You're sayin' the victims were targeted?"

"Yes, which means they're somehow connected. I don't know what the connection is, but I only had access to a single case file, and the same holds true for Skid. As for the state cops, they've got the juice to demand every case file and the experience to find the link. In case I don't stumble on it first."

I looked through the window at a bed of white chrysanthemums. The rain had pushed the blossoms down into the soil, and the petals were spattered with mud. The plants, of course, didn't give a shit, but Rosie definitely would. The chrysanthemums were scheduled to come into the house, cut to make bouquets.

Given Price Sibley's attitude and his violent instincts, I needed some authority to conduct an investigation in the county. The Blockers, Harold and Rose-Marie, were my only real hope, and I found myself approaching their trailer a few minutes before ten o'clock. Samantha Blocker opened the door, as she had on the prior day.

After a curt greeting, Samantha ushered me into the living room where I found Harold and Rose-Marie sitting on the couch, exactly as they'd been on the prior afternoon. They offered an elaborate thanks, in which the Lord was mentioned three times, for the contribution I'd made to Marie's funeral expenses. Respectability after death was as important in their eyes as respectability in life. Maybe there'd be no mahogany casket with silver handles and no parade of limousines, but at least they'd get Marie into the ground and put up a headstone without bankrupting themselves.

"Everyone at the club contributed," I insisted. "It was a joint effort."

This was somewhat of an exaggeration. When I emptied the Stetson I'd left on the bar, I'd found only four hundred dollars.

"Well, you thank 'em," Harold said. "One and all. You tell 'em we're grateful."

"I will."

An awkward silence followed, until Samantha came out of the kitchen with a mug of coffee and laid it on a small table beside me.

"So, what brings you out here?" she asked.

"I want the family to hire me as a private investigator. I'm licensed and have been for a long time."

"What about the sheriff?" Rose-Marie asked. "Isn't that what the sheriff's supposed to do? Investigate?"

Samantha answered for me. "Sibley's got his head up . . ."

"Now you stop right there, Samantha," Harold said. "I know you come here to help, but usin' that kind of language in a Christian household ain't doin' your momma the slightest bit of good."

I broke in before the argument picked up speed. "Samantha's choice of words might have been crude, Harold, but she's right. You know about that new development on 207?" I waited for a nod. "Well, I was out there yesterday, and I watched our sheriff round up a dozen workers. Most of those men don't even own cars, and no woman in this county would stop on the road for any one of them. Without doubt, the killer's local."

Rose-Marie was first to speak. "I don't mean to challenge you, Rooster, but why can't you just investigate? If that's what you want to do? Why do you need us?"

"Mom's trying to say that we can't afford to hire a private investigator," Samantha broke in. "Things bein' what they are."

"As to the first question, my license doesn't give me the right to investigate as I please. If I haven't been hired, I'm just another citizen interferin' with the police in their own investigation. But I'm not lookin' to make money here. I just need the legal authority and one dollar to seal the deal."

"And you think you can find the man who killed my daughter?"

I was sorely tempted to lie. I admit that. But the sorrow deeply embedded in Rose-Marie's pale gray eyes brought me up short. The Blockers deserved the truth.

"Right now, I'm out to stir the pot, see if there's any meat at the bottom. Where that will take me, I do not know. I wish I did, Rose-Marie. I wish I could lay my hands directly on the man who did this to Marie. The way it is, though, I can only promise to try."

I chose that moment to break out Gilmore Ellerbee's mugshot, which I passed around. Harold and Rose-Marie both shook their heads after a glance, but Samantha flicked her gaze to the front door. Whatever she had to say, she wasn't about to say it in front of her parents. A moment later, my dollar fee in hand, I headed for my truck.

Samantha followed me out, and we stood on the tiny porch for a moment while she organized her thoughts. Then she raised her eyes to mine and said, "That man in the photo, Gilmore Ellerbee? I went to high school with him."

I nodded agreeably. "What was he like, Samantha?"

"He was beyond creepy. I don't believe there was girl at the school who didn't find him staring at her one time or another. And don't ask me what he was thinkin' while he watched. I'm a free spirit, but not that free."

"You're sayin' that you know this from personal experience?"

"Hell, yes." Samantha folded her arms across her chest, the gesture seemingly protective. "This happened at a spring dance in my junior year. After a couple of hours, I snuck out of the school for a cigarette, which I did pretty often in those days. There was a tree there, across from the athletic field, and I used to get behind it so you couldn't see the glow of the cigarette from inside the school. Ellerbee, the son of a bitch, was hiding near the entrance to the gym, which, of course, I didn't know till he was walkin' right at me, a smile on his face and a hard-on in his pants. Excuse my French."

"Did he touch you?"

"You think I was fool enough to give him a chance? I had a can of pepper spray in my purse and I unloaded right in his face. Believe me on this, Gilmore took off real quick. He didn't bother me again, either. But that's not what I have to say. See, my sister knew all about Gilmore, and I'm tellin' you, sure as there's a God in heaven, she wouldn't have stopped her car for that creep if he was hangin' from the branch of a tree."

CHAPTER FIFTEEN

The rain had slackened by the time I headed back into town, passing between fields and forests softened by a pale gray fog. My destination was a sorority house on the university campus, Omega Delta Phi. One of the victims, a student named Cary Thompson, had lived there as a new pledge for the six months preceding her death. My expectations weren't high, but I was sure the students would talk to me. I'd begun my security business by providing services to the fraternities and sororities at Ole Miss, and I continued to advertise the club in the campus newspaper, *The Daily Mississippian*.

To me, the four-thousand-acre campus at Ole Miss had always seemed more like a wealthy suburb than a school. Lawns and trees separated almost every building from its neighbors. Landmarks like Ventress Hall and Rowan Oak, once the home of William Faulkner, abounded. The university's very first building, The Lyceum, erected in 1846, had been preserved. It stood almost at the center of the campus and now served the chancellor.

According to Faulkner, "The past is never dead. It's not even past." That may not have been the case in cities like New York where change was a way of life, but it was surely true in Mississippi. I don't know if it's a good or a bad thing, but in my home state, we are—beyond any doubt, reasonable or otherwise—tradition bound. We do not forget.

That was probably why most of the students at Ole Miss belonged to one or another of the fraternities and sororities strung along two streets: Fraternity Row and Sorority Row. The dwellings they occupied were not simple houses. In sharp contrast to the brick dormitories reserved for those who shunned the Greek system, fraternity and sorority houses were sprawling affairs, antebellum in style for the most part, and set on spacious lots.

Omega Delta Phi's two-floor house was no exception. Columns running the length of the wood-frame building supported a roof that overhung a long porch. The surrounding yard was carefully maintained, the lawn recently mowed. Even flowerbeds that had grown sparse as fall progressed were meticulously weeded. A flag-stone path leading to the front door, though wet, was free of mud.

The young woman who opened the door when I rang the bell flashed a welcoming smile. I suspect that she knew me from the club, although I couldn't remember her name or even her face. I asked for the house mother, a middle-aged woman named Mae Williams. House mothers ruled the sororities, a tradition as old as the Lyceum, which is why I'd been kissing their asses for as long as I could remember.

"Good afternoon, Rooster," Mae said when she finally came out of her den.

"Afternoon, ma'am."

"Well, I see you're dry. Did the rain finally stop?"

"It did, and I believe it'll clear by nightfall."

"I hope so. We're sponsoring a Rebel Rally in the Grove tomorrow morning."

The Grove was a ten-acre wooded park in the center of the campus. On game day, thousands of students gathered in the Grove to urge the team on. Rallies during the week were also common, especially if cosponsored by a fraternity.

"Well, Rooster, what brings you to our door this afternoon? Another party?"

The question was reasonable. I commonly rented out the restaurant or the club for private parties. But my answer brought the polite chitchat to a close.

"I've been retained by Marie Blocker's folks to investigate the death of their daughter, and I was hoping to speak to a few of the girls who knew Cary Thompson."

"It's about time somebody showed up." Mae drew a deep breath, then repeated herself. "It's about time."

"The sheriff hasn't been here?"

"His deputies paid a visit the day after Cary's . . . after the incident. They spoke to a few of the girls and we haven't seen them since. I tell you, Rooster, in all candor, some of the questions they asked were indelicate and entirely uncalled for. Now I was raised to a certain standard, but I found it hard to remain polite."

"I'm real sorry to hear that," I said, "but I'm not surprised. If Price Sibley was better at his job, I probably wouldn't be here."

Mae Williams took the hint. She could accommodate me or refuse me, her choice. Twenty minutes later I was seated in a parlor as old-fashioned as it was plush. Eight young women surrounded me, including Cary Thompson's roommate, a sophomore named Liz Di Bono.

I stuck to the basics, and the women responded freely, often commenting on each other's comments as they filled in the gaps. I learned that Cary was relatively old-fashioned and not given to risky behavior, a more-or-less average girl who got along with her sorority sisters without attracting much attention. Never a flirt, she had a steady boyfriend, the son of a man who owned a fifty-thousand-acre farm near Calhoun County to the south. Cary was returning alone from a Sunday afternoon visit to the farm when she vanished from a back road. Her car was found with the engine running.

The boyfriend's alibi was solid. He'd remained at home with his parents and four siblings after Cary left for Oxford. Every member of the family could honestly swear to this because they'd assembled in the backyard for a spirited game of Wiffle ball that lasted until it became too dark to see. By then, Cary had been gone for hours.

I let the stories play out, then asked about the days and weeks before Cary disappeared. Did Cary report anything unusual in her life? Anything? Had they, themselves, noticed anything unusual, on or off campus?

"Do you mean," one of the girls wanted to know, "like creeps hangin' around?"

"Exactly like creeps hangin' around."

But aside from a general belief that all males were on some level creeps, no individual displaying unusual creepiness had crossed their paths. At that point, I thanked one and all for their time, then allowed Mae Williams to show me to the door where I again expressed my thanks.

As I unlocked the truck, a young woman crossed the lawn from the back of the house, coming in my direction. I recognized her as Liz Di Bono, Cary Thompson's roommate. She was a small girl, stunningly attractive, with large brown eyes and frosted hair the color of honey.

"Rooster," she said, the expression on her face earnest, "may I talk to you for a minute?"

I wanted to tell her that she could talk to me for a week, but managed to control myself. "Sure, go ahead."

"Well, you asked about Cary, if anything new was happening in her life."

"That's right."

As Liz began to speak, a blush rose from her throat into her cheeks. "I don't suppose there's a good way to say this . . ." She hesitated again, as if expecting me to supply the next sentence. When I didn't, she looked down. "Cary and her boyfriend started having sex about a month ago. I know that doesn't seem like a big deal in this day and age, but Cary's parents are very religious.

They're fire and brimstone religious, according to Cary, and she was real scared they'd find out. Like, if she became pregnant."

"Did she?" I asked, knowing that might give her boyfriend a motive.

"No, but she decided to use birth control, which was like a big deal, at least to her." Liz shook her head. "After someone's gone, you find yourself wishing you'd paid them more attention while they were still here. So, I know she went somewhere to get a prescription for birth control pills about a week before she disappeared, but I don't know exactly where."

CHAPTER SIXTEEN

Twenty minutes after leaving Omega Delta Phi, I pulled up in front of Oxford Workouts, Barbara Michael's gym on South Lamar Boulevard. Located across from the U-Haul dealership, Barbara's prefab building was little more than sheets of metal siding riveted together. The interior was marginally more attractive, but just marginally. Oxford Workouts was a no-nonsense gym. You came to sweat and groan. You were expected to leave exhausted.

The interior space was divided into three large rooms separated by temporary dividers. The dividers were high enough to provide a degree of privacy, but didn't come within six feet of the ceiling. Barbara commanded the room on the north where she taught everything from jazzercise to belly dancing to step aerobics. Virtually all of her clients were leotard-clad females who didn't care to be evaluated.

The central portion of the building was given over to routine workouts. The equipment included treadmills, stair steppers, strength machines of all kinds, and a decent selection of free weights. This is where I spent most of my time, at least when I wasn't getting my ass kicked by a ranked MMA fighter named Codie Shuffield.

Codie ran a two-hour boxing class three evenings a week in the southern end of the gym. He had a gym of his own as well, Oxford Kickboxing, where he taught self-defense classes to kids and adults willing to accept the occasional black eye and bruised ribs. At Barbara's, he taught white-collar boxing to a mainly up-scale clientele from the university. I was the exception, a would-be tough guy who could in no way provide Codie with a challenge.

Codie wasn't around, which was just as well. I was in need of a hard, fast workout that afternoon, not a beating. I outweighed Codie by thirty pounds, but rarely laid a glove on him. Not only was he much faster, but he seemed able to anticipate every move I made.

Gyms had long been special places for me. Call it a legacy of my football years, but I felt as comfortable around a weight pile as I did in my own bed. At the time, I was bench pressing more than four hundred pounds, and I was damn proud of it.

When I came through the door, gym bag in hand, I found Barbara at the reception desk. A smile softened her sharp features as she looked up from the magazine she'd been reading.

"What happened to Rachael?" I asked. Rachael Vernon usually worked reception.

"Rachael's out back, taking a cigarette break."

"A cigarette break? I thought this was a health club."

"That's why she's out back."

Barbara wore a two-tone leotard, green and red, the colors running to alternate arms and legs. I studiously kept my gaze above her throat, but not without an effort. Most of the women in Mississippi, especially the coeds at Ole Miss, try to project a certain delicate vulnerability. Frail Southern flowers, that's the tradition, and as I've already said, we're tradition-bound in Mississippi. But not Barbara, whose no-nonsense personality reflected her general businesswoman's attitude. The bottom line was the bottom line, and no amount of sweet-talking or eye-fluttering could change the numbers.

I started to ask Barbara about the business but held my peace. In better times, she'd be teaching a class. I smiled at her remark, then started for the locker room. She stopped me with a question.

"Bears or panthers?"

"What?"

"Women. You can divide them into a pair of camps. Women attracted to panthers and women attracted to bears."

Though I'd never thought of myself as a bear, I knew I wasn't a panther, not at six one and 240 pounds. "What about refrigerators with legs?"

"Ah, now you're getting kinky."

If I remembered right, kinky was right up Barbara's alley. Once again I started off to the locker room, but Barbara wasn't through.

"She's not coming back, right?" Barbara asked. "To Oxford?"

"You mean Vera?"

"Yeah, Vera."

"Vera came here to pay her dues, not to live." I hesitated, but although Barbara's gray eyes continued to study me, I didn't read a challenge in her gaze. "Maybe that's what I wanted, a relationship with a definite end. It's what I'm good at. But the truth is that I don't really miss her."

Barbara's gaze finally shifted when she looked down at an open ledger on her desk. "Stop by the office on your way out," she said. "And have your credit card ready. Your dues are overdue."

I worked out for the next sixty minutes, going at it hard. I needed to burn off a little steam, and I didn't have a lot of time. I began with a twenty-one-minute run on a treadmill, covering exactly three miles, steady as she goes. Calisthenics followed: sit-ups, push-ups, and squats interspersed with various stretching exercises. I knew most of the other patrons well enough to greet, but I stayed to myself. When I shifted over to the weights, I worked with the Nautilus equipment instead of the free weights I normally used, moving from station to station almost without pause.

By the time I hit the one-hour mark, my arms and thighs screamed for rest, but my thoughts had centered. If Gilmore Ellerbee resided in the county, I'd find him. Maybe he wasn't the man who killed Marie and the others, but his failure to register was a crime in itself. Skid would chew him up and spit him right back into Parchman. Another rapist out of circulation.

I showered and dressed quickly. There was work to be done out in the county, and I wanted to get to it as soon as possible. I only remembered Barbara's demand as I approached the front door. Rachael was behind the reception desk by then. She saw me hesitate, then pointed to the office.

"Barbara asked me to remind you about the fees." Rachael paused long enough to shift a wad of gum from one cheek to another. "You know, she who must be obeyed."

I didn't see it exactly that way, but I headed for the office without debating the point. Truth be told, I was damn tired of sleeping alone. Vera Califano wasn't coming back to Oxford and I really didn't care. It was time to move on.

Barbara's office was empty when I entered, but not her private shower from which she emerged after I called her name, clad in a pink terrycloth bathrobe. The look in her eyes was speculative, but oddly sad.

"You'll have to excuse my appearance, Rooster," she said. "I've got a business appointment later and I felt the need to freshen up."

What she'd freshened up were the carnal memories I had of our prior relationship. But that would have to wait for later on. I took out a credit card and handed it over.

"Say, Rooster," Barbara said as she ran my card through her terminal, "I hear tell you're investigatin' Marie Blocker's murder."

"The Blockers hired me."

"Are you gettin' anywhere?"

I had no idea what to say and I compensated by showing her Gilmore's photo. She shook her head, then asked the obvious question. "Is this the guy?"

"At this point, I only want to talk to him. He's a convicted rapist who failed to register as a sex offender. Skid's looking for him too." I gave it a couple of beats, then said, "Any chance you might come by the club tonight?"

"Whatever for?"

I turned the question over for a moment, then went for it. "Push-ups, squats, leg raises, and every kind of abdominal exercise you can imagine." I slipped the card into my wallet and signed my name to the receipt. "I don't care what you teach me, as long as it's advanced."

CHAPTER SEVENTEEN

I made a brief stop at my apartment where I changed into jeans and a T-shirt. Then I threw a leather vest bearing the Velvet Hammer MC colors over the T-shirt and headed off to a remote house on the southeastern edge of the county near Coon Creek Lake. A man named Lamar Howard, called Ink because his body was covered with jailhouse tattoos, lived in the house. At one time, Ink had commanded the Hillside Henchmen, an outlaw biker gang. That was before—fueled by more different narcotics than he later remembered—he plowed his chopper into a tree. Though a bit worse for wear, the tree still rose alongside Highway 9, near Pontotoc. Not Ink Howard. Ink was paralyzed from the waist down and would never rise again.

Back about ten years, when Velvet Hammer was up and running as a bike club and a business operating in several states, we'd naturally attracted the curiosity of one percenters like Ink Howard. Were we rivals in their various illegal enterprises? Could we be intimidated? Did our success represent an opportunity they could exploit?

One percenters like Ink generally eased into first contacts, probing for weakness. If you showed fear, they'd take it a step further, especially if you had something they wanted. At the time,

I'd taken the only course open to me. I'd made it clear at the outset that I wouldn't be disrespected. One biker refused to take the hint, a low-ranking asshole from a minor league club. Maybe he was stoned, or maybe retarded, but when he ordered me to get on my bike and get lost, the beating I put on him was meant as a lesson for all. I broke his jaw and dislocated his right shoulder, both after he was more or less helpless.

I'd met Ink for the first time on the night he and six buddies turned up at the club wearing Henchmen colors. This was back when he still had his legs. First thing, I invited him over for a drink. I'd heard of the Henchmen, a local gang with ties to much larger gangs. Ink knew of Velvet Hammer as well, but not because we were excessively fierce. Handling security for top-line rockers was cause enough for celebrity.

"I want you to know that you and your boys are welcome at the club," I told him toward the end of the conversation. "Your money's as good as anyone else's."

Ink had smiled, revealing a mouthful of bad teeth, a badge of honor with some bikers. "Long as we don't get out of hand? That the point you're comin' to?"

"I won't let anyone fuck with my business . . . no more than you'd let anyone fuck with yours. In fact, the way I understand things, we're not competing. This is about respect, which I understand to be a two-way street."

I considered all this as I piloted my bike over the twenty miles of roads between Oxford and Ink's place. The rain had stopped completely, and the sky was marked by wispy clouds that drifted slowly from south to north. I made my way along Highway 7 to 9W to 428 to 331. The roads became smaller, less traveled, and more poorly maintained as I proceeded, until I was finally riding on dirt roads. Eventually I found myself on a narrow track leading through a pine plantation, easing around puddles left by the rain. The track dead-ended in a large clearing with a ramshackle house set at the back. The siding on the house hadn't been painted in decades, and patches of tar marked the home's roof where shingles were missing. The odor of pine sap was overwhelming.

Ink was outside, in his wheelchair, when I rode up. He was bare chested, despite the lingering chill, the better to show off the tattoo that dominated his chest, a Madonna-like figure holding a demon child on her lap. There was a legend beneath the tattoo: MOMMA TRIED.

I parked my bike and walked across the yard, taking my bearings as I went. To my right, the largest bulldog I'd ever seen lumbered to its feet and slowly approached. The dog was fastened to a tree by a chain with links big enough to anchor a cargo ship. The animal stopped when the chain gave out but didn't take its eyes off me. Near a small porch leading to the front door, an Econoline 350, no more than two years old, had been equipped with a hydraulic wheelchair ramp. I pegged its value at above forty grand. Maybe Ink hadn't retired after all. The van was worth more than the house.

"How do, Rooster?" Ink said as he waved me to a chair next to him. "Kind of you to visit."

Though my visit had nothing to do with kindness, I nodded before sitting down. Perhaps twenty feet away, a young woman sat in a worn rocking chair she'd positioned in full sunlight. I wondered why Ink had chosen to sit in the shade, but then I caught a glimpse of his dilated pupils. Coke? Speed? Ink's capacities were the stuff of legends, and I didn't blame him for taking advantage of whatever consolations were available.

"That there is Miss Cassie. She's my caregiver."

Cassie nodded to me, and I nodded in return. She was young, attractive, and most likely a relative of some kind. When I turned back to Ink, he'd taken a beer from the cooler next to his chair and was holding it out to me.

"Thanks," I said as I pulled the tab. "How's your momma?"

Catherine Howard had been confined to a nursing home for the past two years, the result of Alzheimer's. Ink was close to his mom, perhaps because the last time he was in prison, she'd been the only one to visit.

"She's poorly, Rooster, and gettin' worse. Sometimes she recognizes me, but mostly she don't. Docs say there ain't no fixin' it. Gotta take it one day at a time."

"Sorry to hear that."

Ink shook his head. "We all rot in the end." He drained the beer can he held, then asked, "How 'bout you, Rooster? How's Rosie Bell?"

"Still a ball of fire."

"Good to know."

I wasn't taken with his sincerity. Ink had a swastika tattooed on the left side of his neck and an iron cross on his forehead. But we were in Mississippi, where politeness was a way of life, especially among country folk. For the next five minutes, we chatted about the club. Ink wasn't big on classic blues, but he loved Kirk Smithhart, a bar band rocker if there ever was one. I told him Smithhart would play Rooster's Blues House that very night and he nodded.

"I don't believe I ever mentioned it," I told him, "but I'm a private investigator licensed by the State of Mississippi to investigate just about anything anyone pays me to investigate."

Ink reached into the cooler and took out another beer. He offered one to me, but I shook my head. There was something about Ink's condition that inspired me to remain completely sober.

"And why would a private investigator licensed by the State of Mississippi be investigatin' a man in a wheelchair?"

"He wouldn't," I replied, "unless you've become a serial killer in your old age."

"Well, outside of mutilatin' a box of Cheerios from time to time, I believe I can plead innocent to that charge. But tell me what you're doin' here, if I'm not a suspect. Not that you've caught my attention."

I appealed to instincts I knew he'd understand. In his world, an attack on one Henchman was an attack on all.

"Marie Blocker. The latest victim? She worked at the club. I consider her to be family."

"Marie, yes. I seen her on TV this morning. Recognized her right off from the club. Friendly girl, if I remember right, the one with the big smile."

"She did have a big smile, Ink, but she looked something like this after a sadistic rapist got through with her." I took one of the autopsy photos I'd copied after Skid left the squad room and laid it in his lap. The photo had been taken just after Terri Crawford was stretched out on the table, before the pathologist got started. I didn't have to explain anything to Ink, and I didn't try. Ink was surely familiar with knife wounds, and Terri had been sliced over and over again. His tongue worked across his lips as he stared down.

"Mother fucker," was all he could find to say.

"Yeah, that sums it up real nice." I took the photo and returned it to my pocket. "That woman you see there, her name's Terri Crawford. She was the first victim, but I have a strong feeling Marie doesn't look much better. Anyway, her parents hired me to look into her killing, which makes it nice and legal. For some reason, they don't trust Price Sibley."

"Can't imagine why. Our sheriff's got integrity written all over his face. He's an example to the entire community."

We both smiled. Sibley was generally believed to be corrupt, and the way I figured it, Ink was probably one of the corrupters. I took a moment to describe what the autopsy photos revealed, the cutting, the bite marks, the strangulation. Rapists were generally despised by other criminals, and commonly attacked in prison. In Ink's world, you could kill for gain or honor, but not for fun.

"There's two things I'm sure about," I said. "You look at where the bodies were left, scattered all around the county, you have to figure the killer knows the back roads. That makes him local, Ink, maybe somebody we both know."

"And the second thing?"

"The boy didn't start at this level. He built up to killin', and he's most likely been convicted of a sex crime and been to prison."

"If I catch you right, you're askin' me to name likely candidates."

"No, I didn't come here askin' you to pick names out of a hat. But you know the players in Lafayette County, and I'm hopin' you'll think on it. Plus, it occurs to me that we have a common interest here." I waited until a sly smile crossed his face. "Me, I'm hurtin' because too many young ladies are afraid to step out at night and my club's half-empty. You? Well, the city council, right now as we speak, is askin' the mayor to ask the governor to send in the state police. You can see as how that wouldn't work out for you."

Ink raised his beer can, and I tapped it with my own, then drained it. Time to go.

"One more thing," I said as I unfolded Ellerbee's mug shot. "I'm tryin' to locate this man specifically. His name's Gilmore Ellerbee."

Something flashed in Ink's eyes, peeping through the veils of whatever chemicals ran through his brain, a hesitation while he considered the consequences. The hesitation was brief, barely a flicker, and I might not have noticed if it hadn't vanished so fast.

Ink handed me the photo and watched as I returned it to the inner pocket of my vest. "Never seen him before," he declared. "You say the boy grew up in Lafayette County?"

I hadn't, but I answered his question anyway. "He did, as it turns out." I rose to my feet and tossed my beer can into a pile behind Ink's chair. "I appreciate your hearin' me out. And by the way, Jay Lang'll be in next Thursday. In case you're in the market for shit-kicker blues."

Jay Lang and The Devil's Due was another of Ink's favorite groups, but he didn't react to what I'd hoped was good news. He looked thoughtful instead, thoughtful but determined.

"One thing I need to mention, Rooster. Now ain't the best time to go nosin' around the county. Understand, I don't mean to disrespect you. You and me, we're friends, and I'm hopin' we'll remain so. But the way I feel, you should let me do the lookin'."

I held my ground for a moment, towering over him and his wheelchair. That I'd attack him was impossible and we both knew it. Still, I didn't feel as if I could just walk away. That would be a violation of one of my basic principles. Never show fear to a growling dog.

"I appreciate the offer, but the way it is with me, the way I'm made? I believe I'll go wherever the fuck I want. No disrespect meant. Have a good day."

Ink dropped his hands to his lap. "Now, there you go, indulgin' that hot temper of yours. I'm not sayin' you don't have reason to be upset. In fact, if I had the son of a bitch who killed Marie and them other women . . ."

I broke in. "Those other women would be Terri Crawford, Sonia Sanchez, Cary Thompson, Tanesha Brown, and Janice Coulter."

"Like I said, Rooster, if I had the man here, I'd kill him myself." He tapped his knees. "Or get someone else to do it." Maybe he expected me to smile, but I didn't, and he continued on. "Now, I'm thinkin' back to the first time we met. At the club? If I recall right, you're the one who told me there wasn't no competition between my business and yours. Now I'm tellin' you there are rocks out here that don't need turnin' over. Keep in mind, rattlesnakes sometimes make their homes under rocks."

Ink turned away from me, to Miss Cassie in her rocking chair. Though she must have heard our conversation, she'd been so quiet I'd barely noticed her.

"Time to get indoors, Cassie," he said. "Before the skeeters come out to feed."

CHAPTER EIGHTEEN

I had another stop to make before I headed for the club, but I took my time going about it. Ink had been fully supportive before I mentioned Ellerbee's name, then he'd backed off, then he'd threatened me. I had to take the threat seriously. Ink might be confined to that wheelchair, but he could dial up whatever muscle he needed. Still, he'd gone about warning me off in the wrong way. You can't wave a red cape in front of a bull and expect the animal not to charge. Ink had all but admitted that Ellerbee was in the county. At least that's the way I understood his attitude.

At one point, I passed a cluster of tiny homes, shotgun shacks for the most part, close to where county roads 444 and 459 intersected. A registered sex offender lived in one of the homes. I don't know what I expected as I slowed, maybe a neon sign reading EVIL LIVES HERE or SERIAL KILLER INSIDE. Instead, I found three kids, two boys and a girl, playing in a dirt yard.

I continued on, riding from one corner of the county to the other, until the rush of the wind and the clatter of the engine and the rumble of the exhaust merged into the howl of a raging fire. I was neither running away nor running toward the fire. I was inside. The illusion gradually died as I skirted Oxford, staying to the north. I hadn't let it slow me down. I'd been there too many times before, the effect sometimes triggered by no cause I could name.

I powered on toward the southeastern shore of Sardis Lake. Created by a dam on the Tallahatchie River, the lake, fifteen miles long and less than three wide, was shaped like a cigar. Hundreds of Oxford residents had camps near its shores, anything from a trailer parked on a narrow lot to homes covering thousands of square feet. I didn't have a camp of my own, but I'd fished the lake and the Tallahatchie River to the north many times, pulling serious bass and crappie from its waters. So had thousands of people from Lafayette and the surrounding counties. On holiday weekends, there were enough jet skis on the lake to staff a decent-sized invasion force.

Fishing was not on my agenda that afternoon. I was headed for the home of Brentlaw Buckman's daddy. The Brentlaw Buckman Blues Band had been crisscrossing the South for years, appearing at one small venue after another, including Rooster's Blues House, as they awaited their big break.

Music ran in the Buckman family, as it did in many southern families. Brentlaw's daddy, Ezekiel, was an old-time fiddle player who stopped in at the club from time to time, often sitting in with one band or another. Zeke had made a living playing bluegrass for decades, but had no trouble whatsoever with the blues. The younger musicians respected his skills, and I welcomed him personally whenever he showed up. But my visit on that day had nothing to do with music. The Buckman family's pedigree ran back to the colonial era. I wanted to lean on their knowledge.

I pulled up before Zeke Brentlaw's house at four o'clock. As I parked my bike, a dog rose from the grass and hobbled toward me, a bluetick hound. The bitch's muzzle was gray, her eyes watery, and her gait unsteady. I scratched her head and she dropped to the grass.

"Howdy."

I looked up to find a middle-aged woman in jeans and a western shirt standing on the porch. "Afternoon, ma'am. My name is Rooster Feathers, and I'm hopin' I came to the right house. Is this the Buckman place?"

"Rooster? Zeke's told me about you. Says you run the best club in Mississippi. Can't beat your place for a good time."

"I appreciate that, ma'am . . ."

"You call me Jordan." She took a step back. "C'mon up and set yourself. I've got lemonade in the fridge, or a beer if you'd prefer."

"Lemonade would be fine, Jordan."

"I assume you've come to talk to Zeke. I'll just fetch him."

Five minutes later, the Buckmans, husband and wife, made an appearance. I took the lemonade Jordan offered, but she didn't go inside, merely stood there smiling. All the better.

We chatted about Brentlaw and the band for few minutes. Brentlaw was currently in Florida playing a series of clubs strung across the Panhandle. He'd return at Christmas, as he did every year, to pass a little time with his parents, siblings, and numerous relatives. I took that bit of information as a hint. Why not book the band in advance? I didn't bite, though. I'd hire the band when I heard from Brentlaw.

"So, tell what you come all this way for," Zeke finally said.

"I'm lookin' for someone, a local, lived all his life in the county." I unfolded Gilmore's photo and passed it to Zeke and Jordan.

"That there is Gilmore Ellerbee," Zeke said.

Jordan confirmed the ID a moment later. "As I live and breathe," she said. "That's Gilmore. It gives me a chill, just the sight of him. You know, I worked at the school, in the kitchen and the cafeteria, so I knew the boy pretty well. Strange don't begin to describe him."

"You say you're lookin' for Gilmore?" Zeke asked. "Because I thought the man to be in prison."

"He's out," I said, "but nowhere to be found."

"No surprise, not to me. The Ellerbee family's pure trash, Rooster, the whole clan. Been trash goin' back generations."

"Two things, Zeke. Ellerbee's required to register as a sex offender and he told officials at Parchman that he was headed back to the county. But he never showed and he never registered. If I can find him, the police will put him back in prison."

Zeke snorted as he shook his head. "The man's relatives are in prison, too. Fact, the whole family's been in jail once or twice, and that includes Gilmore's momma. The woman served six months in County for passin' bad checks."

The basic question, why didn't Ellerbee register, went unasked because I knew the Buckmans couldn't supply an answer. It could have been the inability of criminals to follow rules of any kind, or even sheer stupidity. But neither explained Ink's reaction when I'd mentioned Ellerbee's name.

My cell phone chose that moment to pour out the opening notes of "Backwater Blues." I glanced at the caller ID screen and found my contractor's name. This was the same contractor I'd been trying to reach for days now.

"I apologize for being rude," I said, "but I need to take this call."

Zeke and Jordan didn't have a lot of choice because I stepped down off the porch and walked a few feet into the yard. The old dog came up to sniff my leg but found nothing of interest and soon returned to her nap.

Paul Baddour, the contractor in question, hadn't called to apologize for being out of touch. His tone, in fact, was nearly gleeful as he delivered the bad news. The sinks I ordered for the new restaurant were on back order at the warehouse and wouldn't be available for three months. If I wanted to remain on schedule, I'd have to come down to the jobsite and choose different sinks from a warehouse catalogue.

Not only did I want to remain on schedule, my loan from the bank depended on it. I told Baddour that I'd come by in an hour, then turned back to the Buckmans and shrugged. "Business calls, but I thank you kindly for the hospitality."

As I turned, Jordan stepped to the porch railing. "You know, Rooster, I believe I might have seen Gilmore. Maybe last month. I was down to the bank at Abbeville when an old car drove past, a

Lincoln. Now the reason I noticed the car is because it was hangin' low to the ground, like someone took out the springs."

"And you say Ellerbee was inside?"

"I didn't recognize him right then, but now that I think on it . . . I don't believe I'd say so under oath, but, yes, I feel like the man drivin' was Gilmore Ellerbee."

CHAPTER NINETEEN

I placed a call to Annie-Fay Keefer before I started off. The call went right to voice mail, and I left a simple message, inviting her and her husband to visit the club that night, all expenses paid. The implications were obvious enough. I wanted information her boss didn't want me to have, and I was hoping that Annie-Fay, who despised Price Sibley, wouldn't give a damn.

By the time I reached Highway 7 and turned south toward Oxford, my thoughts had centered on the sink crisis. Specifically, I wanted to know if the new sinks would cost more than the old because the suddenly back-ordered sinks had been purchased at a generous discount. I'm not a trusting man, except with people I know well, and I didn't know Greg Baddour at all.

A few miles down the road, I picked up a tail, a sheriff's car. It trailed me for about a minute before the deputy inside lit his flashers. He followed it up a moment later with the siren. As I wasn't speeding, hadn't drifted across the center line, and my taillights were in working order, I was naturally unhappy with this turn of events. At another time in my life, I might have tried to outrun the cruiser. No more. I was a businessman now, with a lot to protect. I pulled over.

135

First thing, I got off the bike, which weighed nearly seven hundred pounds. Then I simply stood there with my arms at my sides as the deputy got out, a young white man who had to be in his early twenties.

"What can I do for you, deputy?" I asked. "Bein' that I wasn't breaking any laws when you pulled me over."

"You can stand quiet for the next few minutes until the sheriff arrives." The deputy's tone was even, but his right hand stayed alongside his holstered weapon. I was a lot bigger.

"Does that mean I'm under arrest?"

"And you can shut your smart mouth, too. You're stayin', and there ain't nothin' more to say on the subject."

We were separated by about twenty-five feet of flat ground, and I was nearly certain I could cross the gap before the deputy brought the semiautomatic into play. I was surely tempted, the right to go about my business unmolested by government being pretty basic to my understanding of the American way. But this was a fight I couldn't win. Nor would it bring me any closer to finding Marie's killer.

Sibley arrived as I considered my options. He came up slowly before pulling to the side of the road, then got out even more slowly. Once again, he rose to his full height, squared his shoulders, and threw out his chest. The gesture reminded me of a tom turkey challenging a rival in a cornfield.

Tyler Hardin climbed out as well, his perpetual smile, something between a smirk and a sneer, firmly in place. I shifted to face them.

"You can get back to work," Sibley told the deputy.

"Yessir."

I watched the deputy slide into his cruiser and drive away. Behind me, the margin on this side of the road gave way to a stand of shagbark hickory, red oak, and ash. Before me, passing cars and trucks slowed for a better look.

"Get on the ground, asshole," Tyler Hardin said. When I merely stood there, he repeated himself. "Boy, you best get on the ground, and I mean right now."

I shook my head, certain that I'd be stomped if I complied. "Tyler, you want me on the ground, you're gonna have to put me there."

When Hardin's left hand dropped to the Taser on his belt, I took an almost involuntary step toward him. He responded by pulling a Glock .40 caliber from its holster.

"I won't tell you again. Get on the ground."

I waited three or four seconds, then said, "Me getting on the ground voluntarily ain't gonna happen, Tyler. So, you need to put that gun away or pull the trigger, one or the other."

Hardin's lips tightened into a straight line. I knew the man to be brutal, especially when turned loose by Sibley, but I also knew that he wasn't that bright. Now that he'd pulled his weapon, the cars behind him had all but stopped. So, what to do? Commit a public murder? Or lose face? The issue was too complex for Deputy Hardin, and it was his boss who finally decided.

"That's enough, Tyler," Sibley growled. "Go back to the car."

Hardin flinched at the sound of his boss's voice. For just a second, his relief showed in his face, but then he assumed his customary sneer as he obeyed orders. Sibley watched until his deputy was safely behind the wheel before taking a step in my direction, then another, then another, until our chests touched. He stared down at me for a long moment before he finally spoke.

"Rooster, I know I'm getting' forgetful, what with my advancin' years and disabilities, but I recall tellin' you to stay out of the county."

"No, sheriff, you're still holdin' it together. You did confine me to the Oxford city limits."

"Then tell me, because I'm curious by nature, why you didn't heed my words."

"Why? Well, for the first thing, America was still a free country last time I looked, and a man could go any damn place he wanted if he didn't break any laws. For the second thing, I'm licensed by the State of Mississippi to conduct investigations, and I've been hired by the Blocker family to investigate the death of their daughter. I'll show you my credentials if you want."

Sibley's breath hissed out of him. His eyes closed briefly, then opened. "Listen up, boy," he said. "I don't need a civics lesson from a piece of white trash raised up by a black-ass nanny. No, sir, I do not." He jabbed a finger into my chest, jabbed it hard. "Now you might be an important man back in Oxford, what with all those punk students comin' to your club, but out here in the county, I'm the only law there is. You won't get a third warning." He jabbed me for a second time. "Go home and stay there. Don't test me again."

I managed to stop the words on the tip of my tongue. I did not say, "Next time you see Ink Howard, give him my best." No, I watched Sibley drive away, then hopped on my chopper. I needed to see about some back-ordered sinks. First things first.

CHAPTER TWENTY

Alma-Beth Patterson sat behind the small desk in her small office at the Women's Division of the County Health Department, her small, sympathetic smile firmly in place. The young woman on the far side of the desk appeared somewhat bedraggled, as if she'd dressed hastily and forgotten to apply any makeup beyond a quick smear of pink lipstick. Her hair's natural color was dark brown, as revealed by the two inches of root showing beneath the platinum-blonde dye. It, too, appeared a bit disheveled. Her name, according to the preliminary appointment form, was Jennifer Smith.

"Now, honey, you don't have to be shy with me," Alma-Beth instructed after several minutes. "You just tell me whatever it is that needs tellin'. Believe me, I am not here to judge you. I'm here to help you."

Jennifer finally raised her chin far enough for Alma-Beth to note a pair of light-blue eyes streaked with red. Most likely, the girl had spent time in her car, tears falling, before she found the nerve to come inside.

"I'm just not sure," Jennifer said. "Maybe it's nothing and I'm wasting your time."

"I'm a nurse, Jennifer, so why don't you let me decide?" Alma-Beth reached across the desk to pat her client's hand. "Tell you what, let's try this. To guarantee privacy, we'll keep this strictly between the two of us. I won't write anything down, not one single word, unless you give me permission."

"I understand, but this is just so embarrassing, Nurse Patterson."

"Uh-uh, Jennifer. Nurse Patterson won't do a'tall. You call me Alma-Beth. No need to get formal. And as for embarassin'? Honey, I've heard pretty near everything there is to hear more times than I care to count. Now, why don't you start off by tellin' me a little about yourself. Are you in school?"

Jennifer Smith nodded once. Yes, she was a junior at Ole Miss, but she had her own apartment, paid for by her parents. Initially, at her mother's insistence, she'd taken a roommate, but the roommate had moved back home and now school occupied Jennifer's full attention. Her major was pre-law, but with a strong minor in chemistry. Chemistry was part of her life strategy because huge areas of patent law required knowledge of chemistry, while the potential for employment in law firms serving various pharmaceutical and chemical companies was vast.

"My grade-point average is 3.9, which makes me a cinch to get into one of the big law schools, like Yale or Princeton."

"That's great, Jennifer, and I'm happy for you. It sounds like you don't have a care in the world. But that ain't true or you wouldn't be sittin' across from me."

The girl shook her head. "I only wish it was."

Alma-Beth watched the small muscles in Jennifer's face as they relaxed, one by one. It always happened this way, once you got them going. That was Alma-Beth's special skill, convincing the lost and frightened to believe that her intentions were kind and her concern genuine.

"I'm a careful girl, and I haven't had many affairs," Jennifer confided. "But I always used protection when I did . . . when I did sleep with someone. Which wasn't a lot, I swear."

Again, Alma-Beth patted her client's hand. "I'm not here to judge you, Jennifer. Believe me."

"Right, I understand." Jennifer swiped at her eyes. This was the painful part. "About two months ago, I went to a fraternity party. Do I have to name the fraternity?"

Alma-Beth smiled and shook her head. "We're not the police here. You just tell me what you want to tell me."

"OK, well the truth is the party started early and I had a lot to drink. Too much, obviously, because when . . . when some of the girls started exposing themselves—you know, their breasts—I got caught up in the moment. Like I couldn't control my behavior the way I usually could, and the next thing I knew, I was in a bedroom with this boy and he didn't have protection and . . ."

Jennifer Smith took a deep breath and said, her voice on the edge of despair, "I think I have a sexually transmitted disease. God, don't let it be AIDS."

* * *

The girl's problem wasn't AIDS, as Alma-Beth, a licensed practical nurse, well knew. The symptoms of AIDS didn't manifest themselves in a couple of months. And she probably didn't have an STD, either. Most likely, given her symptoms, she had a common urinary tract infection unrelated to her indiscretion. But Alma-Beth had completed Form 10-B-22 anyway, noting Jennifer's age, gender, address, home and cell phone numbers, etc. Then she'd written out a referral to a sympathetic doctor, a woman, and handed it over, along with a few reassuring comments. Now she stood in the department's parking lot, smoking a cigarette, waving to Jennifer as the girl drove away in a shiny red Highlander. Only after the SUV turned a corner and disappeared did she take out a small notepad, write down the vehicle's plate number, then retrieve her cell phone. A moment later, her brother answered the phone.

"I'm thinkin' this is good news."

Monroe's tone was impatient. The man was itchin' to go, of course, like he was always itchy these days. Like there was someplace he was reachin' for that he couldn't get to. Alma-Beth had welcomed her brother when he came out of prison. The demand that she care for him had come from her mother only a day before the woman died. And there was the other thing, too, the menace. Better to keep this bulldog fed.

"Well, here's the good news, Monroe. A girl come in tonight, twenty years old, lives alone. She ain't the best-lookin' woman at

Ole Miss, but she's well-built. Comes from an important family, or so she says. Her daddy manages a casino in Gulfport. Owns a big piece of it, too."

"And what's the bad news?"

"The girl may have a social disease. She's on the way to a doctor we use. I'll get a report within a week."

Monroe paused for a moment, then said, "Alma-Beth, I believe I'll take advantage of the wait by having Sneak put a trackin' unit on her vehicle."

"Fine with me. Now, I have to get back to work."

"Anything else comin' in?"

"Not unless you've taken an interest in the morbidly obese great-grandmother sittin' in my office." Alma-Beth waited for Monroe's laughter to subside, then added, "But you'll appreciate this girl we're talkin' about. Her name's Jennifer Smith and she speaks proper. She ain't trash like us."

When he responded, Monroe's tone was so cold that his sister shivered on the other end of the phone. "Alma-Beth," he said, "by the time I get through with Jennifer Smith, she won't just be trash, she'll be garbage."

CHAPTER TWENTY-ONE

I got back to the Square at eight o'clock, stopped at the restaurant for a catfish dinner, then headed upstairs to the club. Blind Mississippi Morris, born Morris Cummings, had already claimed the stage when I stepped into the room.

Born into a musical family in 1955, before the folk music scene exploded, Morris hailed from Clarksdale where I was born. He grew up with the delta blues of men like Mississippi John Hurt and R. L. Burnside, Fred McDowell and Robert Johnson. Now, sixty years later, Morris's harmonica, though amplified, reached back through the history of the blues to its earliest days in the cotton fields and the marshes of the delta.

I stopped just beyond the doorway. Out of respect, surely, but also because the wail of a blues harp is among the loneliest sounds music has to offer. On that night, it carried me right back to Marie Blocker. Marie was lying in a refrigerated cabinet at the ME's office in Jackson, her body twice cut to pieces, by her killer and by the pathologist who performed the autopsy. It couldn't get any lonelier than that.

Annie-Fay Keefer and her husband were seated at a table, eyes half closed, letting the music wash over them. They were entranced, as were the rest of the sparse audience. Morris wore a vested, sky-blue suit, white Kangol cap, and dark, dark glasses that covered his eyes. He swayed back and forth as he played. Unable to see the audience, he had only the music to guide him.

I finally crossed to the bar and had H-Man fetch me a bottle of Jack Daniels. When he came back, I poured myself a double and squeezed a few drops of lime into the glass. I'd had a good day for an amateur, good enough to draw a few conclusions. They were obvious conclusions, to be sure, and probably unrelated to the killer who'd been terrorizing Oxford. I weighed them anyway.

The deputy who flagged me on Highway 7 had obviously been looking for Rooster Feathers. Once he found me, he'd been instructed to detain me until the sheriff arrived. Was all that attention due to an insignificant confrontation at the Blockers' home? Or had Ink called Price Sibley because I'd asked about a man named Gilmore Ellerbee? I was picking door number two—from Ellerbee to Ink to Price Sibley—and that's the way I intended to play it until proven wrong. Ink and Sibley were running a game, and Ellerbee had a part to play. The nature of the game? That part was easy because there was only one game in the county big enough to attract our duly elected sheriff.

According to rumors that began to circulate early in the year, several large meth labs, turning out dozens of kilos every week, had opened in the back country. Where did they get their chemicals? Who did they sell to? I didn't know and really didn't care to find out. Richard Nixon started the War on Drugs eight years before I was born. In the light of the war's obvious failure, I was pretty much convinced it would still be ongoing when I faced judgment. Keeping drugs out of the club had defined the extent of my concern. Until now.

One thing I was pretty sure about. There was no way a high-volume meth lab could operate in the county without the cooperation of the Henchmen. And that was only if the lab wasn't theirs to begin with. For some time, I'd assumed that Ink was retired, his criminal life over, but the modified van in his front yard argued otherwise. So, what would he do if he came to believe that Ellerbee had sliced those woman? I'd looked into Ink's eyes after he examined the autopsy photo. He'd kill him, no doubt.

My thoughts drifted back to Ink's reaction when I mentioned Ellerbee. How were the two connected, if they were connected at all? I couldn't imagine the creep who'd confronted Samantha Blocker and Ink as friends. No way, no how. But I could imagine Ink using Ellerbee in some capacity, perhaps to mule drugs or work in one of the labs. That meant, if I wanted to find Ink and have that conversation I longed to have, I needed to move fast.

I looked up just as Morris launched into "Rollin' and Tumblin'," a classic blues that reached so far back nobody knew its origins. The tune had been covered by hundreds of musicians, including Muddy Waters and Bob Dylan. I'd heard the song played almost as a dirge, but Morris was doing it up-tempo that night.

I rolled and I tumbled, I cried the whole night long
I rolled and I tumbled, I cried the whole night long

When I rose this morning, momma, I didn't know right
from wrong

Ten minutes later, finally done, Morris wiped the sweat from
his brow with a blue handkerchief, smiled at the applause, then
announced a short break. I turned my attention to Annie-Fay, remembering her many complaints about Sibley and his department.
According to Annie, the county, along with the science of policing,
was undergoing rapid change. Meanwhile, Sibley ran the job the
way he had when he first took office. For example, there were only
two computers in the department, both antiques, and neither was
able, beyond a search for criminal records, to communicate with
the many state and federal databases available to law enforcement.

I'd listened politely in the past, but I knew Annie-Fay had an
agenda of her own. As one of two blacks in the department, and
the only woman, she had no hope of promotion under the present
regime. Sibley's relatives would inevitably come first. On the
other hand, if Sibley were replaced by somebody more forward
looking—somebody like Oxford Police Chief Thad Carson—her
fortunes would surely improve.

Annie-Fay approached the bar a few minutes after Morris left
the stage, carrying a pair of empty Budweiser bottles. She laid the
bottles on the bar, then signaled H-Man for refills before turning
to me.

"The word's out on you, Rooster. If any of us sees you, we're to
call it in."

"Been there, done that. Me and Deputy Hardin had a bit of a confrontation this afternoon."

"He rough you up?"

I shook my head. "Tyler's a punk, Annie-Fay. You don't lie down, he turns tail."

"What about Sibley?"

"Too many witnesses. This happened out on Highway 7."

Annie-Fay took one of the bottles offered by H-Man and sipped delicately. "Don't sound like you're plannin' to back off."

I shrugged. "Let's talk sex offenders."

"My favorite topic."

I recited the names of the registered offenders given to me by Skid, the viable ones. Annie-Fay was familiar with the entire list, including offenders too old or too sick to commit crimes. She visited their homes occasionally, like many of the deputies, just to let them know the department hadn't forgotten them.

"There's one man, though, who's off-limits." Her smile became suddenly provocative. "That would be a rapist named Mathew Monroe."

"And why is that?"

"Monroe lives with his sister, Alma-Beth Patterson, who works for the County at the Department of Health. My supervisor, Henry Osborne, told me that Alma-Beth's makin' sure her brother rides the straight and narrow. The public has nothing to worry about."

"You believe that?"

"Hell, no."

Blind Mississippi Morris, led by his guitarist, Brad Webb, chose that moment to approach the bar. "Is that you, Rooster-man?"

"It is, Morris. How you been?"

"Still wakin' up on the right side of the grass, Rooster, and still got breath enough in my body to blow my harmonica."

I hugged him, as I always did when he played the club, ignoring the sweat. The man was a national treasure.

"Is it always this slow, Rooster?" Webb asked.

"'Fraid so, and it will be until the killings stop." I gestured to Annie-Fay. "This is Deputy Sheriff Annie-Fay Keefer. You drive drunk in Lafayette County, she'll be the one to lock you up."

H-Man slid two Coronas across the counter, and Greg picked them up. "I look forward to it, ma'am," he announced before heading out to the balcony with his boss and mentor.

As they passed through the doorway, I turned to Annie-Fay. "Tell me about Mathew Monroe."

"Monroe did five years at Parchman for a sexual assault. He cut a deal before trial, Rooster. In return for a nine-year sentence, he admitted to his guilt, a blessing for the victim who would other-wise have to testify. He's still on parole."

"You ever deal with him personally?"

"I stopped him once for running a stop sign. The man had the eyes of a snake and the shit-eating grin of a child who's just pulled the wings off a butterfly. But he was real polite, Rooster. Took his ticket, thanked me, and drove away."

CHAPTER TWENTY-TWO

Annie-Fay excused herself and returned to her husband. I waited until she was seated, then instructed H-Man to charge their tab to my personal account. That done, I let my eyes wander across the club. I was thinking the killer might be in the club right now, but that was unlikely, given the size of the crowd, and I failed to uncover any likely candidates. I did, however, notice Boyd Jessup sitting in the back next to a woman I didn't recognize. A widower with three children, two of them still in school, he'd run with Velvet Hammer in the early days.

Boyd shared a history common to much of the deep South's rural population. His family had share-cropped in Lafayette County for a hundred years before the system vanished in the course of a single generation. Now, at harvest time, instead of whole families, harvesters that can do the work of fifty families move across the fields like alien landing craft in a bad sci-fi movie.

The son of a sharecropper turned out after a final accounting, Boyd was a bricklayer, and a good one. But he'd been struggling for years, every job temporary, the competition for those jobs ferocious, the downtime long enough to make "getting ahead" as unlikely as it had been when the Jessup family chopped cotton. Still, men like Boyd were seasoned survivors. They'd have a vegetable garden off to one side of the house, a chicken coop in back, and maybe a pig they'd been fattening up since early in the spring. They'd hunt and fish as well, with the family eating everything they killed or caught. A buck taken in early fall went a long way to seeing a family through the winter.

I walked over to Boyd's table as Morris sounded the opening notes of "Killing Floor Blues." Boyd smiled as I came up, revealing a missing tooth on the right side of his mouth.

"Evenin', Rooster, how are you gettin' along?"

"Doin' the best I can with the little I have, Boyd."

"Join the club." He gestured to the plump woman sitting alongside him. "This here is Laura-Jane. We got hitched about a month ago. Now, Laura-Jane was brought up in a family of preachers, but I ain't holdin' it agin her. No, sir, I'm tryin' to broaden her horizons by takin' her out to hear some devil's music."

I nodded to Laura-Jane. She was about the same age as Boyd, with dark eyes and short, straight hair that she'd pushed back over her ears.

"How do, Rooster. Hope you're not payin' attention to this old fool. His mouth runs off even when he's not drinkin'."

"Don't worry, Laura-Jane. I've known Boyd too long to be influenced."

Laura-Jane smiled, but her husband spoke up first. "We're off to Texas," he announced. "Ain't no future for the kids here. Laura-Jane's brother works in the frackin' fields, out near Corpus Christi. He says he can get me on with a Danish company by the name of Statoil, so I guess you could say I have officially launched myself into the international marketplace."

Laura-Jane gave Boyd a little shove. "This is Boyd's way of mockin' my brother," she said.

"Swear on the Bible, Rooster, that's just how he talks. Like he's Donald Damn Trump. But I don't mind. I just need me a chance, and I can't find one in these parts."

I didn't have anything to add. The man's reasoning was right on point. The university was the largest employer in northern Mississippi, and by a good margin, but it could in no way accommodate all the Boyd Jessups in Lafayette County.

"Boyd, do you mind if I ask you a question?"

"Fire away."

"You ever hear of a man named Gilmore Ellerbee?"

Laura-Jane raised a hand. "Sneak Ellerbee? Sure have."

"You said, 'Sneak'?"

"That's the name he goes by, and you can trust me on this. The name fits the man, and has since the man was a boy. My middle girl was at the high school with Sneak. He was the kind of creep, if you saw him comin', you moved on before he got to you. Ain't nobody I know was surprised when he got sent off to prison for rapin' that woman."

"You see him recently?"

"Matter of fact, I did. Maybe a week ago, at the Package Store in Water Mill. Loadin' up on cheap bourbon."

"You sure, Laura-Jane?"

"Sure enough to do my browsin' on the other side of the store."

CHAPTER TWENTY-THREE

Laura-Jane had nothing to add. She didn't know where Ellerbee lived or how he passed his days. She only knew that men like Ellerbee were fated to spend most of their lives in prison, and avoiding them was her life's ambition. I listened to her for a few minutes, until she had no more to say. Then I thanked her before returning to my little corner at the end of the bar. Twenty minutes later, as Morris concluded his second set, Barbara Michael walked into the club. Somehow, my perverted mind flashed back to Vera Califano, the first time I'd seen her. Vera was standing out on the Square, microphone in hand, looking so young and eager that I was instantly drawn to her. Only later, in bits and pieces, did I discover her charmed life. Vera had grown up in the suburbs of Chicago, her father a dentist and her mother a high school teacher. She'd never been sick a day in her life and had never held a job before graduating college. Her reward upon graduation was a spanking-new Toyota Rav-4, which she still drove, and she'd emerged from college debt-free, in contrast to former classmates who struggled to make their loan payments.

Barbara's face spoke to a different set of circumstances. Raised after her mother's passing by a father who drove an eighteen-wheel-er cross-country, life hadn't offered Barbara Michael a whole lot of freebies. Hers was a bootstrap childhood, and it showed in the intensity of her gaze and the shallow laugh-lines extending from the corners of her eyes. She'd earned her body, too, which could only be described as sleek. Without doubt, she'd outlast me at any competition requiring cardiovascular fitness. I'd seen—or heard, really—Barbara conduct three classes in a row, her voice barely straining as she instructed her students.

Barbara and I had already begun to drift apart, the parting nearly complete, before Vera came on the scene. Oddly, though we remained friends at the gym and on horseback, neither of us chose to speak about the end of the affair. Still, I definitely felt some measure of regret, especially after I realized that Oxford was only the first stop on the Califano Express. Vera was going places, and I would not go with her.

Barbara Michael's eyes were the soft brown of freshly turned earth. They fastened on me as she approached, a half smile playing on her full mouth. I let my eyes wander over her outfit, as I was surely meant to do. Barbara wore jeans and a red-and-white western shirt, its top buttons open, over an Oxford Workouts T-shirt. A black leather vest with silver buckles at the hem completed the ensemble.

"You look great," I said. "What are you drinkin'?"

"An old-fashioned."

"And the whiskey?"

"Jameson."

When H-Man brought her drink, Barbara sipped and sighed. "I needed that, Rooster. I've been half the night with my accountant, and the news . . . the news ain't good."

I gestured to the fifteen people in the room. That was another thing about Oxford after the killings began. Even those brave enough to venture out generally went home early.

"Join the club."

"But you're opening a new restaurant. You're expanding."

"Only because I signed a contract before the killings began."

Barbara raised her glass: "Here's to luck. Good, bad, or indifferent, if you wait long enough, it's bound to turn."

"Amen."

We chatted for the next few minutes about mutual friends, the Crays, a couple now in the middle of a divorce. Though both had cheated, somehow their friends had formed two camps. Either Hal Cray or Edna Cray was despicable, there was no middle ground. Ordinarily, neither of us would care much one way or the other, but the Crays had three children, the oldest all of eight, and they were being torn apart by a custody suit made extra vicious by each side having plenty of ammunition.

From the Crays, we turned to our horses, Little Harry and Scarlet, and from there to the fortunes of the Ole Miss Rebels. We were still at it, engaged in polite conversation, when Mississippi Morris finished his last set and H-Man called for a last round. Not one of the ten or so patrons still in attendance heeded my bartender's call. This was the middle of the week. Time to pack it in. I paid

Morris off a few minutes later, the amount a good deal less than he deserved. But that was the nature of the biz, and we both knew it. He thanked me, ditto for Brad Webb, and the pair returned to the road. Barbara stayed close, and I found myself searching for a polite way to invite her upstairs without my lecherous intentions becoming too obvious when she abruptly changed the subject.

"Rosie Bell took my evening class in step aerobics and we had a talk afterward," she informed me. "She told me you're looking for Marie's killer on your own, just like I thought."

"Not just Marie's, Barbara."

"But you're lookin' for this maniac on your own?" She waited for me to nod, then said, "Rosie's worried. What if the killer sees you coming? Do you really think he'd hesitate to kill you?"

"Probably not . . ."

"Then why are you doin' this? You're a successful businessman, for God's sake. Why do you have to play Lone Ranger?"

"The Lone Ranger? No, no. The Lone Ranger was a damn Yankee. I'd sooner be Silver."

"Silver?"

"Silver was the Lone Ranger's horse."

My pitiful attempt at humor fell as flat as Wile E. Coyote after a thousand-foot drop onto the desert floor. "Maybe I'm upset because hard-working women like you have to live behind locked doors and windows but still don't feel safe. Maybe I have to be out there because I don't know who's next. You? Rosie? One of them."

I gestured to the women in the room, servers and customers, but Barbara wasn't buying my argument.

"Bullshit, Rooster. You like to live dangerously. You like to be out there, testing the edge of the razor."

"Is that an accusation?"

"Only if thinking you're invincible is a character flaw."

"You mean it's not like I was getting paid?"

"I mean it's not like you're competent or that you have backup. Most criminals think twice about murdering a cop, but that doesn't apply to you. Always remembering, of course, that the man who slaughtered those women has nothing to lose." She gave me a chance to consider a set of facts I couldn't deny, then added, "Rosie's certain the state cops will take over the investigation within a few days, a week at most. Bringing all their resources with them. There's just no reason to risk your life."

"Skid Tisdale gave me the identical lecture on Sunday."

"But you didn't listen."

I tried to make a joke of my answer. "Actually, I'm usin' myself as bait. Come and get me before I find you."

Barbara leaned forward and kissed me softly on the cheek. "I have to leave," she said. "I've got an early class tomorrow."

I wanted to put my arm around her, wanted to draw her in, even knowing it was the worst move on the board. In my life, women have always done the choosing, starting with Rosie Bell. I watched Barbara stride across the room and head down the stairs. I was thinking, as I listened to her footsteps, that I should have described my progress thus far, or declared that finding a man named Gilmore Ellerbee would be a positive contribution to the welfare of Lafayette County, even if he had nothing to do with the killings. Instead, I turned to Aaron Cloninger, the club's manager. I told him to lock up when he was through, then headed for my apartment.

CHAPTER TWENTY-FOUR

I went online first, to check my emails. Among the usual collection of spam ads and routine notices, I found an email from Vera Califano, sent that afternoon. She missed me terribly but was busy, busy, busy. The network expected her to work two stories a day, covering fires and murders. Newbies, of course, had to prove themselves, and Vera intended to "exceed expectations." She used the word "indispensable" three times but never said "see you soon."

After a few minutes, I turned away from the computer and dialed Skid Tisdale's cell number. He answered on the third ring, his voice sounding over the blare of an air horn and the hum of traffic.

"Detective Tisdale," he said.

"Detective Feathers," I replied.

"Ah, Rooster. I thought it might be this asshole lieutenant who's commanding the late tour. So, what's doin'?"

I'd caught Skid sober after midnight, a rare occurrence for which I was grateful. "Ellerbee's in the county," I said. "I've got two people who've seen him going about his business."

"Which is what?"

"That I can't say for sure, but the way I figure, if he was treading the straight and narrow, he would have registered." I changed the subject abruptly, a cop trick Skid had used on me in the past. "What do you know about meth labs out in the county?"

"The county ain't my province, Rooster, but as long as you're askin', there's a few labs out there runnin' wide open. I spoke to my daddy the other days. He says that in his day they was growin' weed mostly or runnin' whiskey stills. Guess times have changed."

"And so has the money, Skid. The pot of gold just keeps on growin'. You have any idea who's runnin' the show?"

"The deputies I know at the jail won't talk about drugs. I believe they're most likely under orders to keep their mouths shut. But I did get this from an informant I've been cultivating for a year. The Henchmen run the labs and make deliveries. They're the face of the operation."

"All right, thanks. But I need you to do me a favor."

"For you, Rooster, anything that doesn't interfere with my immediate goal."

"Which is?"

"A place on my girlfriend's couch, with my right arm around her shoulder and two margaritas sitting on the coffee table in front of us."

Somehow, I wasn't surprised. "Didn't you tell me that you have connections at Parchman?"

"No bosom buddies, Rooster, but there's a woman supervisor who's civil and helpful. That's a rare combination in the world of penology. Why do you ask?"

Scott Michael

"There's another offender on your list, Mathew Monroe. He and Ellerbee were inside at the same time. Can you find out if they knew each other?"

"I can ask." Skid breathed into the phone for a moment. "Look, Rooster, if you have anything solid, you should turn it over to me."

At that point, I might have told him about the little progression I'd worked out, from Sibley to Ink to Ellerbee. I didn't.

"I have nothing, nothing at all, linking Ellerbee to the killings. And I haven't found him yet, either. When I accomplish any one of those goals, you'll be the first to know."

I left Skid to his own devices at that point and made another call, this one to Dr. Ralph Kowalchek. I wanted to ask him about serial killer teams, if they existed, but his cell phone went directly to voice mail. I'd catch him in the morning.

I don't sleep much on the best of days, and that night was no exception. I drifted off somewhere close to one o'clock and woke up at five. A pot of coffee and a couple of fried eggs with toast carried me through to six thirty when I called Professor Ralph Kowalchek.

"Tell me you have a suspect," he demanded.

"More like a person of interest."

I described Sneak Ellerbee's background as it was described to me, then jumped to the sightings and what these witnesses had to say about Ellerbee's character. I admitted, too, that the evidence was thin. Ellerbee had committed a rape, yes, but there were other rapists living in the county, and a lot more if you included the surrounding counties.

"What about violence, Rooster?" Kowalchek asked. "Did Ellerbee employ excessive violence when he committed the rape that sent him to prison? Was the attack sadistic?"

"I don't know," I admitted, "but a woman I ran into, Marie Blocker's sister, claims that Ellerbee's a total creep and no woman would stop her car for him. I spoke to other people who knew him, and that kind of thinking is pretty much the consensus."

I carried the phone over to a Motörhead poster on my wall. A wolf stared out at me, its fur and fangs bloody. Two metal tusks grew out of its lower jaw. Tipped in blood, they curved upward like scimitars.

"I have reason to suspect that Ellerbee's involved in some other scheme, probably connected to the meth trade, and maybe that's why he didn't register. But I only called to ask a simple question. I want to know if serial killers ever work in pairs."

"The simple answer is yes. Lawrence Bittaker and Roy Norris, Leonard Lake and Charles Ng. The Hillside Strangler turned out to be two men, Kenneth Bianchi and Angelo Buono. If you were more experienced, of course, you could have answered that question in under a minute by going online."

I ignored the last part. "If the simple answer is yes, what's the complicated answer?"

"All serial killers are dangerous, obviously, but now we have a pair operating as a team. Your death, of course, wouldn't trouble them in the slightest. If they see you coming, which they almost certainly will as you stumble along, they'll have plenty of time to plan your elimination. Especially if they conclude that you're not backed up by a police agency of some kind." He hesitated for just a moment before adding, "Death is forever, my friend. Something you might want to think about."

I took that happy thought to heart as I next dialed Rosie Bell. I expected the same lecture, but Rosie delivered good news, at least from her point of view. Bill Rowan, Oxford's mayor, had already spoken to Governor Malcolm Reed. Rowan had suggested a joint task force, with the Department of Public Safety in overall charge, and Reed had agreed. He would get back to Rowan within twenty-four hours with a timetable.

"The task force should be up and running by the beginning of next week," Rosie told me. "At that point, you're required to hand over any pertinent information in your possession and get out of the way."

"You spoke to the mayor about me?"

"And Thad Carson, too. Nobody's faultin' you, Rooster, and right now you're not impeding an investigation. But once the task force gets rollin', they want you in Oxford minding your own business."

CHAPTER TWENTY-FIVE

I was driving my pickup because the weatherwoman on WLOX was predicting afternoon thunderstorms. A .45 caliber semiautomatic lay on the seat beside me, proof that I wasn't altogether crazy. As I drove, I recalled a day on the football field at Northwest Community, a day with our season on the line. I was so eager for the first snap that I couldn't stand still. The opposition's offense included a 230-pound running back who loved contact. He ran over you, not around you. As for me, I wanted the contact as much as he did. As Mike Tyson once said, "Y'all come get some."

Without my GPS, I might never have found Mathew Monroe's home. My route took me north on Highway 7 into Marshall County, then southwest on 310, then onto a totally unfamiliar series of back roads that finally crossed a dirt road that wound deep into a stretch of forested state land. Just as Ink's home was tucked away in the backwoods, Monroe's home was at the end of that road, and most likely for the same reason. Criminals seek privacy.

As I pulled to a stop at the end of the road, I reminded myself that three questions remained to be answered: how the victims were targeted, how they were taken, and the place they were taken to. The last was made especially important because I knew that place wasn't Mathew Monroe's home before I stepped out of the pickup.

The two-story house before me was decently kept, and there was no basement to house a convenient dungeon. What's more, a woman stood outside spraying water on a flowerbed located a few yards from an old Lincoln with badly worn springs. Around thirty years old, she was slim and dark haired and apparently unafraid. Her dark eyes observed me closely and without a trace of panic.

"How you doin' this mornin'?" I stopped ten feet away from her. "The name's Rooster Feathers, and I apologize for interruptin' your morning."

"That's all right. I wasn't up to much anyway." She shut off the hose and dropped it. "Name's Alma-Beth Patterson."

"Patterson? I believe my GPS unit has failed me. I'm lookin' for a man named Mathew Monroe."

"That would be my brother." Alma-Beth smiled for the first time, a quick flash of small white teeth. "Monroe ain't home just now, but it's sure hot out here and I've got a pitcher of sun-brewed tea in my fridge. Why don't you grab a little shade while I fetch us both a glass?"

I nodded agreement, then watched her sashay into the house. She took her time about it, as if she hadn't a care in the world, as if she didn't mean to alert her brother, who might or might not be at home. But she was right about it being hot, and I took her advice, thinking as I stepped into the full shade beneath a handy oak that she hadn't inquired into my business with her brother.

I recalled once asking Skid why suspects talked to him instead of demanding a lawyer. The answer, he told me, varied from man to man, but most commonly they just wanted to know how much the cops had on them. Were the detectives close or just sniffing around? Did they have eyewitnesses, fingerprints, DNA? Was there a snitch out there, pointing the finger?

Alma-Beth reappeared a few minutes later, bearing two glasses on a round Coca-Cola tray. I accepted one and took a more-or-less mandatory sip. Sweetened with honey, the tea was excellent.

"So, Rooster, if I'm not bein' too bold, tell me what you want with my little brother? I'm assumin' you're not police."

"No, ma'am, not a cop. I'm a private investigator hired by the Blocker family to investigate the death of their daughter. If you remember, Marie Blocker was slaughtered."

I left it like that, with just the one word—slaughtered—hanging out there like a wriggling night crawler on the end of a hook. Alma-Beth didn't even blink.

"I believe you're diggin' in the wrong patch if you think my brother had a part to play in that nasty business. The sheriff's deputies are out here every other day, one or another of 'em, 'specially since them killings started. Monroe can't hardly move without somebody comin' round to check on him."

"So, where is he now?"

Alma-Beth replied quickly, and I was certain she'd anticipated the question. That was all right, too. "Monroe's over to his parole officer, most likely peein' in a cup."

"He's on parole?"

A sudden gust of wind passed through the tops of the trees in the surrounding forest, reminding me of just how isolated we were. Alma-Beth shivered and hugged her arms to her chest. Her tiny giggle seemed genuine, but her eyes were dying out, the embers fading.

"Now, I believe you're deceivin' me." She was smiling now. "I believe you already know the answer to that question."

I returned her smile. "Well, you got me there. Say, you wouldn't know a man named Sneak Ellerbee, would you? Sneak and your brother were imprisoned about the same time at Parchman, and I was wonderin' if they knew each other on the inside."

"Never heard of a Sneak Ellerbee."

"Well, let me show you his picture. Maybe you've seen him without knowin' his name." As I reached into my pocket, I glimpsed a shadow move behind a curtain on the second floor. I didn't react. "See, Ellerbee's the man I'm really after, not your brother. I was just hopin' they ran into each other."

Alma-Beth took the photo and gave it a long look before shaking her head. "Nope, don't recognize him." Then she hesitated for a moment before asking a question. "Do you think this is the man who's been killin' those women?"

"I wouldn't go that far, but two people have seen him, so I know he's in the county and I mean to run him down. I mean to run him down and ask him that very question."

"It's a free country, Rooster, and you can ask whatever you want. But I can tell you without any doubt that my brother was sittin' at home on the night Marie Blocker disappeared. Reason I know is because the station we was watchin' issued an Amber Alert. I couldn't believe it, not another one, and I recall lookin' over at Monroe and askin', 'When is this gonna end?'"

I left Alma-Beth standing in her yard as I drove off, along a badly maintained dirt road cratered with muddy potholes. Alma-Beth's lie, that deputies regularly monitored her brother, didn't trouble me all that much. She might have lied for any number of reasons. And she hadn't slipped up when I told her that I knew Sneak and Monroe had been in Parchman at the same time. Her eyes didn't narrow with suspicion or widen in surprise. I'd been expecting her to become angry at some point. Who was I, not even a cop, to question her about her brother? Or to imply that he killed for fun? But Alma-Beth hadn't become angry, most likely because she'd been warned about me and had time to arrange her answers. Still, that last question, when she asked me if I thought Ellerbee was the killer, betrayed an obvious concern.

If my asking whether Ellerbee and her brother knew each other at Parchman set her off, she'd reacted to a bluff. I'd yet to hear from Skid, and Parchman was an enormous prison with thousands of prisoners. But Sneak and Monroe were two good-old-boy rapists from Lafayette County, and there was an excellent chance they'd known each other, at least as acquaintances, before they went to prison. The county has exactly one lower elementary school, one higher elementary school, one middle school, and one high school. Alma-Beth was perhaps thirty. Sneak was twenty-five. I didn't know Monroe's age, but Alma-Beth had referred to him as her younger brother, so he had to fit in somewhere.

From Ink to Ellerbee to Monroe to Price Sibley. The connections were too strong to deny. But whatever I might think of Ellerbee and Monroe, I couldn't imagine Sibley or Ink snatching women off the street. And I still hadn't answered any one of the three vital questions. I didn't know how the victims were targeted, how they were taken, or where they were kept before they were finally murdered.

I was too lost in thought by then to be truly aware of the road ahead, despite its many hazards, and it was only by luck, good and bad, that I ran into a pair of these hazards at the same time. First, my left front wheel dropped into one of the road's deeper potholes and the truck dipped sharply on the driver's side. A second later, a bullet crashed through the windshield, destroying the rearview mirror as it passed over my right shoulder. The unmistakable crack of a rifle followed. I was under attack.

I slammed on the brakes just in time to avoid a second attempt on my life. This time the bullet kicked up dirt on the road fifteen feet in front of the truck. My brain screamed at me: do something, do something, do something. The demand didn't leave a lot of room for the nature of that something, but my instincts took over. I snatched up the .45, opened the door, and rolled onto the dirt as a third round cut through the windshield. This time I registered a muzzle flash in the trees on the far side of the road about fifty yards ahead.

I fired off three quick shots in the sniper's general direction as I crossed the road and flung myself into a thicket of young maples that reached out to scratch my face and arms. The pain was entirely welcome, and I barely reacted when another shot rang out. The shooter was a hundred yards away, firing into a dense forest. The odds against a bullet missing every tree trunk between us were too high to calculate.

Rifles are powerful weapons, much more powerful than handguns, but hard to wield in a dense forest. You can't butt them up against your shoulder and still swing the weapon, not if you're also moving. You have to shoot from the hip, and that's a skill few men have mastered, or even tried to master. I had the advantage here and I started forward, moving from tree to tree, stopping to listen, looking for any movement in the deeper shadows. I didn't know who tried to ambush me—Sneak, Monroe, or even Alma-Beth— and I didn't care. I only knew that if I got my hands on whoever it was, I'd resolve a lot of questions in a big hurry.

Suddenly, off in the distance, I heard a distinct hum that I couldn't place. It disappeared so fast I couldn't be sure I'd heard it at all. But then I heard something else, the angry chuck-chuck-chuck of a red squirrel, followed by the call of a songbird. Both sounds came from directly ahead of me. The shooter had, at the very least, changed positions.

I maintained caution, though I moved a little faster, until I finally discovered a marshy logging road marked with the wide tire tracks of an ATV. For a minute I stood there, certain the trail, if I followed it, would lead back to Monroe's house. I won't say I wasn't tempted, but the opportunities for an ambush were too great. I'd been saved by a pothole, a form of salvation unlikely to occur twice in the same day. I went back to my truck.

The windshield was a spider's web of intersecting cracks that spread from a pair of small holes, and the rearview mirror was gone, sheared off at the base. One of the bullets had impacted the seat in the back of the crew cab. The other had passed through the small rear window. I had to brush glass off the seat before I got into the pickup and started the engine. Though I felt a need to get out of there, I left the transmission in park until my heart finally slowed. Then I smiled, thinking of how much I'd enjoy describing my afternoon to Skid. Say over a double bourbon and a thick steak. Funny thing about life, the closer you come to an abrupt end, the better it gets.

CHAPTER TWENTY-SIX

In light of the afternoon's thunderstorms, now passed, and the generally wet conditions—raindrops still dripped from the trees on the edge of the yard—Mathew Monroe dumped a good four ounces of kerosene on the charcoal briquettes before lighting them. The flames shot up eight feet when he threw in a match and stepped back, pleased with the effect. Overhead, ragged black clouds drifted to the south, while an intermittent breeze, still mild for now, hinted at cooler weather. The October heat wave had ended.

Monroe watched the flames slowly die, thinking what didn't die was the flame in his gut. They'd dumped Marie Blocker three days ago, and the need had already begun to swell. Within a week he'd be on fire, from toes to nose, with the heart of the inferno concentrated about midway.

What to do? Monroe needed to get out of Dodge, especially with a Wyatt Earp named Rooster Feathers riding the fucking range. But that would entail a long, long delay before he snatched another toy off the street. Could he bear it? Because the temptation, when the hunger came hard upon him, was to throw caution to the wind and grab the first bitch that took his fancy. He was too smart for that, way too smart. Right?

Alma-Beth came out of the house as Monroe considered his options. She carried a plate of raw chicken legs and a bowl of homemade BBQ sauce on the same Coca-Cola tray she'd used to carry Rooster's iced tea earlier in the day. As she started across the yard, the sound of approaching vehicles brought her to a halt. Motorcycles, more than one, gearing down as they negotiated a muddy road made even muddier by the afternoon rains.

"Monroe?"

"What you want, Alma-Beth?"

"You hear that?"

Monroe cupped his ear, then turned to his sister and smiled. "That'd be Ink, I expect. Come to frighten me."

"Are you scared?"

"Can't say that I am, girl. Can't say that I am."

Ink made a grand entrance. His van, first, then six motorcycles, two abreast. The van drove straight onto the yard and stopped with its nose facing Monroe, twenty feet away. The bikes fanned out on either side of the van, also facing Mathew Monroe. Each of the riders was equipped with a long gun, a rifle, or a shotgun, jammed into a leather scabbard. Each wore the colors of the Henchmen.

The display was impressive, and Monroe had to admit it, but patience was a game Monroe had learned to play in prison. He didn't intend to challenge Ink or his boys, and he had no illusions. Ink had only to give the word, and he, Mathew Monroe, would die on the spot. Alma-Beth, too.

The hydraulic ramp on the back of the van slowly unfolded until the lip of the ramp hit the ground. Then the rear doors opened, banging against the ramp's support, and Ink descended in a motorized wheelchair. He zipped around the side of the van, the chair bouncing on the uneven turf, and came to within ten feet of Monroe. Close enough, what with the tattoos, to appear somewhat menacing, despite the useless legs.

Alma-Beth was first to speak. "I'm afraid my brother's forgot his manners, Ink, so I'll say good evenin' for him. How you doin' tonight?"

"How you think, Alma-Beth, havin' to drive all the way out here when I got better things to do?"

In fact, Ink's place, in the county's southeastern corner, was about as far away from Sardis Lake as you could get and still be in Lafayette County. Which was the way Ink wanted it, a long-distance relationship, just in case some cop took Sneak down on his way to Memphis. The stakes were big now and getting bigger every day.

"If you ain't here on a social visit, Ink," Monroe said, "then exactly why did you come?"

"I come because I had me a visitor couple days ago. Man named Rooster Feathers, owns that blues club down to Oxford. Did you happen to run into him?"

Monroe shook his head. "The blues don't interest me all that much. I prefer my music on the more optimistic side. But I did hear of the man and his club."

"What about Sneak?"

"Can't speak for him."

"And he ain't here?"

"He's out drivin'."

Alma-Beth broke in. "That's what he does. Sneak, I mean. The boy spends most of his life behind the wheel."

Ink glanced at the Lincoln parked twenty feet away, then turned back to Monroe. "Monroe, you did say you never met this man? Rooster Feathers?"

"Never laid eyes on him, to my knowledge."

"Well, thing about Rooster, he's pretty tough. You know what they say, it ain't the size of the dog in the fight, it's the size of the fight in the dog? You ever hear that one?"

Monroe's eyes were fixed on Ink's, neither man willing to look away. The confrontation had become personal. Mathew Monroe didn't like jumping through hoops, though he'd jumped through many thousands on behalf of the screws at Parchman. He'd had to take it then and he had to take it now, given Ink's escort. But all things come to he who waits.

"I've heard that said a time or two, Ink, about the dogs."

"That's good because Rooster Feathers? Well let's just say he's a damn big dog and he's got about as much fight in him as any man I know. You tangle with Rooster, he's just gonna keep on comin' till you near put him in the ground. Plus, the man headed up Velvet Hammer awhile back, so he's got plenty of backup if he needs it. But that ain't the worst. No, the worst is that Rooster thinks he's doin' the Lord's work, routin' out the evildoers amongst us. Man like that can't be discouraged."

Ink finally looked away, glancing at his men from right to left, as if measuring their value.

"I don't mean to be disrespectful," Alma-Beth said, "but I don't understand how this changes what we're doin' together."

Though Ink would have liked to roar out his response, he didn't have the lung power and he went the other way. He lowered his voice, forcing Monroe to lean forward.

"Rooster come to me a couple days ago. Told me that he was a private investigator and he was investigatin' the death of Terri Blocker. You know who that is, Monroe? Terri Blocker?"

"One of those women who disappeared. The deputies found her dead a few days ago."

"That's exactly right. Now I told Rooster I didn't know nothin' 'bout that. Told 'em I hadn't even heard a rumor. Told him if I heard anything, even a word, I'd let him know. Then, just about the time he's getting' ready to leave, he pulls out a mug shot and asks me if I recognize the man in the photo. You know who that man was?"

"Me?"

"Not you, Monroe. Sneak. He showed me Sneak's photo. Now, why would Rooster have that mug shot, which he could only have gotten from the cops? Was Sneak involved in kidnappin' those women? I mean, if the man's always out drivin', like Alma-Beth said, he might be doin' anything. But maybe it doesn't matter, because like I said, Rooster's lookin' for Sneak, and he ain't the type to give up."

Monroe recognized the invitation. Sell out your partner, sacrifice him to the greater good. Rooster was looking for Ellerbee and wouldn't stop. Eliminating Ellerbee would eliminate a link in the chain connecting the man to Monroe, Ink, and Sibley. Talk about a fool's errand. If you hid the body, Rooster would be lookin' forever.

"Ink," Monroe said, "I didn't have nothin' to do with those women, and I don't believe my partner did either, but . . ."

"Shut the fuck up, Monroe, and listen close. Just now, I'm decidin' whether or not y'all are jeopardizing my operation. And it ain't only me. There's men I have to answer to, investors you might call 'em, who put up a lot of money to get us goin'."

Ink didn't use Price Sibley's name, but Monroe understood well enough. And he also realized that Rooster Feathers had engineered this confrontation. It came as a revelation and stirred up a wave of hatred that burned in his throat. If Ink knew about Rooster's visit this morning, Mathew Monroe and his sister would already be dead.

"This conversation we're havin, Ink? I feel it ain't right. It's disrespectful. You hired me and Sneak to do a job, and we've done it without a single hitch. Now you're half-accusin' me of bein' some kind of serial killer. And you're doin' it in front of my sister."

Ink's eyes, which weren't all that wide open to begin with, narrowed further. "You don't like workin' for me? You wanna go your own way?"

"Not really, but you hired me, Ink, and I guess you can fire me. I wouldn't hold it against ya."

"I'm glad to hear that, Monroe. But y'all have a job comin' up tomorrow night. You remember, right?"

"I do."

"Well, if I was you and Sneak, I wouldn't be late with the delivery."

Monroe didn't challenge the threat. Instead, he simply watched as Ink climbed the ramp, as the doors closed, as the ramp pulled back into the frame, as the van and its motorcycle escort drove away. When he could no longer hear them, he turned to the pile of smoldering coals. As he spread the briquettes out until they covered the bottom of the grill, Sneak Ellerbee stepped out of the woods, rifle in hand. Sneak nodded to Alma-Beth before speaking.

"You know I couldn't take all of 'em out, right? If they made a move on ya?"

Monroe thought for a moment, then said, "But you could have taken out Ink? You could have pushed the back of his head through his eye sockets?"

"I could have, and easy, too, the man bein' in that chair and all."

"Well, that's enough, Sneak. That's enough for me."

CHAPTER TWENTY-SEVEN

Skid filled in another piece of the puzzle when I met him at Rosie's on Tuesday morning. He was contemplating Rosie's surefire hangover cure when I walked in, a banana milkshake laced with a raw egg and plenty of hot sauce. Although Skid was too polite to refuse (and maybe a little too sick), he couldn't quite bring himself to touch the glass, not with the egg white floating on top. He looked up at me, his expression vaguely hopeful. Maybe my appearance would distract Rosie long enough for him to dump the concoction in the sink.

"Now, Skid, you drink that," Rosie said, dashing all hope. "And maybe next time you'll stop drinkin' before you kill another few million brain cells."

"You ever take this cure, Rooster?" he asked.

"I have, and I'll tell ya, I vomited so long and hard I forgot all about my headache."

Rosie's tone foreclosed a negative response. "Take yourself to the kitchen, Rooster, and pour yourself a cup of coffee. Have a biscuit, too."

I did as she ordered. Rosie and Skid were great friends, and she'd already agreed to support him for chief should Thad Carson move on. He'd drink the cure because it would please her, though it wouldn't do him the slightest bit of good. Inside the kitchen, I buttered a biscuit, added a dollop of Rosie's homemade blackberry jam, and chewed thoughtfully until I heard Skid cry out.

"Oh, my God. Oh, my God."

Probably the hot sauce.

I returned to the living room a few minutes later and took a seat in an armchair. At that point, I might have reported the attempt on my life. I didn't, instead directing my question to Rosie.

"Tell me what's up with Governor Reed? Are we still on schedule?"

"Just a little hitch, Rooster. Thad Carson's pitching a fit. According to Thad, if the state police make an arrest, the Public Safety Commissioner will claim the credit. Likewise for Governor Reed. They'll portray the Oxford PD as a bunch of hicks who couldn't find a lost cat. As we all know, Thad's set on runnin' for sheriff. That won't happen if people think he's incompetent."

Skid took a long pull at a mug of coffee near his elbow. "That's true," he said, "but so what? Nobody expects politicians to play fair, and gettin' a serial killer off the street has to come first. On the other hand, if we could resolve this on our own?" He looked directly at me, his expression intense, despite the vein-streaked eyes. "Let's just say there'd be a feather for every cap: mine, Carson's, Rowan's, even Rooster's. And by the way, Rooster, you were a hundred percent right. I called down to Parchman. Monroe and Ellerbee were cellmates for almost two years."

I thought of Ralph Kowalchek's improvised profile. In his opinion, the kidnappings and the murders and everything that happened in between were the product of long-term planning fueled by intense fantasies. Sneak and Monroe in the same cell, passing those long nights by themselves? Surely they'd fueled each other's obscene desires. Surely they'd inspired each other. What they hadn't done, of course, not even for a split second, is reflect on the humanity of their victims.

Skid's news came too late to be helpful. Without answering any of the three main questions, I'd already put Monroe and Sneak together. My problem was that I had no idea what to do next, except wait to discover what—if anything—fell out of the tree I'd been shaking for the past few days.

Waiting and hoping were not my strong points. Maybe that's why I eventually focused on the third question. Where were the victims taken? If I was right about Monroe and Sneak, I couldn't imagine their dungeon to be all that far from their home. They'd want to keep their sex toys handy, in case they felt a sudden need. But there were thousands of camps around Sardis Lake, including many that were rarely used and hundreds that had been abandoned for decades. Once deer and duck seasons got under way, the area would be swarming with hunters. For now, the forests were pretty much deserted.

* * *

I spent most of the afternoon in the office because I had an unusual deal with Paul Baddour, my contractor. I paid the costs of the materials, but he did the purchasing. The deal was good for me, but it depended on the honesty of the vendors who sold the material and my careful scrutiny of each and every expense. Early on, I'd visited the major vendors, introducing myself as I made two things clear. I'd be the one signing checks, and I could change vendors at will. I worked out discount rates, demanded price sheets for every manufacturer, and checked every expense above twenty-five dollars against those price sheets. The scrutiny had paid off more than once, but it was time consuming and I'd been putting the job off for the past two weeks.

Three hours later, around dinner time, I headed down to the club where I found Marty Martin and a man called Rocky at the bar. Both had ridden with me when Velvet Hammer provided event security.

Marty Martin was Marty Martin's real name, the name on his birth certificate, and too good to change. Rocky was in his twenties when he earned his street name, a product of his career in the ring. The man trained hard and fought often but lacked speed and talent. Five years later, when he retired with a 9–20 record, his sole claim to fame was that he'd never been knocked down.

I was glad to see them, as I was always glad when old friends showed up. We exchanged manly hugs and fist bumps, and I announced that I'd buy the next round. Then I introduced the subject of Ink Howard. I didn't have to take it further. Both knew of the meth labs and Ink's involvement with them. The Henchmen were there to protect the operation and arrange transportation to market, but they definitely had partners. One of them, according to the story going around, was Sheriff Price Sibley.

"Ink came to me about six months ago," Marty told us. "He wanted me to mule shipments into Memphis." Marty Martin stood a couple of inches taller than me but didn't weigh more than 190 pounds. The man was all whipcord, with deep lines on the side of his face and a sprinkling of old acne scars running beneath his eyes. He had a reputation for being steady, quiet, and reliable.

Rocky was Marty Martin's polar opposite. All torso, he had enormous shoulders and a belly to go with them. His head was shaved so close that his scalp gleamed, but his thick beard reached to the top of his chest. I'd been nervous with Rocky from the beginning. As an employee, the man was reliable enough, but I sensed that he could cross lines I didn't want my employees to cross. Then I discovered that he was making collections for a Memphis loan shark.

I called Rocky right after I found out, and we met in a ratty bar near Clarksdale. This was Rocky's home turf, and I was careful not to insult the man. Velvet Hammer provided security for serious people, I explained. These serious people liked the colorful display we put on, what with the choppers and Velvet Hammer colors on our leather vests. But they also expected us to be respectable, if not actually tame.

"I'm not makin' any judgments, Rocky, and I'm not tellin' you what to do. But I can't have you arrested for breakin' some mark's legs, either. Call me a pussy, but I have an image to protect."

The choice was no choice at all for Rocky. His loan shark provided steady work. I called him, at most, once a month. We shook hands, went our separate ways, and remained friendly whenever we met.

"Why didn't he use one of the Henchmen?" Rocky wanted to know. "They'd jump at the chance."

The answer seemed obvious to me, though I kept my opinion to myself. Protected by Sibley, Ink's meth labs operated freely inside Lafayette County. Only when the drugs left the county, when they were on their way to Memphis, running through Tate and Desoto Counties, did any serious threat exist. Ink didn't want anyone close to him arrested. If someone had to go, best to keep him at a distance. Call it plausible denial.

"The man pressed me pretty hard, like I was supposed to be intimidated," Marty Martin explained, "but I refused. See, most of my life, I about had nothin', my parents bein' drunks like they were. But I just got married, and now I have a stepson and a stepdaughter. They're good kids, the both of 'em, and Hailey's a good woman. I don't wanna do nothin' to mess 'em up. They deserve better."

I turned the conversation to Monroe and Sneak at that point. Both knew Monroe, but neither had ever heard of Sneak Ellerbee.

"Reason I'm askin'," I said, "is because I think one or the other is mulin' for Ink. I also think these two boys are responsible for the killings. I'm talkin' about the women: Marie Blocker, Terri Crawford, Sonya Sanchez, Cary Thompson, Tanesha Brown, and Janice Coulter. You boys listenin' yet? Because there may come a time when I need some help."

Kirk Smithhart and his band were in the house that night. Smithhart was a killer guitarist whose music edged closer to rock than to traditional blues. Like Eric Gales, he could bring an audience to its feet yet still amaze you with his technical skills. In fact, I would have had a hard time choosing between the two, even if I was stupid enough to make the attempt.

Kirk began his set with an instrumental, "Sleepwalk." He eased into the simple melody, drawing out its seductive qualities, his tone so insinuating it raised the hairs on the back of my neck. This was how you wanted your lover to call you into the bedroom. But I had no real appetite for music that night. I couldn't keep my mind off the mess I'd so willingly embraced, and my attention continued to jump from Ink to Sneak to Monroe to Price Sibley. I gained no insights, only sensed that some part of my brain was sorting the bits and pieces, fitting them together, taking them apart, looking for something I'd missed, a conclusion I'd failed to reach.

I finally went upstairs about nine o'clock, to do exactly what, I couldn't say. Then Annie-Fay Keefer phoned. "We made an arrest tonight," she told me, "in the killing of Janice Coulter. A drifter named Jake Creel."

"Do you think he actually did it?"

"Well, I'm not usually given to rush decisions, but you might take a second to consider this part. First, Jake Creel's been committed three times because of mental illness. Second, he finally signed a confession after a fourteen-hour interrogation. Third, he's from Texas, not Lafayette County. Fourth, he doesn't drive."

"All right, I get the point. What about physical evidence?"

"Blood in the abandoned shack he calls home."

"Janice Coulter's?"

"Won't know that for a couple of weeks, when the DNA results come back. Human, though. Definitely human blood."

"What about an alibi?"

"Rooster, when Jake Creel's not busy talkin' to himself, he pours enough cheap wine down his throat to pickle a horse. He couldn't account for his last five minutes."

CHAPTER TWENTY-EIGHT

With nothing better to do, I settled in front of my computer, a bottle of Jack at my elbow. I accessed Google Earth, then pinpointed Monroe's house and worked outward from there. Sardis Lake was a quarter-mile to the south, but dense forest marked much of the area to the east, west, and north. There were farms to be sure, some of them large, but for the most part, the monitor revealed only a mottled green blanket that smothered the ground.

I kept zooming in and out, maybe looking for a house with a D-for-Dungeon on its roof, until my diligence paid off. Halfway through my second drink, I discovered a number of shadowed lines running through the map.

In another part of the country, the lines might have been creeks, but here the land was very flat. We had lots of marshes and small ponds, but moving water was pretty rare, and these lines traced curves too perfect to have been cut by water. They had to be roads, or the remains of what once were roads, now shielded by the upper branches of bordering trees.

I suddenly realized that I'd used similar roads and trails many times, to hunt and fish, and I kicked myself for not having remembered they were out there. The oldest of them were likely cut by settlers as much as two hundred years ago. I knew because I'd stumbled on the remains of a homestead reduced to its foundations and a few stacked chimney stones more than once. But most of the abandoned roads I'd hiked were old logging roads. All of northern Mississippi, every inch, had been logged at one time or another, in some places many times. The roads cut to get the logs out of the forest were gouged from the topsoil, creating sunken roads that remained sunken long after they stopped being used.

Find an abandoned structure at the end of one of these roads and you could work undisturbed, you could take your time, you could listen to the screams and pleas of your victims without fear of being overheard. You could enjoy every single second.

I poured myself another drink. I'd narrowed the possibilities to only a few hundred. How long would it take me to explore every one of those gray lines running through the forest? I rejected my first answer, several lifetimes. With a little effort, I told myself, I could narrow the possibilities. Some of the forest roads stopped and started without touching a county road. Others came relatively close to a farmhouse, and many were sure to be impassable.

The least I could do was check them out. That, of course, would mean riding the back roads of Lafayette County, which would considerably elevate the chances of my running into Sibley and his attack dog. An alternative occurred to me at that point. Why not snatch Monroe? Why not take him to some isolated area and do to him what he'd done to Marie Blocker? If his confession included details that could only be known to the killer, how I'd obtained it wouldn't matter. I wasn't a cop and Monroe wasn't entitled to a lawyer. I might go to jail, of course, if I seriously injured the man, but what's a few months in prison to a successful, if small scale, entrepreneur?

On that happy note, I headed off to bed.

Rosie called at nine o'clock as I sat down to breakfast on the following morning. The governor and the mayor had decided to let the arrest of Jake Creel play out in the courts. They were content to remain on the sidelines. Mississippi Public Safety Commissioner Bobby Stapp would not be riding to the rescue.

I told her that the dominoes were ready to fall, that all they needed was a small push, a push that only a law enforcement agency could provide. Rosie was having none of it. I was preaching to the choir.

"Rooster, are you fool enough to think I'm the one with the juice here?" She hesitated for just a moment. "Well, you can surely trust me on this. I am the low girl on this particular totem pole."

"Did you at least try?"

"I'm hopin' my ears deceived me. I'm hopin' that wasn't a note of sarcasm I detected in your voice."

Talk about running into a brick wall. Rosie, of course, was right, and I believe that one part of me was actually pleased by the news. Now the entire burden fell on me. I wouldn't have to share. At another level, I'd given all of them—Ink, Sneak, Monroe, and Sibley—fair warning. I was coming after Sneak Ellerbee, and I wasn't giving up until I ran him down. Sneak had committed a serious crime when he failed to register. Faced with prison, no one, least of all Mathew Monroe, could assume he wouldn't talk, at least about his drug activities.

My phone rang for a second time as I considered the possibilities. I checked the caller ID: Harold Blocker, Marie's father. But Harold wasn't on the other end of the line when I answered. Instead, I heard the voice of Samantha Blocker, Marie's sister.

"I have some bad news for you, Rooster," she said.

"Join the club."

"What?"

"Never mind. Just go ahead."

"Price Sibley came by this morning and talked to my folks. He told them he had a man in custody, a drifter named Jake Creel, and that Creel had confessed to one of the murders."

"I know all of this, Samantha."

"He also said it's only a matter of time until Creel's charged with killing Marie. He said they already have evidence and they're still investigatin'. My parents thanked him, but then he said that you were interferin' with the investigation and they needed to fire you. He wasn't nice about it, either. Sibley said he would have made an arrest days ago if it wasn't for you."

I looked down at my breakfast, thinking I shouldn't have doused my eggs with ketchup. It looked too much like blood.

"Do they believe him, Samantha?"

"They say that they do, but . . . Look, Rooster, my parents go to church every Sunday. They pray for the Lord to protect them from all the devils that roam the earth, doing Satan's work. Well, Price Sibley's one of them devils, Rooster, and my folks know it."

"Then why are they firing me?" I asked, though I knew the answer.

"Because they have to live in this county." She hesitated long enough to take a breath. "Anyway, Daddy's too ashamed to call, so he asked me to do it. It's not like I wanted to, or like I agree, but you're fired and there ain't a damn thing to be done about it."

I slipped my .45 into a shoulder holster before I left my apartment, then dropped a pair of loaded magazines into the front pockets of my jeans. A few minutes later, I was on my bike and headed for Sardis Lake where I scouted the edge of the road leading to Monroe's house for the second time, again looking for a place where I could remain out of sight and still observe anyone going in or coming out. Then I began to ride the main highways in search of the faint trails I'd noted on the map last night.

The job proved a lot harder than I expected, not least because I didn't have the map in front of me. But I did find abandoned roads and trails, their entrances half hidden by the brush. I explored the ones that were passable, running over rough ground, forcing my bike through the woods when the mud was too thick to chance. My chopper weighed seven hundred pounds. If it dropped onto firm ground, I could pick it up. But thick mud, topped by six inches of water, presented a risk I refused to take.

Many of the trails I explored had been used before, mostly by ATVs. I remember becoming excited the first time I saw tire tracks in the dirt. I followed that particular road until it dead-ended at an isolated pond. As I sat astride my bike, staring out at the water, a small perch broke the surface, chased no doubt by something large and hungry.

Persistence is my specialty, always has been. I kept on going, only heading back to Oxford as the sun began to drop and the shadows deepened. But I didn't return to the club. I headed for the gym, very much needing to burn off my frustration. At that point, I couldn't bear to sit still.

I came through the door as Barbara came out. She smiled when she saw me, a warm smile, or so I concluded at the time. She was genuinely glad to see me, but she was also in a hurry.

"How do you know when your doctor's an extortionist?" she asked as she slid by.

"I don't have a clue."

"When your gynecologist threatens to cut off your birth control if you cancel your next appointment."

CHAPTER TWENTY-NINE

Alma-Beth Patterson had a cigarette in her hand as she stepped through the door of the brick building that housed the Lafayette County Health Department. She lit the cigarette as she crossed the walkway and stepped onto the parking lot. I watched her eyes close momentarily as she dragged the smoke into her lungs, then open again as she blew the smoke into the chilly air. The temperature had dropped into the forties and was still on the way down.

I let Alma-Beth enjoy her smoke for a few moments as I rehearsed my pitch. Given the consequences, I knew I wouldn't reach her on the first round. My only aim was to set the hook and let her run with it.

Alma-Beth's eyes darted to me as I stepped out of the shadows on the far side of the lot. For a moment, I thought she'd run, but she stiffened as her expression first became defiant, then amused.

"Nothin' better to do?" she asked.

"Just wanted to catch you alone for a few minutes."

"And why would that be?"

"Maybe I'm smitten."

Alma-Beth's laugh was far from pleasant. "I s'pose you have a ring in your pocket, ready to propose."

"No ring." I gave it a few beats, then said, "You ever hear of a woman named Karla Homolka?"

"Is this a test, Rooster? Do I get a gold star for the right answer?"

"Karla Homolka was a Canadian, married to a man named Paul Bernardo. Now Paul, he had a wanderin' eye and he liked 'em young. He just couldn't keep it in his pants. In fact, he didn't appear to be trying, so Karla decided to go along to get along. She offered up her fifteen-year-old sister as a sacrifice. That would be Tammy Homolka, a virgin at the time."

"How do you come to know all this, Rooster? Are you some kind of shrink, maybe one of them FBI profilers? Or are you only a run-of-the-mill pervert?"

"I had me a hunch, Alma-Beth, so I went on Google and did a search for male-female serial killer teams. Found Paul and Karla, and others as well. I suppose it's a case of anything you can do, I can do better."

I stopped abruptly. Alma-Beth was staring into my eyes, her own filled with a hate that cheered me considerably. "You think I'm crazy?" she said.

"I don't exactly know what to make of you, not yet. But here's what they did, Alma-Beth. I'm talkin' about what Paul and Karla did to Tammy. First, they fed Tammy an animal tranquilizer, along with alcohol, which put her to sleep. Next, they took turns raping her, videotaping every thrilling moment as they proceeded. But then Tammy woke up after about an hour and ruined the fun by fighting back. Paul and Karla couldn't have that. They dosed her with halothane, an anesthetic. That put Tammy out, so they got the video camera running and returned to raping her. I don't know what might have happened if Tammy survived, but sometime that night she choked to death on her own vomit. Unfortunately, her passing was ruled to be accidental, which allowed Karla and Paul to murder at least two other girls, one fourteen and one fifteen, before they were caught."

"What does this have to do with me?" Alma-Beth's voice shook, but she still managed to get the words out. "I'm not a pervert, and I swear I never touched a girl in my life."

"Well, you probably wouldn't have wanted to touch this one, either. Not after your brother got through with her. Here, take a look."

I passed her a photo of Terri Crawford taken by the medical examiner when she was first stretched out on the table.

"Meet Terri Crawford, your brother's first victim," I said. "The photo was taken before a pathologist opened her up. Understand? One hundred and fifty-two cuts inflicted over a period of three days, all courtesy of your brother and Sneak. Nice guys, right? Her name, by the way, is Terri Crawford, formerly night manager at the Graduate Hotel. She left a husband, two children, a mother, and a father behind. I didn't bother to count the aunts, uncles, and cousins."

"This is bullshit. My brother never touched anyone. And you need to leave me alone before I call the cops. I ain't afraid of you."

I started to laugh but thought better of it. "Just bear with me for another minute, Alma-Beth, because I'm gettin' to the point. See, I started on this whole chain of thought earlier tonight when a woman acquaintance made a joke about her gynecologist cutting off her birth control. Seems like when I heard that, my brain did a little jump to a conversation I had with a friend of another victim, Cary Thompson. She told me that after Cary began to have sex with her boyfriend, she made some sort of arrangement to acquire birth control. I mean, you can see how I put the two things together, right?"

"Fuck you, Rooster."

I didn't resent the comment, since I pretty much deserved it. But it didn't stop me, either. "What finally happened was that Karla Homolka turned on her old man, and they were both convicted. Paul was sentenced to life in prison without the possibility of parole because the Canadians are merciful people and there's no death penalty in Canada. But this ain't Canada, Alma-Beth. We're in Mississippi, where you get the needle for spitting on the fucking sidewalk."

She turned to walk away, but I took her by the shoulder. If she'd fought me, I would have let her go. She didn't.

"I don't expect you to confess here and now, but I do want you to know that you're the answer to a pair of questions. Namely, how the victims were targeted and how they were taken. You work in the Women's Health Division of the Department of Health. One of the services you provide is birth control. It says so right on your website, and it's just natural that Cary Thompson came to you. But again, I'm not askin' you to sign a confession. I just want you to consider the conclusions that authorities are likely to draw when they check the names of the victims against the appointment list at the clinic."

"I didn't have nothin' to do with what happened to those women," she said. "I ain't crazy like that."

I stifled my first response: then how are you crazy? I stuck to the game plan instead. "The victims were taken from their homes or their cars, seemingly without a struggle. What made them open their front doors? Or get out of their cars? Especially after the first couple of victims. I mean, no woman would stop her car out on a back road for a man she didn't know. But we're raised real polite down here, trained from birth. We'd open our doors for a woman or stop our cars for a lady in distress."

"Are you done now, Rooster? Are you all finished?"

"Me? I don't think so, Alma-Beth. I think I'm just gettin' started."

CHAPTER THIRTY

Sneak Ellerbee didn't know exactly when he was going to peel away, only that if he drove the pickup to the rendezvous point near Memphis, the people on the other end, the ones he'd never laid eyes on, would surely kill him. Because that's what he'd do if he was in their shoes, what he'd arrange if he were in Ink's shoes. He and Monroe couldn't be left alive. There was just too much at stake. But first things first. Sneak wouldn't make his move until he was sure that he wasn't being tailed.

Just hours before the pickup arrived, after a long discussion, Sneak had concluded a deal with his partner. He'd rendezvous with Monroe in their safe place only if they took Alma-Beth with them when they left Mississippi. Both men knew they couldn't leave her behind, not alive, and Sneak wasn't about to kill her. Not after all she'd done for them, not after all she'd done for him. And to him, for that matter.

Sneak made a right turn at the end of the dirt road leading away from Alma-Beth's little house. He flipped the radio on, hoping to find a Memphis station. The night sky, without a single cloud, was a bowl of stars jammed so close together they formed a continuous line across the center of the sky. This was good because reception definitely improved on clear nights. On one occasion, he'd pulled in a station broadcasting all the way from Nashville. The Christian Broadcasting Network, unfortunately, but still . . .

Sneak fiddled with the seek button, looking for Jarmin on The Max, but the stations he picked up faded within a few seconds. Until he got closer to Memphis, he'd have to keep his own company. He snapped the radio off and sat up just as a headlight appeared in his rearview mirror, a single headlight, the headlight of a motorcycle.

"Oh, fuck," he said, his voice sounding scared, even to him.

Maybe, he thought, that's exactly what's supposed to happen, the fear showing through, when your future narrows to a few hours. At fucking most. Sneak reached forward and swept his hand beneath the seat until he found the butt of a .357 hidden there. A moment later, the revolver's weight rested in his lap. Six shots in the gun, six more in his pocket. Sneak found himself wishing for a Thompson submachine gun or an UZI with a fifty-round magazine. You could empty an UZI in five seconds.

Sneak imagined himself getting out of the truck, turning to face the oncoming bike, and opening up, the UZI spitting fire into the night, every bullet punching bloody holes in the flesh of his enemy. But the fantasy lasted only a few seconds before he came back to earth. Although he'd possessed handguns on numerous occasions, he'd only fired one a few times. And then half drunk in the woods. Meanwhile, Ink's men had been armed with rifles and shotguns.

In the dark? A handgun versus a long gun? At fifty yards? Yeah, that'd work.

Sneak turned onto Highway 310. He followed the road for about a mile, then took a left onto the less-traveled Callicut Road. As the pickup straightened, he slammed the gas pedal to the floor. The truck's transmission screamed in protest but finally started turning. A minute later, bouncing madly on its worn shocks whenever the road dipped, the Ford's speed topped sixty miles an hour. Still, he barely slowed as he turned onto a gravel road, throwing up a dusty tail that almost obscured the motorcycle's headlight.

Obscured or not, the headlight stayed right there, about a hundred yards back, dropping behind on the curves, making up ground on the straightaways. Sneak gave it a few more minutes, but then slowed. He wasn't going to outrun the bike, and the last thing he needed to do was wrap the pickup around a tree and wake up a cripple like Ink. A cripple in prison, maybe on death row. Resigned, Sneak took out his cell phone. Mostly, he couldn't get a signal out here, but his luck held up this time.

"Alma-Beth," he said when she picked up the house phone, "fetch your brother. Right now, Alma-Beth."

Monroe came on a moment later. "What's got your shorts twisted up, Sneak?" he said, his tone contemptuous, as usual.

"I'm bein' followed is what. By a chopper. Picked me up as I come out the driveway."

"Who do you think it is?"

"Gotta be someone from the Henchmen. Who the fuck else?"

Monroe took his time replying. "If it is, they're only givin' you an escort."

"On a one-way ride, man. A one-way fucking ride. I drop the shit off, they're gonna cap my ass, then come for y'all and Alma-Beth."

Sneak's hand dropped to the revolver in his lap as a stray thought slid through his mind. The odds on Monroe's survival would improve with Sneak dead and gone. Especially if Alma-Beth followed. If Monroe put his sister in the ground, there'd be no one alive to testify against him. Ink would still be out there, of course, but if Monroe had a running start . . .

"The guy that's following you, I don't think he's one of Ink's people," Monroe said. "Ink's big on displays. He wouldn't send one man. He'd send ten."

"If it's not Ink, then who is it?"

"I think it's that asshole, Rooster."

"Following me at three o'clock in the morning?"

"Maybe he caught an attitude, bein' as you tried to kill him."

"No more bullshit, Monroe. You're the one who put the gun in my hand. You're the one who said to go kill him."

Sneak made an abrupt left turn as he drew close to the Tate County border. If Monroe was right and the bleeding heart asshole was the one trailing him, Sneak didn't want to confront the man outside of Lafayette County. He'd need backup, just in case he came out alive, and Sheriff Price Sibley had a lot to protect.

"You there, Sneak?"

"I'm here."

"Well, don't get any big ideas."

But Sneak already had a big idea, or at least a single idea. He wanted to survive the night. Even if they put him in a cage and kept him there for ten or fifteen years before they killed him. Years instead of hours seemed like a pretty good deal at that point. He began to work his way along familiar back roads, the twists and turns seeming almost random, but always working closer to the center of Lafayette County, closer to Oxford. Eventually his route took him south of Oxford, to where Highway 7 widened to four lanes.

As he turned onto the roadway, Sneak tucked the .357 under the seat and drew a long breath, then another and another until his chest loosened up. The one thing he didn't want to do was appear frightened. As he drew a last slow breath, as he felt his shoulders relax, he suddenly recalled a long-forgotten incident. He'd come flying into the yard on his bicycle, maybe thirteen years old, only to find his stepfather at home. Too drunk to go to work, Ethan Vann had yanked his wife into the yard and thrown her into a muddy pool that once served as a hog wallow. He'd beaten the hell out of her, too, and he was still beating her whenever she tried to pull herself out of the filthy water.

Ethan was laughing like a hyena, as he always did when he pounded on his wife and stepson. Maybe that's why he didn't notice Sneak, who piloted his bicycle to the front door, then took a long look at his mother, at her battered and bloody face. Another trip to the hospital, another day in a life as miserable as any that could be imagined.

I could end this, he told himself without really knowing what he meant. But then the meaning became clear. He could fetch Ethan's shotgun from inside the house and blow the man's head off. Simple as that. No one could stop him. The shotgun was kept loaded, and Ethan was fifty feet away. And nobody would blame him. His mom's condition spoke for itself. He'd acted to save her. Good-bye misery.

So, why had he stood in front of that door for a good twenty minutes, until his stepfather finally got tired and walked into the house without acknowledging Sneak's presence? Why had he waited until it was too late, until Ethan Vann was asleep on the couch?

Just a few days ago, on his way to Memphis, he'd told himself to make tracks for West Texas, to leave Monroe and his crazy sister behind. The roof was coming down and there was nothing to be gained by waiting until it smashed his head.

And he'd been 100 percent right, his timing perfect. Talk about a last chance. Talk about a road not taken. And now he felt that Alma-Beth and Monroe owned him. They controlled him. He was bound to them. Their fate was his fate.

Resigned at last, Sneak piloted the truck, cargo and all, through the heart of Oxford to the sheriff's office, located conveniently close to the county jail. As he locked the truck, as he walked through the door, as he approached the uniformed deputy behind the counter, he told himself that he'd been here before. He'd survived once in prison. He could do it again.

"Name's Gilmore Ellerbee," he said as Rooster Feathers came through the door. "This man's been followin' me for the past couple of hours. You'll need to call your boss on this."

"Is that right?"

The deputy wore a sergeant's stripes on his sleeves and a name tag that read Chimes. Well into his forties, he had a belly that hung over his belt and a pair of man-boobs that qualified him for a job at Hooters. Now, he folded his arms over the crease between his chest and his belly, then cocked his head. Sneak assumed the gesture was meant to be intimidating, but the deputy didn't look as if he could get out of the chair, much less kick Sneak's ass.

"Chimes, you don't call Price Sibley, and I mean right the fuck now," Sneak said, "he's gonna kick your fat ass all the way to Gulfport."

The deputy held Sneak's gaze for a few seconds, then looked up at Rooster. "Is this asshole tellin' the truth? Have you been followin' him?"

"Gilmore Ellerbee is a paroled sex offender who failed to register. There's a warrant out for his arrest. Check it out for yourself."

Chimes waited a moment for Ellerbee to deny the accusation, but Sneak only shook his head.

"Call your boss," he said. "This is way too big for you."

CHAPTER THIRTY-ONE

What was it that Barbara told me? One thing about luck, good or bad, if you wait long enough, it'll turn? As I sat in an interrogation room at the sheriff's station, one wrist handcuffed to a massive eyebolt, I suddenly realized that the waiting part didn't have to be all that long. Every now and then, your luck turns on a dime.

The good luck began early in the afternoon when Barbara's casual remark led me to Alma-Beth and her job with the Department of Health. It got better yet when Rocky phoned me twenty minutes after I left Alma-Beth standing there with her mouth open.

"Rooster, I got to ask you one more time," Rocky said. "You really think there's a connection between Sneak Ellerbee and those women been killed?"

I smiled to myself. Last night, he claimed never to have heard the name Ellerbee. "I am, Rocky. I know what they did and how they did it."

"Then why ain't Sneak been arrested?"

"Because I can't find him."

The following silence dragged out, second by second. I could hear Rocky's shallow breathing. He was making up his mind about something and I didn't want to rush him. Rocky wasn't the most honest man in Mississippi, but he surely drew the line at rape and murder.

"There's a load goin' out tonight, maybe two or three o'clock in the mornin'. Sneak's gonna mule it up to Memphis."

"Can you tell me where he's startin' from?"

"From Monroe's place, north of Sardis Lake."

I never asked Rocky how he knew all this because there was only one way he could have known. He'd been drawn to the one percenters, the outlaws, all along. Now he'd joined them. Bad luck for him because he'd go to prison sooner or later, but good luck for me.

I might have called Skid after I hung up, but Skid had no authority outside of Oxford. And I might have called Rosie, who had no authority anywhere. I had plenty of time to think it over. I found a spot within a grove of young pines just after midnight, far enough from the road to remain hidden from the few cars that passed. Though not frigid, the night was too cold for the swarms of mosquitoes that haunt the forests of Mississippi. The chill hinted of the coming winter. Within a few weeks, the leaves would change and the weather turn wet. We'd see hail in January and wake up with frost on the shorn cotton fields. I'd spend another Thanksgiving and another Christmas with Rosie, and another New Year's at the club. All I had to do was survive.

Somewhere after two o'clock, a tan pickup, followed by a chopper, its rider displaying Henchmen colors, turned onto Monroe's road. Less than ten minutes later, the chopper returned, this time with a passenger, and took off toward the southern end of the lake. Barely two minutes after that, I watched the pickup bounce along the rough road. It hesitated at the intersection, then turned north. I also hesitated, but only for a few seconds, before following. My plan was simple enough. Somewhere between the lake and Memphis, I was going to stop Gilmore Ellerbee, even if I had to shoot him.

As it turned out, Sneak had a plan of his own.

I did finally call Rosie, but not until I'd trailed Sneak to Price Sibley's headquarters. And even then, I'd hurried into the station after only a few words, unwilling to give Sneak the chance to run out the back door. But Sneak hadn't taken off. He stood in front of a deputy named Chimes when I made my appearance, demanding that Chimes call his boss.

I pled my case. Gilmore Ellerbee was a convicted sex offender who'd failed to register after he left prison. If that weren't reason enough, a search of his pickup, parked just outside, would turn up large quantities of crystal meth bound for Memphis.

Sneak didn't respond to my accusations. His focus remained on the consequences for Deputy Chimes if he didn't consult his boss.

Chimes pursed his lips as he considered the alternatives. But there wasn't all that much to consider because a phone call to Price Sibley would cost him nothing. Thus after due consideration, Chimes phoned his boss, then listened for a minute before calling in a pair of deputies named Clark and Whitworth. They disarmed me first, then escorted me to an interrogation room and handcuffed my right hand to the aforesaid eyebolt.

"What next?" I asked.

Clark smiled. He looked young enough to be a high school fresh-man, his pitiful attempt at growing a mustache having produced no more than a few wispy hairs.

"Now we wait."

"What about the man I came in with? What about Gilmore Ellerbee?"

"Last I seen him, he was goin' out the front door."

Unlike Whitworth, who promptly fell asleep in his chair, Clark was a talkative man. He told me he'd been up to the club a few times, he and his fiancée, Price Sibley's niece, Mary-John.

"You put on the best show in the county, Rooster."

"I appreciate the compliment, deputy, but would you mind tellin' me why I'm bein' detained? Seems like I haven't done anything to merit this kind of attention."

"That right there, Rooster, it's above my pay grade. Only thing I'm sure of is that you're not leavin' just now."

"But you don't know why?"

"I don't, and I'm not the least bit curious. In this here sheriff's department, it don't pay to ask questions. And I ain't a curious man by nature. Like to mind my own business."

"No exceptions to the rule?"

Clark chewed on that for a minute, then said, "There's times an exception kinda sneaks up on you, but I don't go lookin' for 'em."

"That's good, Clark. So, what if I told you that man who just walked out of here kidnapped, raped, and murdered six women in Lafayette County?"

"If you told me that, which I guess you are, I'd ask you to prove it." Clark laughed softly when I didn't reply, then abruptly changed the subject. "Say, did you hold one of them parties I heard about when Ole Miss played Alabama on Saturday?"

The Saturday in question might have happened in another century, but I nodded agreeably, then said, "The man I come in with? Sneak Ellerbee? Would it surprise you to know that he was drivin' a pickup, a Ford F150, loaded down with crystal meth? That your department could have called in a drug dog and taken a big-time dealer off the street?"

"Hardly nothin' surprises me since I joined up with the department. But, hey, about them parties. Mary-John loves the blues and she loves Ole Miss and she sure does love a party. I know you invited deputies in the past, so . . ."

The man had a one-track mind, which I acknowledged with the most genuine smile I could muster. "Hey, no problem. Next away game, you and Mary-John are officially invited. Show up hungry and thirsty."

"I do thank you kindly . . ."

When Tyler Hardin walked into the small room, Clark's eyes turned dark with what I took to be a mix of fear and loathing. He slid his chair away from the small table I was trapped behind but didn't leave the room. For his part, Deputy Whitworth opened his eyes and looked around. But as his chair was already against the wall, he didn't move.

From outside, before Hardin closed the door, I heard Rosie's voice at a distance. She sounded angry.

"You're just full of yourself," Hardin said. "Thinkin' you're better than us rednecks out here in the county. Just like that uppity nigger who raised you."

"Actually, if you go outside and look around, you'll see that we're in Oxford at the moment."

"And that smart mouth of yours? I do believe I'm gonna have to shut it."

From where I sat behind a small table, Hardin appeared massive, a giant. I suspected that was his intention and that he'd played this game before, played it with handcuffed men.

"I haven't been charged with any crime," I said. "You got no right to hold me."

"How 'bout contempt of cop? Maybe it ain't writ down in the law books, but us rednecks take it real serious."

I watched him unbuckle his gun belt and hand it to Deputy Whitworth. I watched his thin lips widen into a happy grin. I watched him smack his right fist into his left palm. As a show, it was strictly pitiful, and I had the feeling he'd lifted it from some 1940s crime movie. But I went with the cues, shrinking down and turning to my left, the only move open to me because my right wrist was cuffed.

I continued to back off as Hardin took a step toward me, then another, his grin tightening down. I believe at that moment he felt a surging power that compensated for all his many faults. That messy divorce? Where his wife claimed that he smacked her around on a regular basis? Or the fact that he'd twice failed the written exam for the Oxford Police Department before Sibley recognized his talents? None of that mattered anymore. Tyler Hardin's ultimate superiority would now be demonstrated.

I let him come within a step before I uncoiled, driving my left fist into his unprotected lower ribs. Not my best punch, to be sure, because my right hand was still cuffed, but I believe that I made Codie Shuffield proud. It was Codie who told me that a blow to the hanging ribs produces a shock wave of released energy that slams into the liver, resulting in a level of pain that temporarily precludes further combat. In the boxing world, similar punches have resulted in fighters being counted out.

Codie proved to be correct. Hardin dropped to one knee, then rolled onto his belly. I don't know what he might have done when he recovered, nor did I give a damn. It didn't get that far because Deputy Whitworth, now wide awake, pulled his Browning and pointed the barrel at my face. I think he would have pulled the trigger, as much from pure reflex as any calculated decision, if Deputy Clark hadn't intervened.

"I won't back you, John," Clark said, his tone even.

"What?"

"Open your ears, John, because I'm not fucking around here. That woman outside? Standin' twenty feet away from this door? She sits on the city council. Tell me what excuse you'll give the woman for shootin' a handcuffed prisoner from ten feet away."

"He attacked a deputy."

"That don't grant you the authority to execute him."

"You scared, Grant?"

"John, listen carefully because I ain't gonna say it a third time. If you have some kind of urge to spend the rest of your life in a prison cell, you'll just have to pass the time without my company. I won't back your play."

CHAPTER THIRTY-TWO

Ink Howard dropped the cell phone onto his lap and cursed softly. The man on the other end of the line, the man who'd just hung up, Miguel Gonzalez, had spoken matter of factly, though with a heavy accent.

"This *pendejo*, he ain't shown. Tha's bad, *hombre*, for you and for me also."

Ink didn't really blame Sneak. If the man had been stupid enough to make that delivery, he'd already be eating dirt. That's what came of being a weak link. That's what came of being a rapist and a murderer. Sneak's death was much deserved and long overdue, as was Monroe's. Ink had been with many women before his accident, had even played kinky with those willing, but he'd drawn the line at rape, for him and the bikers he ran with.

Once again, the phone in Ink's lap began to ring. He glanced down at the screen and recognized the number. Price Sibley's burner. Ink pressed the phone to his ear. Sibley liked to put on airs, like he was in charge, but he was a straight-out criminal. The only difference between Ink and Sibley, as far as Ink was concerned, was that Sibley had him outnumbered.

"Any sign?" Ink asked without saying hello.

"I went over to Monroe's place myself and spoke to Alma-Beth after I searched the house. She tells me her brother and Sneak took off early this morning. Didn't say where they were off to. Didn't say if they were comin' back. Seems like the house belongs to her, and Monroe was stayin' there on a temporary basis."

"Sheriff, I'm tellin' ya that bitch is up to her neck in this. I've known her goin' way the hell back, and she's always been crazy. You couldn't get nothin' through to her. Talkin' to her was like talkin' to a rock."

"Like I said, we searched the house lookin' for anything con-cernin' those women. We found exactly nothin', Ink, not even a drop of blood. Far as I'm concerned, those boys ain't guilty of nothin'. This is all Rooster's doin'."

Ink glanced to his right and left. A Henchman sat on either side of his chair. Both men were armed, with handguns and shotguns. Cassie sat farther off, in her rocking chair. Ink watched her get up and head for the porch. To make breakfast or get out of the cold? Ink hated to be cooped up in that house. The wheelchair was prison enough.

"Maybe I'll go pay Alma-Beth one them up-close-and-personal visits," he finally told Price Sibley. "Ask the questions in my own unique way."

"Don't do it. We got enough problems without you puttin' a county health worker in the hospital. Anyway, I'm thinkin' that Monroe and Sneak are on the run. They're on the move, and they won't stop runnin' till they get someplace far from Lafayette

County. I've got my people workin' roads all over the county. I'm sure you've got people out too. Ain't no way they could be stupid enough to hang around. If they didn't have our fucking property with them, mine and yours, I'd say good riddance. The way it is, though, it's gonna cost us if we can't make delivery."

Ink didn't argue the point. Yes, Sneak and Monroe had to be in the wind. The real issue was whether or not Alma-Beth knew where they were headed. Ever the optimist, Sneak was betting on yes. That meant the product was recoverable, most likely without Sibley's help. Finders, keepers?

"Ya know what I'm thinkin', Sheriff?"

"What's that?"

"I'm thinkin' we're better off with them gone, product or no product. I'm thinkin' they murdered those women and they did it for fun. I'm thinkin' if they get busted, they'll give us up in exchange for a life sentence instead of the needle. I mean, it ain't like either one of 'em has a conscience."

"I made an arrest for those crimes, Ink. In case you didn't notice."

"I did notice, Sheriff, and I felt right proud when I heard the news. But I'm still sayin' we're better off with Sneak and Monroe gone. As for the money? I'm lookin' at the money as a cost of doin' business. Once things get back to normal, we won't have no trouble makin' it up."

Thirty minutes later, when Cassie emerged from the house bearing a tray, one of Ink's bodyguards, Thump Zain, jumped out of his chair and ran over to offer his assistance. He took the tray and carried it across the lawn to a weathered picnic table. As he put it down, his head exploded.

Ink stared at Thump's body as it toppled over and fell to the ground, as the crack of a rifle, followed almost instantly by a second shot, rolled though the surrounding woods. Ink turned to his left, knowing what he'd see. The man who called himself No-Class Henderson lay on his back, one knee pulled up. His blue eyes were open and his hands clutched the left side of his chest. Most likely, the man was trying to hold back the blood being pumped from his heart, but his shirt and the top of his jeans were already soaked. The man was as good as dead.

Ink was tempted to reach for the handgun concealed in a pouch attached to the back of his wheelchair but restrained himself at the last second. Showing the weapon didn't make a lot of sense while his enemy remained hidden. Maybe later, if he got lucky—if he got *very* lucky—the gun would make a difference. Meanwhile, he still drew breath, though probably not for all that long.

Sneak Ellerbee came out of the woods a step behind Monroe. He walked directly to where Cassie stood with her hands covering her mouth and laid his rifle on the ground. She didn't resist when he led her to a rocking chair and pushed her into it, but her entire body continued to shake, even after he let her go. Sneak had reached the point where he accepted his fate. His fate and his position. This was Monroe's show. He was the star, and there was no changing that fact, just like there was no sharing the spotlight. Sneak had to content himself with the role of supporting actor. If he didn't like the part, he should have taken off when Sibley let him go, should have headed for West Texas. Should have, should have, should have . . .

Sneak felt like he was going insane.

"You wanna tell me what's the point here?" Ink's tone was so matter of fact, he might have been discussing the weather.

Monroe glanced down at the shotgun in his hands. "Let's just say that when I leave a room, I like to shut the door behind me."

"Seems to me that you ain't left the room. Seems to me you're standin' right in the middle of the room. Sibley's got his deputies scourin' the county for any sign of your sorry asses, and I've got my own boys out lookin'. Y'all are lucky you even got this far." Ink shifted his gaze to Sneak. "Sneak, y'all could've been five hundred miles away by now. You realize that, boy? Monroe here is leadin' you into the grave, not away from it. What kind of leader is that?"

"Go ahead, Sneak," Monroe said. "Tell him."

Sneak stared at Monroe for a moment, then glanced at No-Class Henderson, who'd stopped moving. Having just killed two men, Sneak didn't fear Monroe at that particular moment. "Just get it done, man. We ain't got all day."

"You in a hurry, Sneak?" Monroe didn't wait for an answer. He faced Ink squarely, his gaze tightening down. "Men like you, Ink, they always choose the obvious. They go with the odds. Like, what were the chances that I'd turn up on your doorstep, that I'd take out your bodyguards, that I'd be standin' in front of y'all right this minute? Pretty small?"

"Pretty stupid is how I'd have to put it."

Monroe gestured to Ink's bulldog. The animal was standing at the end of his chain, his nose pointed at a trail of spatter extending from Thump Zain's body.

"That dog ain't no more good to you at the end of that leash than your boys were sittin' in them chairs." When Ink didn't dispute the point, Monroe went on.

"Two days ago, you came to my house and disrespected me with my sister watchin'. Like you wasn't a drugged-out cripple in a wheelchair. Like you were better than us. How's that work for you right now, Ink? You still feelin' superior?"

Ink responded with a bitter laugh. "I ain't feelin' superior, man. But not because of you. That son-of-a-bitch, Rooster Feathers, he beat us both. And he didn't have to do nothin' but stir the pot and let us hang our own selves."

"You may be right about that, but Rooster ain't here, and you are."

"Fuck you, Monroe. You kill me, the boys will never stop lookin' for you."

"Ink, you got that backwards. They'll never stop lookin' if I leave you alive, but you'll be forgotten ten minutes after you're in the ground. Now if I showed myself, the Henchmen would have to kill me as a matter of honor. But they won't waste no energy lookin' for me, not when there's all that money to be made." Monroe finally gestured to Cassie in her chair. "Whatta ya say, Sneak? One more for the road?"

Sneak tried to shake his head, tried to say, "No, no, no. We have to get out of here." But the words died in his throat and his head never moved. Instead, a flame rose in body with the suddenness of a lit propane torch. The flame touched every cell as it fired his imagination. When Cassie jumped out of the chair and started to run, he caught her by the hair and threw her to the ground. He asked himself a simple question as he stared down at her. Why the fuck not? Because there was no escape, not anymore. Ink was 100 percent right. Him and Monroe? They were crazy to come here, crazy to hang around. Why not add one more crazy to the list?

Ink answered that question by reaching for the pistol in the pouch behind his wheelchair. It was now or never. His hand snaked behind the chair, slid into the pouch, groped for the gun's handle. Instead, he found a pint bottle of bourbon, then a box of tissues, then . . .

"Monroe," Sneak shouted, "watch out."

Monroe spun on his heel, then grinned as he drove the butt of his rifle into the side of Ink's head. Ink's hand came out of the pouch empty as the wheelchair went over, spilling him onto the dirt. Blood poured freely from the wound in his scalp, soaking his hair and dripping onto his shoulder, yet he remained conscious.

"Ink, you need to accept the fact that you're a damn cripple. Tryin' to play the hero just makes you look more pitiful than you already are." Monroe knelt to pluck the semiautomatic from the pouch. He tossed it to one side and rose to his feet.

Cassie made a move then, jumping to her feet, a hopeless gesture. Sneak wrapped his right arm around her chest, pinning her hands. He held her that way until she topped struggling.

"Whyn't you let her loose, Monroe?" Ink managed to prop himself up on one elbow. "Cassie ain't done nothin to y'all."

"Are you maybe suggestin' that she's one of those innocent-type victims?" Monroe smirked as he waited for a response that never came. "Well, you could be correct on that one. Little Cassie might be as pure as the driven snow. But I'm not, Ink. I'm not innocent, not at all. Too bad for you and her both."

Monroe drove the butt of the rifle into Ink's face for a second time, then a third, then a fourth, over and over again, throwing off bits of bone and brain every time he lifted the rifle above his head. He didn't stop until Ink's skull was a shapeless, bloody mass. Then he turned to Sneak, wordless for the moment.

"You want me to fetch the Lincoln?" Sneak finally asked.

"Nope." Monroe gestured to Ink's van with its tinted windows. "Everybody and their grandma's lookin' for the Lincoln. Me and you, we're gonna travel in style. Bring the bitch."

CHAPTER THIRTY-THREE

Sibley and his deputies held me in that room for nearly three hours, until seven o'clock, before a lawyer hired by Rosie was allowed inside. Landon Lake IV had patrician roots that extended all the way to the original Jamestown colony in Virginia. His family, in the way of southern families, claimed to have fought in every American war, though he'd skipped his own. Tall and impeccably slender, Landon wore an expensive suit that draped, more than fit, his body, and a bow tie big enough to be a scarf. His honey-brown hair curled across the tops of his ears, each strand precisely placed, while his posture somehow managed to be erect and languid at the same time.

"Mr. Feathers," he said as he closed the door behind him, "it's good to meet you."

Lake didn't introduce himself or extend a hand. The last part would have been useless anyway because my right hand was still cuffed. As for the first part, I suspect Landon Lake simply assumed that I already knew his name. Which, in fact, I did. But he wasn't some sort of exalted patrician, even if his ancestry reached four centuries into the past. Lake's father and his father's two brothers had filed for personal bankruptcy within days of his son's passing the Mississippi bar exam. All were partners in a failed scheme to revive a cluster of dead oil wells in western Oklahoma. The irony was that these same wells, subjected fifteen years later to the fracking process, were now productive.

If the Lake family could have maintained their leases, they'd be among the wealthiest families in Mississippi. They hadn't, and the clan had been struggling ever since. Which is why Landon practiced general law, anything from writing wills to representing common criminals like Rooster Feathers.

"You come to set me free, Landon?"

Lake managed a thin, cold smile, probably at my use of his first name. "I have good and bad news for you. First, the bad news. Our sheriff is determined to charge you with obstruction of justice. He claims you impeded a murder investigation. The good news is that you'll be released in Ms. Bell's custody without having to make a court appearance or post bail."

I think I was supposed to jump for joy, or maybe express my undying gratitude for Landon's efforts on my behalf. Instead, I leaned back in my chair and said, "Tell Price Sibley to go fuck himself."

"Pardon me?"

This time I said it loud enough to be heard outside. "Tell Price Sibley to go fuck himself."

"Please, that's quite unnecessary."

"You don't get it, Landon. Sibley's not offering me a break. The asshole wants to keep me quiet."

"Explain."

"If I'm released in Rosie's custody, whatever I do affects her political career. That's enough to shut my mouth. But I'm not biting. You go tell Sibley that ten minutes after I'm arraigned and post bail, I'm gonna hold me one hell of a press conference. It won't be hard to arrange since I've had just about every reporter on the Oxford Eagle over to the club at one time or another. Personally, I think they'll be right interested when I tell them about a convicted rapist named Gilmore Ellerbee who was released from prison just about the time the murders started. They'll like the twists, too. First the one about that same Gilmore Ellerbee, who failed to register as a sex offender, being inside this very building last night. The second about how our sheriff personally released the man and he's now running around Lafayette County, maybe hunting up another victim."

Landon waited until I finally shut up, then stuck one hand in a pocket. He'd spoken slowly to begin with, but now drew out every syllable. "These accusations, Mr. Feathers, I don't believe they'll help your case. Keep in mind, you have assets and you can be sued for libel."

"Not if I'm telling the truth. Not if my word is backed up by the sheriff's own security cameras."

"Is that what you really think?" Landon's thin mouth turned down. "Mr. Feathers, in this country anyone can be sued for anything, and mostly it's the attorneys who win."

He had a point there, but I was too pissed off to listen. "You just deliver the message, Landon, and let me worry about the consequences."

As it turned out, no consequences materialized, though I was held for another three hours before Deputy Clark unlocked the handcuff that chained me to the wall. "You're free to go, Rooster Feathers," he told me. "No harm, no foul."

I resisted an urge to smack him by reminding myself that he'd stuck his neck out when his partner wanted to shoot me.

"That party invite still out there?" he asked.

The totally unexpected question finally grounded me. I didn't exist in some alternate universe. The Earth was still turning and I had two businesses to operate. "What's your first name?"

"Clark."

"Clark Clark?"

Clark flashed me a boyish grin, a grin full of mischief, and I sensed a deep reservoir of basic intelligence beneath the aw-shucks exterior. The kid knew how to conceal his hole cards.

"My momma," he explained, "had an unusual sense of humor."

More or less desperate, I made a pit stop in the men's room before I joined Rosie in the lobby. She led me outside, then had me follow her Camry to her house. Though I expected a lecture in the parking lot, she contented herself with a bit of advice.

"Take time to think, Rooster. The shortest distance between two points isn't necessarily a straight line."

I immediately flashed back to the Ole Miss–Alabama game when Ole Miss tried to run into the heart of the Alabama defense, a hopeless task. I continued to think along those lines as I fired up the chopper and dutifully followed the woman who'd raised me, as I ate the breakfast she prepared, as I drank her coffee, as I described the sequence of events that left me in an interrogation room, one step from being executed.

"I had him, Rosie. I had Ellerbee right there, and Sibley let him go."

"Why?"

"You want the simple answer?" I didn't wait for a response. "Sibley's a silent partner in a wide-open meth operation being run by the Henchmen. Ellerbee and a man named Monroe work for the operation, muling drugs into Memphis. They also dabble in kidnapping, rape, and murder. I'm talkin' about Ellerbee and Monroe."

"Can you prove any of this?"

I went on to connect Alma-Beth's Patterson's job at the Department of Health with Marie Blocker and Cary Thompson, insisting that Alma-Beth played the role of facilitator.

"A woman?" Rosie's tone was a mix of shock and outrage. "You really believe a woman could have done those . . ."

"I'm not sayin' that she participated, but there are plenty of examples of male-female serial killer teams where the female took part. There's even a videotape of one, Karla Homolka, raping her own sister. So, yes, it can happen. But what Alma-Beth did after the kidnappings doesn't matter. Alma-Beth made it happen. She provided the targets and she was there when they were taken. There's just no other explanation for why Marie Blocker stopped her car late at night on a back road. And we can prove a lot of this by examining the appointment list at the Department of Health."

"Did you tell any of this to Skid?" Rosie wanted to know. She was stacking the dishes and pans in the dishwasher, her back to me, and her tone was deceptively neutral. "Or anyone in law enforcement."

"I didn't."

"Why not?"

"Time. Medical records are confidential, and Skid would have to get a search warrant to look at that appointment list. That means he'd have to go before a judge and demonstrate probable cause, which we didn't have."

"Isn't that something for Skid to decide?" She raised a hand. "No, forget that. If memory serves and my brains haven't gone the way of my eyesight, our mayor attended your party less than a week ago. Is there any reason you couldn't have gone directly to Bill Rowan with all this information? And isn't it possible that Rowan, armed with this information, could have appealed to the governor?"

I hated to be cross-examined, hated it with a passion, especially when my prosecutor relied on 20-20 hindsight.

"Rosie, once I found out that shipment was headed for Memphis last night, I decided to take a shot. I planned to stop Ellerbee as soon as he left Lafayette County and the protection of Price Sibley. I even had a little speech prepared for the deputies who responded when I called 911. 'In the course of conductin' a legal investigation under my authority as a licensed private investigator, I discovered the identity of a convicted rapist, Gilmore Ellerbee, who failed to register as a sex offender. That man is standing in front of you right now, ready to be arrested. And, by the way, I also have reason to believe that there's a large quantity of methamphetamine concealed in the pickup truck that Ellerbee's drivin'.'"

I let out a breath I'd been holding for the past eight hours, only to have fatigue settle in as the tension eased. I'd taken my best shot, but it wasn't good enough. Sneak had outplayed me, and by a wide margin. Was I beaten? Ellerbee and Monroe were surely on the move, from Ink and Sibley as much as from me, and I had no idea how I'd catch up with them.

"But you're right, as usual," I added, "and maybe I'll give Thad a call. Only just now I need some sleep before the club opens tonight. You don't mind, I'll use the spare bedroom. Sure as judgment, if I go back to my own apartment, someone's gonna hit me with a problem I'm too tired to solve."

"And you've already got enough problems?"

"Goodnight, Rosie."

CHAPTER THIRTY-FOUR

I took refuge that night in the blues, as I had many times in the past. James "Super Chikan" Johnson and the Fighting Cocks took the stage a bit after eight and immediately launched into "Sunshine Boogie." One thing about Super Chikan, he knew how to entertain. He'd chosen a guitar made from a shotgun for his first number, a guitar he'd made himself. But the man fabricated all of his guitars, creating them from gas cans, cigar boxes, ceiling fan motors, a Harley-Davidson gas tank, painting the bodies, adding big glass beads that glowed under the stage lights.

Super Chikan's appeal went beyond the music and the guitars. He was a natural storyteller whose background screamed Delta blues. The son of a sharecropping family at the end of that era, he'd been assigned the task of minding the chickens when he was too young to go into the cotton fields. Not fast enough to catch them, he learned to speak their language, clucking to them when he wanted them back in the coop. Did it work? Did he really learn to speak chicken? Did it matter, when he could hold an audience spellbound with this and a dozen other stories?

Super Chikan had one other thing going for him. He was the nephew of Big Jack Johnson, one of the greatest bluesmen to ever touch a guitar. Big Jack died a few years ago, but he played my club many times before he passed. Better yet, on occasion he allowed me to sit in. I play just enough bass not to make a fool of myself, but working with someone like Jack always had me nervous beforehand. I didn't want to mess things up, not in front of a musician I deeply respected. So, one afternoon before he was due to perform, I called Big Jack about the chord changes in a tune we'd do that evening.

"Play with your heart, Rooster," he told me. "Play with your heart."

***

I found myself reasonably content, listening to Super Chikan wail as I sat on my customary perch at the end of the bar, a bottle of beer, a rare steak, and a bowl of country green beans in front of me. My contentment stemmed from a conversation I had with Mayor Bill Rowan an hour earlier. Tomorrow morning, at eleven, I'd meet with Rowan and Thad Carson in Rowan's office, there to lay out the results of my private investigation, including—especially including—Price Sibley's involvement in the meth trade.

By then, I'd convinced myself that the immediate threat was over. Sneak and Monroe could run, but they couldn't hide. Once the cops accumulated enough evidence to indict them—and that would happen in the very near future—their faces would appear on every TV screen in the country, on the front page of every newspaper, on thousands of websites. There's no escaping that kind of publicity.

On stage, Super Chikan and Lala Craig, who did high-energy keyboard solos that brought fans to their feet, had worked themselves into a frenzy on "Shoot That Thang." I closed my eyes and allowed the music to run through my veins, the way it had when I was a child. Johnson was working the upper registers of his shotgun guitar while Lala and the bass player, Heather Valduto, maintained a boogie-woogie beat that drove the tune relentlessly forward. When the band finally ground to a halt, I took a deep breath before opening my eyes. That's when I discovered Barbara Michael sitting next to me.

Without deciding to, I leaned forward and kissed her lightly on the mouth. Barbara didn't pull away, but she didn't wrap her arms around my neck either. Her mouth moved slightly, not quite achieving what I hoped was a smile. When I looked into her brown eyes, I detected a faint, encouraging glow.

"I'm safe now," I told her. "The bad guys are on the run and there's nothing left for me to do."

"Are you telling me they got away?"

"The dominoes are falling. It's only a matter of time before they're all on the ground. But there's no role for me anymore and I'm startin' to feel good about it. Real good."

Barbara wore a pale blue sweater and white slacks, both of which emphasized her sleek figure. Her baby-blue earrings matched the color of the sweater, as did the nail polish on her fingers. It was the perfect moment for a ballad, for me to take her into my arms on the dance floor.

Unfortunately, Super Chikan wasn't about slow, sexy ballads. His music virtually screamed roadhouse, and when he sounded the opening notes of "Hookin' Up," the small crowd began to clap.

"Where is Luther Vandross when you need him?" Barbara wanted to know.

"One flight up?" I suggested.

Barbara merely nodded as she slid off the stool. Once again, a woman in my life had made the decision. I didn't mind, and I followed her up the stairs, the view from behind at least the equal of that from the front. Vera Califano crossed my mind as we came through the door, but only long enough for me to finally admit how stupid I'd been to ever become involved with the woman.

I didn't own a Luther Vandross album and I didn't want to bother going online, so I chose a Ben Webster album cut many decades in the past, Music for Lovers and Thieves. Webster's tenor sax could scream as loud as any of Super Chikan's homemade guitars, but on these cuts he played low and slow, his sultry tone as insinuating as the most exotic perfume.

My plan, going in, was to echo Ben Webster's approach. Start with a drink, wine if Barbara wanted it, accompanied by slices of peach pie. Perhaps we'd dance, holding each other close, exchanging slowly escalating kisses until . . .

Plan B went into effect after the first kiss and we were in the bedroom, bare-ass naked, doing our absolute best to destroy the mattress and box spring within a few minutes. Fortunately, when I'd purchased the set, I'd chosen well and they stood up to the abuse. The sheets and comforter, on the other hand, took a serious pounding before we finally collapsed.

Spent in every sense of the word, I dropped back on the pillow, sweat dripping from my hair onto the pillowcase, my chest heaving. Barbara hadn't changed. She knew exactly what she wanted, and I was more than happy to make the effort, her satisfaction reward enough. As for my own satisfaction, the issue was never in doubt.

Funny thing about peach pie, it tastes even better as an aperitif than as an appetizer. I'd just about finished mine when Barbara finally asked a pair of questions that had gone unasked for a long time.

"What happened, Rooster? Why did we lose it?"

As I'd asked myself this question many times, I had no trouble supplying an answer that relieved me of all responsibility.

"You're askin' the wrong person. I've always thought it was you who walked away. As I remember, it wasn't a very emotional parting because we never had a major fight. More like you'd taken a good look and found me wanting in some aspect or other. Which, by the way, I freely admit to be a valid judgment."

Barbara's laugh was genuine. I'd hit the nail on the head. "I couldn't figure you out, couldn't get to the bottom. You're a successful businessman. That much can't be denied. But there's something wild in you as well, something you've never tamed, maybe something you don't want to tame."

"And that's why you walked away?"

"Did I really need another good-old-boy with an advanced death wish in my life?" She sat up, poked me in the stomach, then said, "But you were supposed to chase me. You were supposed to show me how much you wanted our thing to work out. You didn't, Rooster. You didn't show me, by word or deed, that you actually gave a damn."

Having no defense, I stared at Barbara for a moment. Funny thing about women. Somehow, they can sit stark naked on a bed and maintain a serious conversation without taking into account the effect of that nakedness on the male libido. Clothed, Barbara was beautiful. Naked, she was stunning. I watched her eyes narrow and her smile widen as she studied me. When she finally spoke, her drawl was so thick, she might have been Scarlett O'Hara in *Gone with the Wind.*

"Why, Rooster, I do believe that you've failed to follow this conversation. I believe you're distracted and confused. Tell me what I can do to focus your attention?"

I watched the rise and fall of her breasts as she spoke, but I didn't follow my first instinct. I didn't grab her. Instead, I ran the tips of my fingers along her cheek and the side of her neck and her shoulder. She pressed my hand to her face, kissed the palm, then came to me, her body seeming to flow into mine. I told myself that I'd do it right this time, but had no idea what that entailed beyond taking my time, beyond exploring every inch of her body, including her toes. Especially her toes. Somewhere along the way I admitted the obvious. I liked and admired this woman, now and in the past, a lot more than I ever liked Vera Califano. My relationship with Vera had been little more than a foolish attempt to recapture my high school years. What I wanted and really needed was a woman, not a girl, and Barbara Michael fit that bill perfectly.

CHAPTER THIRTY-FIVE

I was halfway between awake and asleep, in that dreamy state where awareness and focus have yet to meet. Propped on an elbow, I was observing the rise and fall of the blanket covering Barbara Michael, listening to the soft whistle of her breath. The moment had no urgency, only a warm contentment so all-consuming that I answered the phone without checking Caller ID.

"Rooster, it's Annie-Fay."

"Annie-Fay?"

"Yes, Deputy Sheriff Annie-Fay, in case you forgot."

"It's six o'clock, Annie-Fay."

"Right, Rooster, it's six o'clock in the damned morning and I've been up all night. Now, if you're too busy to hear what I have to say, you could always hang up. But the way I understand things, I'm the one doin' the favor."

Barbara sat up in bed, temporarily distracting me. By then, I knew Annie-Fay's news would be anything but good.

"I'm sorry," I said, "and you're most definitely right. I apologize." I covered the phone with my palm and spoke to Barbara. "It's Annie-Fay Keefer."

"I've only got a minute, so let me get to it," Annie-Fay said. "Ink Howard is dead, along with two of his biker buddies. The buddies were shot, probably with a rifle given the size of the exit wounds. Ink Howard was bludgeoned to death. Rooster, it looked like his head was run over by a tank."

I stood up at that point, fueled by a shot of pure adrenaline that sent my brain spinning like a hamster's treadmill. There was only round and round and round. Yes, it might have been a rival gang, or one of Ink's lieutenants pulling off a coup, or even Price Sibley's work. Not that I believed in any of those possibilities, or that I wanted to ask the question that would define my own responsibilities. I didn't want to ask that question, but I had no choice.

I laid a hand on Barbara's shoulder, then said, "Ink had a helper, a caregiver. I think her name is Cassie. She . . ."

"Missing, Rooster. This went down yesterday in the morning at Ink's house. Cassie Howard was there at the time. Now she's missing, along with Ink's van. We found a car, by the way, a Lincoln belonging to Monroe, near the main road."

"Shit."

"I'm actually calling about Cassie. We've been to Monroe's house. Correction, make that Alma-Beth Patterson's house. She claims to own it."

"Wait a second. Are you telling me that Alma-Beth is still around?"

"Yes, and she was cooperative all the way. Let us search the house and the outbuildings, answered every question. But she's sayin' her brother and Sneak haven't been home for a couple of days and she doesn't know where they are and she's really, really worried."

"Do you believe her?"

"Does it matter? She let us search and we found nothing."

Barbara continued to stare up at me, her gaze so judgmental that I wanted to hide. But there was no hiding from this.

"You said you were callin' about Cassie. Does that have something to do with me?"

"Rooster, I have to ask this question." Annie-Fay's tone, by then, was cop cold. "Do you have any idea where Cassie Howard might have been taken? I don't have to explain the consequences if you lie here."

Her tone didn't bother me because I knew I could answer the question honestly. "I have no exact knowledge of where these guys take their victims. I've been assuming it's close to the house, but I could easily be wrong."

Annie-Fay sighed into the phone. "This is bad, Rooster. This is really bad." She hesitated, but I had nothing to say, nothing at all. "I gotta go," she finally said.

That's what I told Barbara as I began to dress: "I gotta go."

"Without tellin' me what's happening?"

I explained as I put on pants and a denim shirt, as I pulled on my socks and slid my feet into a pair of hard-soled boots, as I fitted the shoulder rig over my head and shoved my forty-five into the holster, as I opened a gun safe and removed a Remington .12-gauge autoloader and a box of double-ought shells, as I strapped a cartridge belt to my waist and filled it, even as I brushed my teeth. The story wasn't all that pretty because it included a few of the details uncovered at Terri Crawford's autopsy, but it had to be told.

Barbara didn't interrupt, but I couldn't read her expression. Maybe she was simply trying to absorb the information. Monroe and Sneak, the killers. Alma-Beth Patterson, who facilitated the targeting and the kidnapping. Ink Howard, a meth dealer, now dead. Price Sibley, who might have put a stop to the killings if only his department had organized a competent investigation.

"I met her, Barbara. I mean Cassie Howard. She can't be more than eighteen, a quiet girl who sat by herself in a rocking chair."

"And you think you can save her?"

"Maybe."

"Does that mean you know where she is?"

"It means I know someone who might be able to tell me."

I walked over to the window and glanced outside. The sun had yet to crack the horizon, and the Square was shrouded in gray, predawn light. I watched a police car, a Ford, cruise slowly down the street in front of the courthouse. It stopped at one point and the window rolled down. Moses Hemm, who'd been sweeping the sidewalks in front of the stores for many years and who called everyone boss, strolled over to the cruiser, his attitude casual. He leaned in to exchange a few words with the cop behind the wheel, as he probably did almost every day, then went back to work.

"Are you talking about . . . what's her name?"

"Alma-Beth Patterson?"

"Yes, Alma-Beth. What's the plan, Rooster?"

I just assumed Barbara was asking me how far I'd go to secure the answer I wanted. I was tempted to show her a few of the autopsy photos, then ask how far she'd go to save Cassie Howard. I didn't. There was no point.

"She'll kill me if she gets the chance," I told Barbara. "So there's that to consider right out of the box. And her brother might be home, her brother or Sneak Ellerbee. There's something else, too."

"What?"

"Where did Sneak and Monroe take their victims? That's the one question I never answered. Right now, I'm hoping they took Cassie to the same place and that Alma-Beth can tell me where that place is. But they might not have taken her to their killing ground. They might have stuffed her in Ink's van and taken off for parts unknown. Given their head start, they could easily be a thousand miles away by now."

I added a pair of handcuffs to my kit, then headed for the door, hoping Barbara would follow me, that she'd bestow on me the kiss that fair maidens in books always bestow on the heroes. She didn't.

CHAPTER THIRTY-SIX

The sun had yet to clear the tops of the trees as I drove north on Highway 7 in my pickup. The pickup's windshield and rear window had been replaced, but the rearview mirror was still missing and the bullet hole in the rear seat was a potent reminder of what might have happened, what had almost happened, what could still happen.

Not that I needed a reminder. Monroe and Sneak had nothing to lose, nothing at all. They were going down and they surely knew it, as they surely meant to use the little time they had left to create as much havoc as possible. Ink proved that. Cassie proved that. Killing Rooster Feathers would prove that, too.

The sky to the east was draped by long, heavy clouds running north to south. I watched the sun play with the clouds, turning the edges a fiery orange that faded to charcoal at the centers. The display seemed to mock the gravity of the mission. And not just the obvious, that the sun would continue to rise, the Earth continue to turn, utterly indifferent, whether I lived to be a hundred or died that afternoon. The splendor, the beauty, would also be there, every morning, every night, even if there were no eyes to see it.

I shook those thoughts out of my head. Talk about cut-rate philosophy. I had this life, this one life, and I meant to keep it. I told myself to watch the road. I told myself that Sneak and Monroe weren't the only enemies out there. Price Sibley was out there too. Price didn't want Sneak and Monroe captured. He wanted the pair dead and buried where their bodies would never be found. Right beside Rooster Feather's?

By now, Sibley had to be desperate. Another kidnapping? Another murder? Another body in a ditch? According to Annie-Fay, Sibley had been relatively gentle with Alma-Beth. True, he'd conducted a search, but then he'd left, apparently taking Alma-Beth at her word.

I asked myself what Sibley might have done if Annie-Fay and the other deputies weren't around. What if only Sibley and Tyler Hardin had been present to witness the interview? I couldn't imagine Sibley not wanting to catch up with Sneak and Monroe, and I couldn't imagine him wanting any witnesses to what he'd do to Alma-Beth. Nor could I imagine him wanting Alma-Beth around when he got through with her.

Add one more grave to the bottom line.

I passed a sheriff's cruiser a few minutes later, going the other way. I didn't recognize the deputy behind the wheel, but he glanced in my direction as we passed. I half expected him to slam on the brakes and come after me. Would I resist? Given the stakes? But he kept on going, his taillights slowly diminishing until they disappeared around a bend in the road. I didn't think, or even hope, that Sibley had forgotten me. Only that I might be one more element than he was prepared to handle at the moment.

The sun had risen high enough to clip the treetops but had yet to reach the ground by the time I turned off Highway 310 near Blackwater. Only occasionally broken by cotton fields, the narrow lanes were surrounded by hardwoods that had thrown their branches across the road, so that at times I felt as if I were driving through a tunnel, my life gradually narrowing. That was all to the good, because I'd had enough. The game had to end.

I turned onto the road leading to Monroe's house without passing another vehicle, then pulled to a stop. No way did I intend to drive right up to Monroe's door, maybe tip my hat and say howdy. I'd approach on foot. But I needed to hide the pickup because of Price Sibley, a true wildcard. At some point, he'd pay a second visit to Alma-Beth. If I were still there, I didn't want him to know it in advance.

Fifty yards in, I came around a bend to find the track last taken by my would-be assassin. It had rained two days ago, but the track looked reasonably passable. I shifted into four-wheel drive, low range, and backed onto the trail, pushing through the muddy depressions until the pickup was hidden. Then I got out, the Remington in my hand.

The urge to take off at a run was nearly irresistible as I made my way through the forest. I had to force myself not to think about Cassie, about what was likely being done to her. The rage sure to follow those images would not be productive. I needed to keep my wits about me, as I needed to keep the road within sight or risk becoming hopelessly lost.

Like any kid, I grew up believing that Indians could move in absolute silence, even though a forest is littered with dry leaves and small branches. If true, it was a hell of a trick because I'd spent a lot of time in the woods, yet every step I took sounded, in my own ears, as loud as the crack of rifle. But I kept going, moving from tree to tree, stopping to listen, until I came to the edge of Alma-Beth's yard. Bathed in sunlight, the back of the house glowed. Like a prize, or a trap? One thing certain, the house wouldn't come to me. I'd have to cross the empty yard, a killing ground if I'd ever seen one.

I stopped to formulate some sort of plan but couldn't come up with anything close to foolproof. A check of the windows revealed only the curtains shielding the interior. Coming across the yard, I'd be an easy target for anyone standing even a few inches behind them. There were no potholes to save me at the last second, not unless I tripped and landed on my face, an eventuality not likely to extend my life span.

Before I could implement the only tactic available, to dash across the yard to the back door, a deer, a buck, stepped out of the forest about twenty yards away.

The buck wasn't all that large, but at this time of year, shortly before the rut, he was in magnificent condition. The six points of his antlers gleamed, as did his chestnut coat, and his strut moved him across the lawn as though he were walking on the tips of his hooves. He finally stopped within thirty feet of where I crouched, his breath steaming in the early morning chill.

I forced my eyes to the windows in search of a moving curtain, but the windows remained blank and empty as the deer lowered his head to the ground and began to feed. If I moved, of course, I'd spook the deer, who'd then go crashing through the woods. Panicked deer make a lot of noise. But I couldn't stay there, either. I had to get into the house.

The buck solved the problem for me. He jerked his head up, raising his nose until his antlers grazed the top of his back. His nostrils twitched rapidly as he tested the breeze and his tongue lolled from the side of his mouth. He wasn't smelling danger. No, he'd caught the scent of a doe, an odor he couldn't resist. I watched him strut across the lawn on stiff legs and disappear into the forest.

A few seconds later, I was at the back door. I listened for a moment, my ear to the wood, before trying the doorknob. It turned easily, too easily. Leaving doors unlocked may be a badge of honor in Mississippi, but not under these circumstances. Still, I had no choice. I put the barrel of the shotgun against the door and pushed it open. It swiveled silently inward to reveal an empty kitchen. From just past the door on the other side of the room, I heard the sound of a television playing at low volume.

I tiptoed across the kitchen, stopping at the far door for a moment, then turned inside to find Alma-Beth Patterson seated on a couch, her back to me, a revolver in her lap, watching Judge Judy administer theatrical justice. There was no one else in the room.

I stepped forward, two quick steps, and laid the barrel of the shotgun against her back. "Mornin', Alma-Beth."

"Mornin', Rooster," she said without taking her eyes off the TV screen. "I'm glad it turned out to be you."

CHAPTER THIRTY-SEVEN

Alma-Beth's position was simple enough. Better me than Price Sibley or a Henchman out to build a reputation by avenging his exalted leader. I could have disputed that position as I plucked the revolver from her lap, as I popped the cylinder, emptied the shells onto the floor, and tossed the gun into a corner. I didn't.

"Your brother here, Alma-Beth?"

"Uh-uh."

"How about Sneak?"

"He ain't here either."

"They off playin' with their new toy?"

Alma-Beth chose not to answer the question. "That Judge Judy," she said, "has surely got a nasty mouth on her. It's a wonder somebody hasn't slapped her right in her face. I would if she spoke to me like that."

This was a line of conversation I ended by putting a load of 00 buckshot into the television set. Before the appearance of flat screens, the set would have imploded. As it was, I settled for a four-inch hole in the center of the screen and a scattering of digital circuitry on the rug.

"That was real mean, Rooster. What am I gonna do here all alone without a TV?"

"I asked you a question, Alma-Beth." I walked around the couch to stand in front of her. "I asked you if Sneak and your brother are having fun with a sex-toy named Cassie Howard?"

Alma-Beth pointed to a sampler on the wall to her right: **HOME IS WHERE THE HEART IS**. The letters were tomato red and neatly stitched, but the white background had yellowed with age.

"My momma done that," she said. "Handed it to me three days before she passed over. Told me to watch out for my brother."

"Is that what you mean to tell a jury? My sainted mother, who's now in heaven with the angels, *made* me do it? I get no joy from playin' the pessimist, but somehow I don't see that workin' out to your advantage."

A small voice, one I'd been able to ignore thus far, suddenly opened up full volume. Take this bitch outside, it insisted, and put a rope around her neck. Throw that rope over a tree limb and yank on the free end until you get what you want. No way, this voice insisted, will Alma-Beth die for her brother.

"I want you to listen to me for a minute," I told her. "If what I say is true, don't respond. Just keep silent. That way it's not a confession." I waited until she nodded, then continued. "Of the five previous victims, at least four, and most likely all of them, had an appointment with you at the Department of Health shortly before they disappeared."

I stopped again, leaving Alma-Beth plenty of room for denial, but she didn't speak. "Now that's quite a coincidence, but maybe not enough to convict you, not without physical evidence. So, where will that evidence be found? In the hellhole where your brother plays with his victims. Their DNA, your brother's DNA, and Sneak's DNA will all be recovered." I hesitated for just a second, then tossed the dice. "And your DNA too. Right?"

My bluff met a wall of resistance. Alma-Beth's dark eyes were as blank as buttons. Still, I glimpsed something at their base, something I couldn't touch, the kind of delusion that led a man named John Hinckley to believe that the actress, Jodie Foster, would fall in love with him if he killed Ronald Reagan.

Would self-interest move the woman off her delusions? Would she decide that maybe her momma's mandate didn't include going to prison for the rest of her unnatural life, at the very least? I didn't know, but short of the rope, it was all I had.

"You should know," Alma-Beth said, "that me and Monroe, we're a family. That's all we ever wanted and it's all I thought about while he was down at Parchman. How he'd come out and how we'd make a home."

"Was Marie Blocker part of your plans? Did you figure Tracy Chapman into your little fantasies? How about . . ." I waved my hand, almost in surrender, as Alma-Beth dropped her eyes to her lap. This was a road I could not go down, a road that would not get me to Cassie Howard.

"I don't know nothin' about those women, Rooster. I ain't never been with a woman in my natural-born life."

I eased off a bit, literally, moving back two steps, giving her room. The physical part would come later, if it came at all.

"Remember Karla Homolka?" I asked out of nowhere. "I told you part of her story last time we met. You remember that?"

"I ain't no fool, Rooster. Course, I remember. Thing like that? Ain't no way you can forget."

"Then I'm sure you remember that Karla and her husband were eventually caught, just like you, Sneak, and your brother are sure to be caught. And right soon, too, Alma-Beth. Right soon, these walls are gonna cave in on you."

"I ain't never touched those women. Ain't no one can prove I ever touched those women."

"Did I accuse you of touching them?" I stepped back still farther, until my back was against the wall next to a window. The yard in front of the house was deserted except for a small flock of robins in search of breakfast. The robins, of course, were the perfect alarm.

"Karla's husband, Paul Bernardo, got life, which was the most he could have gotten in Canada. But Karla was offered a plea if she testified against him. Manslaughter instead of murder. Now, I won't lie to you. Karla didn't just walk away. She was sentenced to twelve years in prison, but she was eventually released, even if they did make her do every last second. Supposedly, she's livin' a happy, productive life with her new husband in Quebec."

Alma-Beth's armor was still in place, her gaze still fixed on her lap. It would have been easier if she'd lost her temper. "You should know this," she said. "I had care of Monroe since he was seven, from wakeup until we turned in for the night. I fed the boy. I bathed him. I combed his hair and washed his drawers. And I got myself a nursing degree at the same time. Do you have any idea how hard I worked takin' care of my family? But I couldn't watch Monroe every damn minute. Not if I wanted to put food in his stomach."

"Enough, Alma-Beth, family time is over. Let me finish my story. See, those murders Karla and Paul committed, they were real atrocities. They were horror shows committed in Canada, a country with a very low homicide rate. The Canadian people themselves, the voters, were enraged. As you'd expect, they wanted justice done." I shook my head. "If Karla hoped to avoid passing the rest of her life in cage, she had to do more than testify against her husband, she had to make herself an innocent victim. So, Karla told the cops a familiar tale. How Paul had first beaten her on their wedding night. How he choked her from time to time, how he threatened to kill her if she spoke to the police or if she didn't help him find those girls, how he put a knife to her throat and a gun to her head, how she knew he meant what he said because she saw him kill his victims."

"And that was enough?"

"Like I said, Karla's alive and well, living in Quebec with her husband and her children. But that's not the kicker, not by half. See, after Karla's sentencing, a videotape of Tammy's rape and murder turned up among the evidence collected by the police. It seems Karla, far from the abused victim she claimed to be, eagerly participated in the rape and personally administered the anesthetic that killed her sister. Of course, the prosecutors claimed they'd never seen the tape, but that doesn't matter, not for our purposes.

No, what matters is that Karla's alive and well and not locked up in a cage."

Alma-Beth finally looked up to study me with those blank eyes. "I never done nothin' like what she did. I never touched those women."

"Even better. Monroe forced you to set up his victims, but you drew the line when it came to abuse. In fact, you didn't really know what he did with them because the forensic details weren't released to the press and Monroe never told you. Of course, you were far too scared of him to ask."

I glanced out the window as the robins flew up into the trees, wings flapping too rapidly to follow. The road leading to the house was clear, but I couldn't rule out somebody clever enough to approach on foot. I pulled the shotgun close to my chest just as a yellow cat emerged from the scrub at the edge of the yard. It walked into the sunlight, dropped to its haunches, and began to groom.

Alma-Beth was still looking at me when I turned to face her. "I have another example. Charlene Gallego. She and her husband kidnapped and murdered ten young women, but Charlene got away with fifteen years when she claimed abuse and testified against her husband. So that's two." I hesitated, then pointed to a raised scar on her left arm, maybe four inches long, halfway between her shoulder and her elbow. "Monroe did that, right? He burned you?"

"Rooster, like I have already said too many times . . ."

"OK, fine, no more. But you need to think carefully about your options here. I'm offering you a way out, but if you're not interested . . ." I gave it the required theatrical pause, then said, "Because, Alma-Beth, if you're not interested, if you don't tell me where your brother is right this minute, I'm prepared to do to you what your brother's doin' to Cassie Howard."

I wasn't, not at all, and I knew it when I spoke the words. I'd fought many battles in my life, from one-on-one confrontations in school to all-out bar brawls. My basic claim, that I didn't start these fights, probably wouldn't stand up to close scrutiny, but what I'd never done was act in cold blood. I wasn't a sadist, not even in play in the bedroom. If Alma-Beth refused to cooperate, I'd drag her back to Oxford and turn her over to Skid.

Alma-Beth stared at me, and I thought I registered something like hope in the softened line of her jaw. But when she spoke, I finally realized how convincing she must have been when she first interviewed the victims, and when she lured them out of their cars or into opening their doors.

"Monroe made me have sex with Sneak," she said.

I nodded agreeably. "That wouldn't surprise me, but telling me won't do you any good. On the other hand, telling me where your brother and Sneak took Cassie Howard? Alma-Beth, you'd be a hero."

"You think?"

She smiled for the first time, and something in her eyes clicked shut. She'd worked out a deal with herself, a strategy, and she wouldn't deviate from whatever course she'd chosen. "Well, I don't know anything about that girl you say was kidnapped. But I do know that Sneak and Monroe have themselves an old cabin in the backwoods where they go huntin' and fishin'. They don't own it or nothin', but the place is halfway broke down and nobody ever goes there. 'Cept for Monroe and Sneak."

"How far, Alma-Beth?"

"Real close, Rooster. Just the other side of the main road. Maybe twenty minutes away. Hard to find, though, unless you know where you're goin'."

CHAPTER THIRTY-EIGHT

The back and forth must have exhausted what little patience I had. Alma-Beth was not to be trusted, of course, and her directions were so vague they couldn't be followed in any event. "About three miles" and "look for a tree hit by lightning" simply wasn't good enough. Despite the obvious need for haste, I dragged her into a little room housing an ancient Compaq computer, then sat her in a chair while I loaded Google Earth. The crackle of flames sounded faintly in my ears, and I felt my whole life come together, as if I'd only been waiting for this moment. As if this moment had only been waiting for me.

Too far away from the mainstream for cable, Alma-Beth used a satellite dish to provide a lot more hi-speed Internet service than her computer could handle. Still, we got where we needed to go, using the software to pinpoint the exact location of a small cabin located near a pond.

"You turn in right here." Alma-Beth pointed to one of those hazy lines I'd discovered earlier. The trail curved through unbroken forest for nearly a mile before it gave way to a clearing that included the cabin and pond. I estimated the nearest farmhouse to be at least three-quarters of a mile to the northwest.

"It's pretty rough by the main road," she said, "but it opens up once you get inside."

I might have asked how she knew this if she'd never visited the cabin, but I didn't have time. I dragged her through the back door and into the woods, then handcuffed her to the trunk of a sapling, a red oak that rose to a height of about fifteen feet.

"You can scream for help if you want to, Alma-Beth. You're close enough to the house for someone to hear you. But if you do call for help, you better pray the ear on the other end doesn't belong to Price Sibley."

I turned and walked off, headed for the main road and my pickup. Alma-Beth let me get about thirty feet away before she called out.

"Them women didn't have to stop," she told me. "They didn't have to open their damn doors, either. It was their own choice, Rooster. It was their own fault."

The trail Alma-Beth pointed out was, as she claimed, only a few miles distant from the house. It ran off Emmett Meeks Road, just south of Blackwater Road. I might have reached it in fifteen minutes, including the walk to the pickup, but I never intended to come in through that trail. I couldn't be sure of Monroe's and Sneak's vigilance. Maybe they were totally preoccupied with their new toy, but I wasn't prepared to count on it. Google Earth had revealed another way in, from Tyro-Tacklebox Road to the west instead of Emmett Meeks Road to the east.

At first glance, the approach I decided to make didn't look promising, no more than a series of five cultivated fields broken by stretches of forest. In another age, when cotton was produced mostly by the hard labor of individuals, I wouldn't have gotten close to that cabin and pond unless I hiked most of the way in. But we lived in a new age, a mechanized age, and those remote fields could not be worked with heavy equipment unless there was a track wide enough to admit that equipment. Cotton harvesters are a lot bigger than pickup trucks.

One obvious hurdle still existed, of course. Don't get lost. There were additional fields leading north and south, and additional tracks leading into them. I wouldn't be up in the air, looking down at a Google satellite photograph but on the surface, traveling over irregular ground and through wooded patches. But I had an advantage here. My Chevy had a compass mounted on the dashboard by a suction cup. I couldn't remember why I put it there, or exactly when, and I'd never tested it. I was comforted, nonetheless.

I punched Skid's number into my cell phone as I guided the pickup to the main road. I caught him at lunch, which was odd, because it was just nine thirty. Then I heard a giggle in the background and stopped asking questions.

"Skid, I've got them. Monroe and Sneak. Probably Cassie Howard, too." As briefly as possible, I detailed the events of the morning, then told him where I'd left Alma-Beth and where I was headed.

"You better wait for me," he said.

"No can do, buddy."

"Then how am I supposed to find you?"

"I've got the latitude and longitude. Took them down off a Google Earth map."

Skid was seriously pissed off, as evidenced by his tone and his choice of words. "You've been a complete jerk all your life," he insisted. "But now you've gone off the deep end. Hey, asshole, there's no water in the fucking pool. You're gonna get yourself killed."

"In that case, do me a favor."

"Yeah, what?"

"Put a twenty-dollar gold piece on my watchband, so the gang'll know I died standing pat."

"Screw you, Rooster. This ain't no joke."

I looked down at the shotgun laid out across the seat next to me. "Nope, Skid, it's definitely not."

I read off the latitude and longitude, hung up, and turned onto Highway 310, the fire now sounding in my ears, loud, insistent. A memory surfaced as I accelerated. I was standing outside on the night of the fire, watching the volunteer firemen. They weren't doing much of anything, the house being too far gone by the time they made an appearance. Rosie had arrived by then and I was holding her hand, my brain reeling as I tried to process something much too big for me. And where was my mother?

I found the farm, the only farm on that stretch of Tacklebox Road, easily enough. The name on the mailbox in front of the farmhouse read PORTER FAMILY, all in caps. On another day, if I wanted to fish the pond, I would have stopped at the house and asked permission. As it was, I drove past the house and a stretch of forest to a field to the north. Flimsy wire fences fronted the field, but I discovered a gap toward the end of the second field and turned in.

The cotton fields of northern Mississippi aren't laid out in nice neat squares and rectangles like the cornfields of Iowa. Instead, they follow irregular patterns, often projecting like fingers into the woods, and often separated by substantial woodlots, or even pine plantations. I don't know why this should be so, but I've never been involved in the cotton industry, an industry dominated, as it had been for centuries, by a relatively small number of families. I only knew as I turned onto a dirt track running along the edge of the clearing, that I had to head east, though not exactly due east.

Without my noticing, a breeze had sprung up sometime during the morning, and the ripening cotton bolls swirled in the field like driven snow. I watched the wind curl through the trees and I knew the leaves and branches had to be rattling, but I heard only the sound of the fire, the fire driving me, the fire that had always driven me. Still, I knew the breeze, coming from the north, would mask the sound of the truck's approach, a good thing, and I reminded myself, though I wanted desperately to slam the gas pedal to the floorboards, to creep along. Even then, I threw up a trail of dust.

I understood the stakes, as I understood the urgency. If not, I would have waited an hour on Tacklebox Road for Skid and whatever backup I could muster. But Cassie Howard's survival also depended on my own survival when I didn't know the terrain and was outnumbered, two to one. The only thing I really had going for me was the element of surprise, and I intended to preserve it.

Thirty minutes later, I stopped before a wall of trees that probably, but not certainly, marked the easternmost field of the Porter family's cotton farm. I didn't hesitate, certainty or not. I picked up the shotgun, checked to make sure there was a round in the chamber, and got out of the truck. If I was right, the pond should be just on the other side of the woods, with the cabin perhaps a hundred yards away.

The adrenaline coursing through my veins and arteries demanded action. I wanted to run, maybe give out a rebel yell worthy of a Civil War battlefield as I charged through the woods. I refused to give in, picking my way over fallen trees and around blackberry thickets. I stopped, too, every twenty or thirty feet, stopped to listen, to look. The forest was quiet around me, the birds and squirrels silenced by my presence, but the breeze, now in my face, sang its own persistent song.

The surrounding trees were mature for the most part. They threw deep shadows that made the clearing beyond this patch of woods all the more apparent while I was still fifty feet away. I dropped down to basically crawl on knees and elbows to the tree line. Ahead of me, I saw a small pond, its surface reflecting the intense blue of the late-morning sky. A cabin stood on an angle to the pond, one end of its roof caved in, with a tan pickup, the very pickup I'd trailed into Oxford the night before, parked between the two.

Now all I needed was a plan.

CHAPTER THIRTY-NINE

I think, as I stared at an empty front window in the one-story cabin, that I was hoping Sneak and Monroe would simply amble into the clearing. To smoke a joint, take a leak, or merely stare up at the cloudless sky in appreciative wonder. I don't know what I would have done in that case. Shoot them both? Without warning? Armed or unarmed? Would I cut the bastards down and spare Mississippi the expense of a trial and the cost of all those death row appeals?

This train of thought was a waste of time and I knew it. But I couldn't stop imagining the two of them lying motionless in the dirt. And I didn't have to imagine very hard. I'd been hunting since I was a boy, and the way I thought of it at that moment, there was little difference between a dead serial killer and a dead hog.

Unfortunately, the cabin door remained shut and the window empty, which meant I'd have to get inside, despite the house being almost dead center in a circular clearing that I'd have to cross, a clearing two hundred feet in diameter.

I intended to make a blind approach if I could find a side of the house without a window. My best hope, again, was the element of surprise—that and a shotgun that could do tremendous damage in close quarters. But I couldn't see either side of the house or the back from my current position. I had to move.

I made my way toward the pond, staying well inside the tree line, covering fifteen or twenty feet at a time. Although every crack of a twig seemed to me as loud as a gunshot, I continued on until I was looking at the side of the cabin lying closest to the pond. The roof here was badly damaged, possibly by a fieldstone chimney that had toppled backward at some point, scattering stone and mortar. All good news, because the siding, though scarred, was unbroken. And there was no window to be found.

Satisfied, I crouched behind a fallen hickory, using its trunk and withered leaves for cover. I could imagine myself crossing the open ground at a dead run, coming to a stop with my back against the house. I could also imagine myself shot down from behind before I covered half the ground. Were Sneak and Monroe both in that cabin? I'd come to accept the fact that Monroe was far from stupid. The whole scheme, from the initial targeting at the Department of Health to the disposal of the bodies, demonstrated meticulous planning on someone's part. I'd stood alongside Sneak at the sheriff's office and knew that someone could not be him.

Would Monroe protect himself against intruders? The answer to that question was simple enough. He would, if he could. But the cabin had no power, which pretty much precluded any sort of digital alarm. My time in the security business had familiarized me with just about every commercially available security system on the market. Yes, I could rig some sort of system to run on batteries alone, but without power those batteries couldn't be recharged. Would it be possible to use a car battery to charge the 9-volt batteries common to security systems? Maybe so, but I didn't think Monroe had the expertise to bring it off. No, if anything, Monroe had reverted to something much more primitive. If anything, he'd posted a sentry.

How likely? Now that Monroe knew he was being hunted by Price Sibley and the Henchmen and Rooster Feathers? Too likely for me to ignore because one thing hadn't changed now that I'd come within a hundred feet of the cabin. In order for Cassie Howard to survive, I had to survive.

I looked around, this time at the woods that marked the edge of the clearing. The basically flat terrain meant that anyone stationed in the trees would not have a full view of the clearing. The single exception was a heavily wooded hill, no more than twenty feet high. Probably, when the pond was originally dug out many decades before, the debris was simply piled up on one side. Then nature had taken over, as nature inevitably will, providing excellent cover and the only decent vantage point to be found.

Despite the need to survive, I had to act fast. What was probably happening inside that cabin demanded haste. I devised a simple plan on the fly. I was going to climb that hill from the back and survey the surrounding woods. If I found no threat, I'd come down the front of the hill and approach the cabin from its blind side. From there I'd work my way to the front door and kick it in. I hoped to find a single room inside, as was common in older hunting cabins, but if not, I'd have to adjust. One thing certain, the window of opportunity for Sneak and Monroe to surrender peacefully would be very short.

The breeze was still up and still blowing in my face as I circled the small hill, a piece of good luck as it turned out. I was passing through a stand of hemlocks halfway around the hill when a familiar scent, mingled with the scent of pine, caught my immediate attention. Someone not far away, somebody on that hilltop, was smoking a joint.

I grew more and more confident as I came around the back of that hill and the seductive odor of burning weed grew stronger. Carried on a stiff breeze, it was easy to pin the source to the top of the hill. I didn't know who was up there, Monroe or Sneak, but I was certain that he was facing the cabin and the road beyond.

A stoned-out sentry with his back turned? This was the element of surprise times a hundred.

The footing on the hill was rocky underfoot, though a bit slippery. I held the shotgun in my right hand as I climbed, and used my left to grasp the narrow trunks of well-rooted saplings. The climb seemed to take an hour, with each step carefully thought out, but it was only a matter of minutes until I slipped my head over the crown of the hill to find Sneak Ellerbee sitting in a small niche between a large boulder and a thicket of red buckeye. Sneak was staring out at the clearing, a joint in his left hand, his right drumming against the top of his thigh. Headphones covered both ears, and his weapon, a shotgun, lay against the boulder. Even from twenty feet away, I could hear the music pouring through those headphones. Shit-kicker metal, naturally.

I think I might have yelled without Sneak hearing as I crossed the ground between us, as I slipped my left arm around his throat, as I yanked him up and back until we could no longer be seen from the cabin. My instincts were screaming at me: Kill him, kill him, one down and one to go. I might have done it easily. I had my arm locked around his throat and I was pressing on both carotid arteries. Pressing hard.

Sneak fought me as best he could. But I was much larger and much stronger and he had no more chance of escaping than a mouse from the jaws of a wolf. He passed out in about twenty seconds, and all I had to do was hold on for another two or three minutes and he'd be off to face judgment. What's more, he'd never make a sound and Monroe would not be warned. No, lulled into a false sense of security, not to mention preoccupied, Monroe would be totally unprepared when I came through the door. All I had to do was murder a murderer.

I dropped Sneak after thirty seconds and he crashed into the dirt. As I searched him for a weapon, then unloaded the shotgun and threw the shells into the woods, I watched his chest rise and fall. I tried to ignore the part of my brain that insisted I was a jerk, an asshole, a wimp, and an all-around loser, but didn't altogether succeed.

"Wake up, shithead."

I knelt beside Sneak and shook him until he opened a pair of unfocused blue eyes. Then I got to my feet and put the barrel of the shotgun within an inch of his face. Sneak didn't get it at first. He looked up at me, seeming bewildered by this turn of events. The marijuana probably wasn't helping.

"Do you want to live, Sneak? If not, just shake your head and it's bon voyage, see you in hell."

I wasn't about to pull the trigger and warn Monroe, and I didn't have a plan B, either. But there's something about staring into the barrel of a .12-gauge shotgun that short-circuits the reasoning process.

"Please . . ."

"That's not an answer."

Sneak tried to prop himself up on an elbow, then fell back. "I want to live," he said.

"That's good, Sneak, and you may get to live for a long, long time. You ever hear of a man named Richard Gerald Jordan?"

"Yes, sir. He's on death row at Parchman."

"That's right, and he's been there for thirty-seven years. That could be you, Sneak, if you cooperate." I watched his eyes light up as he considered the possibility. "Now tell me, is Cassie Howard still alive?"

"Yes, sir. Leastways the last time I seen her."

"And how long ago was that?"

"Maybe an hour."

I finally stepped away, giving the man a little room. "You see that shotgun?" I pointed to his weapon, now lying in the dirt.

"I see it."

"Well, it's unloaded, but you're gonna pick it up anyway. You're gonna carry it into the clearing about halfway to the cabin and you're gonna call to your partner. You're gonna tell him that you heard something in the woods, maybe music playing, and you're sure someone's out there. You're gonna ask him to come up and listen."

"What if he don't come?"

"Then I'm gonna shoot you down like the rabid dog you are. One down and one to go. Now, get on your feet."

I watched Sneak carefully as he complied. His eyes had cleared and he was fully alert. Good on one level, but I knew he was searching for a way out. Exposed in the middle of the clearing, there was nothing to prevent me killing the both of them if he succeeded in luring his partner out of the cabin.

"I don't understand none of this," he said. "I don't understand why you just keep on comin'. Ain't nobody done nothin' to you."

I resisted the temptation to ask him what it felt like not to have a conscience, what it felt like to be a freak of nature. "Pick up the shotgun," I told him. "Pick it up and focus. You don't get it right, I'm gonna bury a load in the middle of your back and leave you to die slow."

CHAPTER FORTY

"Monroe, come on out here a minute. We got ourselves a problem."
Sneak had so far complied with my instructions, advancing to the
middle of the clearing, fifty feet from where I was concealed, the
empty shotgun held across his chest and his finger through the
trigger guard. "Monroe, c'mon . . ."

Monroe's face appeared in the window before Sneak completed
the sentence. His forehead was blood-streaked, as was his mouth
and hands. "What the fuck you want, Sneak?"

"There's someone out there. On the other side of the hill. I heard
music."

"Damn, Sneak." Monroe's head vanished, and a moment later he
appeared in the doorway. He didn't walk out to meet his partner,
but only advanced a few yards into the clearing. An AR15 assault
rifle dangled from his right hand and he was stripped to the waist,
his chest and arms, like his face, streaked with blood.

"Tell you what I want you to do," he said. "I want you to go back
up on the hill and stand fucking guard. If this music ain't a product
of your stoned imagination and someone does come along, you
know what to do. As we'll be leavin' soon, there ain't no need to
be delicate." Monroe paused long enough to wink. "Try bein' an

optimist for once in your life. Maybe they'll have a woman along and we'll get two for the price of one."

I took that moment to step into view, the shotgun tucked beneath my arm and the barrel pointed straight at Monroe.

"Just in case you're thinkin' the odds are in your favor," I said, "Sneak's shotgun ain't loaded. It ain't of no more use than a stick."

That's where it started to go wrong, and I think I knew it even then. For one thing, I didn't demand that he drop the rifle. For another thing, I was lost in a burning rage. I wanted to kill him, but I couldn't bring myself to cut him down. I had every right to kill him, given the circumstances, given the weapon in his hand. But I still needed an excuse, something I could tell myself, something I could tell Barbara and Skid, something to ease a conscience the two assholes in front of me didn't possess.

"You gonna shoot me, Rooster?"

"I'm definitely thinkin' on it. Why? You feel like you deserve to live?"

"I do, Rooster. A man like me knows how to enjoy life."

"Speakin' of life, is Cassie Howard still alive?"

"Hell, I'm just gettin' started on the bitch." He was looking straight into my eyes, his stare defiant, though he made no effort to bring the AR15 into play. "Did you come out here alone, Rooster?"

"Don't matter. The Oxford cops have your sister's connection to the Department of Health. Plus, Cassie Howard's gonna point the finger at your trial and there's DNA all over this cabin. You're done." I tightened my finger, pressing down on the trigger, bringing the Remington to the edge of firing. "But I do have one question. Alma-Beth, what was in it for her?"

"Hell, Rooster, she got first licks."

Monroe's laughter boomed across the clearing but stopped abruptly when Sneak stepped toward him. Sneak didn't take it all the way. He stopped about six feet from Monroe, effectively shielding the man. To hit Monroe, I'd have to go through Sneak.

"You're a damn liar, Monroe." Sneak was choking on his own anger, barely able to get the words out, holding the shotgun by the barrel with both hands. "Alma-Beth never touched nobody."

"How do you know that, Sneak? All them hours you was away drivin' or mulin'? Hell, we had us some serious parties, me, Alma-Beth, and whatever boys happened to come round."

"You bastard. Alma-Beth took care of you from the time you were a little boy, elseways you would've ended up in an orphanage."

Monroe winked at me, a mocking sneer firmly in place. His tone, when he spoke, was contemptuous. "Now, Rooster, you see old Sneak here? This is a boy never got laid in his entire life, except it was by force. Then Alma-Beth come along and threw him a few mercy fucks. Ain't no big shocker that the boy thinks he's in love."

Monroe was way ahead of me. He dropped to a knee when Sneak charged and fired two shots that passed through his partner's torso, one narrowly missing me. Then he spun to his left and dashed back into the cabin. With no choice when my only shot missed him, I followed, my legs fueled by a torrent of adrenaline. The element of surprise had disappeared. I had no plan, and no interest in a stand-off.

I didn't hesitate at the entrance but came through at full speed, then stopped ten feet inside, the shotgun moving through a steady arc. I needn't have bothered. An even-money shootout held no appeal for Monroe. He was already through a door at the cabin's rear and halfway across the clearing. I charged through the house and stepped into the sunlight as I brought the Remington to my shoulder. I was built for a shotgun, strong and heavy, and I'd been skeet shooting all my life, but somewhere along the way I'd lost my cool. To the adrenaline, to the sight of Monroe's blood-streaked torso? Maybe both, but I still shouldn't have missed, not at a distance of fifty feet. Yet when I finally pulled the trigger, Monroe, though he seemed for an instant to stumble, melted into the trees and vanished.

I ducked back into the house. I knew what was going to happen next and I had at best a few seconds to prepare. Cassie Howard was crouched against the wall, her legs and wrists bound with duct tape, her mouth gagged. She was badly damaged, so badly that it took all my strength to look at her and remain calm. Still, she was alert, and when I looked into her eyes, I thought I glimpsed, beyond the fear and pain, a reservoir of hope.

"Listen close, Cassie, because we don't have a lot of time." In fact, we didn't have any time before the assault began. As I took out the pocket knife I routinely carried and began to saw through Cassie's bonds, two shots rang out. Both traveled through the back and front walls of the cabin. Neither came close, but the extended magazine on Monroe's AR-15 held fifty rounds. "You and me, Cassie, we're gonna crawl through the front door and into the yard. Then you're gonna get into the woods and find a place to hide. There's help on the way, no matter how it turns out between me and Monroe. Sneak's dead."

Cassie didn't argue, but she did pause long enough to grab a stained blanket and cover herself before she complied. Rounds were coming through the house in swarms, the crack of Monroe's weapon, which would fire as fast as he could pull the trigger, almost continuous. One round struck the door frame as Cassie passed through, scattering splinters that had to sting but that she ignored. She ignored Sneak's body as well, climbing to her feet without being instructed and heading off into the woods. I might have followed, might have sought a defensive position with a good view of that pickup. Monroe wasn't going anywhere without it. If I got lucky, he'd come into the yard without spotting me.

I was much calmer now that Cassie was safe. I wouldn't miss again. But setting an ambush wasn't in the cards. Not after seeing what they'd done to her.

I crawled along the side of the house, to the corner where it met the back. Monroe continued to fire, though more slowly now. I assumed that he was on the move, circling through the woods, but I was wrong. Monroe was firing from a fixed position.

I took this as good news, evidence that my luck had turned again. As I inched around the corner, I let my focus expand until I finally saw the faint muzzle flashes as he fired. In another lifetime, in the movies, perhaps, I would have counted the number of times he pulled the trigger. But the Ar-15's extended magazine held fifty rounds of ammunition, and I didn't have enough fingers and toes for an accurate count. I couldn't wait, anyway, and I didn't want to. I got up, stepped into the open, and fired two rounds at a small space between a stubby oak with a split trunk and a patch of goldenrod.

Some experts claim that 00 buckshot isn't lethal at fifty yards, and I estimated Monroe to be between fifty and sixty yards distant. Other experts disagree, but neither position was relevant to my strategy. Each 00 shell contained nine .33-caliber pellets. Coming through the air, eighteen pellets from two rounds fired off in less than two seconds, Monroe would think he'd been attacked by a swarm of hornets.

I took off for the woods, firing as I went. Monroe managed to pull himself together long enough to get off a single shot that went wild. Then I was in the forest, reloading as I made my way, slowly and carefully, toward Monroe's position. Sightlines were short here, the forest dense with brush and thickets, and I can't say that I'd have found Monroe or that I wouldn't have been shot from cover, if he hadn't decided to help me out. For some reason, he continued to fire the rifle, too far away to have any idea where I was.

If I'd been Monroe, I'd have found cover and waited. He had to know that I was coming for him. If not, I wouldn't have crossed the yard in full view. Though I kept coming, I couldn't fathom his motive until I stumbled on it a few minutes later. The yellowing leaves of a shrub I couldn't name were smeared with dark, arterial blood. Monroe was calling for help.

I took my time anyway. I edged closer until I saw Monroe sitting with his back to the trunk of an oak, firing into the air.

"That you, Rooster?" he called without looking around.

"Yeah, it's me. How you doin'?"

He threw the gun off to one side. "Been better."

I walked toward him, close enough to see blood flowing in short bursts from a hole in his right thigh. "Make me feel good," I said. "Tell me I did that with the first shot. The one I aimed."

"Nah, Rooster. You got me when you crossed the yard. Don't matter anyway, not no more. When I come out of the cabin, I didn't take the time to put on my belt."

"Is that because you were using it on Cassie?"

He shook his head as though ridding himself of the question, then opened his left hand to reveal a pair of shoelaces tied together. "They keep breakin' when I pull 'em tight."

I could save Monroe's life and I knew it. I could take off my belt and draw it tight around his thigh above the wound. Stop the bleeding and he'd live.

"What you did to Cassie," I said, "I don't get it, but I'm startin' to understand how much it means to you. Takin' another victim? Hangin' around, knowin' Alma-Beth might give the whole thing away, which she did? You must've needed your fix real bad, Monroe."

"That's what my momma said, back when she was still alive. Said I didn't have no more patience than a hungry snake." Monroe put the heel of his hand on the wound and pressed down. His face was pale now, but he was still alert. "Why didn't you shoot me? When I first come into the yard? Ain't no one on this earth who'd fault you, what with the rifle in my hands and Cassie in the house. But you decided to let me live, Rooster."

Smiling that dismissive smile, Monroe paused to look up at me. Another win. He knew me better than I knew myself. And he was right. I did make a conscious decision to let him surrender. But that was B.C. Before Cassie. Before I saw what he did to her. As I stared down at him, as I watched blood drip from the cuff of his pants into the forest loam, I heard and I saw. I heard the great roar of a fire, as though I were still inside the house, as if the house were falling down around me. And I saw Marie Blocker's smile, the one that made you feel good about yourself, and I saw it die out forever.

"Now, c'mon, Rooster, be the righteous man I know you to be. Do the right thing here. Tie off the wound."

There were hundreds of possibilities out there, but in the end I chose the simplest. I kicked him in the face, picked up his rifle, and left him to bleed out. The way I figured things, he had about five minutes before he lost consciousness. Five minutes to make his peace with the Lord. Somehow, I didn't think he'd take advantage of the opportunity.

"I enjoyed every minute, Rooster."

Monroe's speech was thick, most likely because his mouth was filling with blood. Still, he had to have the last word. "Every damned second. And that bitch who worked for you? She lasted the longest, Rooster. She outlasted every one of 'em."

CHAPTER FORTY-ONE

The story broke Friday evening on the five o'clock news. By six, the party was ongoing. By eight, the Square reminded me of New Orleans during Mardi Gras. Oxford had come out to celebrate, nearly the whole town from the look of it, the whole town and the whole county. Every hand gripped a plastic cup filled with beer or wine or a cocktail or straight-up moonshine, a technical violation the Oxford Police Department proved unwilling to enforce. I was on the club's balcony at eight, remembering myself on that same balcony the day I first arrived in Oxford, staring at a massive crowd celebrating a home victory. A lot had happened in the intervening years, but on some level I felt almost as divorced from this crowd as I had all those years before.

Our featured bluesman that evening was Christone "Kingfish" Ingram, a sixteen-year-old prodigy who'd played the Steve Harvey and Rachael Ray shows, not to mention the White House where he performed for Michelle Obama. The kid was a great musician, but he wasn't alone. By the time nine o'clock rolled around, Eric Gales, Jay Lang from Devil's Due, Cadillac Funk, and Bobby Rush had showed up, along with a host of sidemen. One thing about musicians, they do love a party, and this party only intensified on the next day when Ole Miss beat the tar out of the Vanderbilt

Commodores. Ten former Ole Miss Rebels showed up that night, including Bo Wallace. Morgan Freeman, a longtime resident who owned the Ground Zero Blues Club in Clarksdale, also made an appearance. Shepard Smith, as well. An Ole Miss graduate, Shepard had gone on to fame and fortune as an anchor on the Fox News Network.

Like I said, I found myself unable to embrace the celebration, despite Barbara sticking close to me throughout the weekend. Barbara was better than good. She looked me in the eye when she arrived on Friday but never asked me what happened. I think she read my reluctance and simply waited for me to open up.

Predictably, I didn't allow the rapid-fire thoughts zig-zagging through my brain to come between me and my businessman instincts. Early on, I dragged a couple of speakers onto the balcony and treated the crowd to a free concert. I figured I might as well because the club was packed and my staff overwhelmed.

Shortly before nine on Saturday night, three men edged into the room. Two wore the colors of the Henchmen. The other was an older man closing in on sixty. He wore a denim shirt and worn jeans and his face was deeply lined and dark, reflecting decades of toil beneath the Mississippi sun. I was instantly reminded of Boyd Jessup.

Barbara looked at me as they approached. "Trouble?"

"I don't think so. If they wanted trouble, they'd get me alone."

The Henchmen gave way to the older man as they edged through the crowd. He came to within a few feet of me, then extended his hand. "My name's Abraham Howard," he said. "I'm Cassie Howard's father."

"Howard?" I smiled as I posed the question. "Any relation to Ink Howard?"

"My nephew."

Howard's grip was firm, as expected. The man was all whipcord muscle. I carefully matched his grip, though I might have gone much further. I outweighed him by sixty pounds.

I glanced at the two Henchmen. "What can I do for you, Abraham?"

"Well, I'm sorry to trouble you." He jammed his hands into his back pockets and settled his weight on his heels. "I just . . . I just have to know what happened. Cassie? She can't talk about it, and I can't say as I blame the girl. But I have to know, and the cops ain't talkin' to me, neither."

Most of Oxford knew I was somehow involved by the time Howard made an appearance. But the cops weren't giving out details and they'd asked me to hold my peace for the time being. That was just as well, because I didn't want to talk about what I'd found in that cabin. Reporters had approached me, but I'd blown them off, an approach that set the rumor mill to running at full blast. The most persistent rumor had me saving Cassie Howard after gunning down Sneak and Monroe in a wild shootout that ended before the Oxford police showed up.

Staring into Howard's gray eyes, I reminded myself that the Oxford cops and the Sheriff's Department had been holding back details from the very beginning. Cassie's father hadn't seen an autopsy report, hadn't read a case file or viewed photos of the dump sites. His imagination had to be running wild. Meanwhile, the reality was beyond imagining.

"I don't have anything to tell you, Abraham. The two men who took your daughter are both dead and your daughter's come home to you. There's really nothing more to be said."

"What about the other one, the sister? Alma something."

"Alma-Beth Patterson. The cops have her and I don't know what she's sayin', if she's talkin' at all. Could be she's lawyered up." That was the truth. I hadn't heard from anyone since leaving the police station, including Skid.

"You're tellin' me that she's involved?"

"Yeah, she's involved, but that's as far as I'm willin' to go. It'll all come out eventually, but you're gonna have to wait."

Howard nodded at me. "I ain't here to find fault, Rooster. You saved Cassie, and I'll be grateful for as long as I draw breath. Maybe sometime later we can get together."

"Abraham, what happened in that cabin doesn't matter anymore. That's over. What you need to do is see to your daughter and her future."

Howard smiled for the first time, a crafty smile through narrowed eyes. "Guess you could say that's exactly what I'm doin'. Cassie's over at Baptist Memorial. They brought up a microsurgeon from Jackson to minimize the scarrin' when he sewed her up. Minimize, right?" His eyes turned inward for a moment, but then he snapped back. "Anyways, Cassie's been wantin' to see you. Must mean a lot to her, because she wouldn't let up till I agreed to come by and ask if you can spare the time."

This was a request that could not be refused. Not with Barbara watching, anyway. I arranged to come up in the morning, but I made one point clear. No media of any kind. If I even sniffed a reporter, I'd walk away. Abraham agreed, shook my hand, muttered his thanks, and turned to leave. As the two Henchmen followed, one of them leaned forward to whisper in my ear.

"You're good with us."

I returned the compliment, leaning in to whisper, "Go fuck yourself."

Five minutes later, I was still fuming when Samantha Blocker, Marie Blocker's tattooed sister, walked up to me. I introduced her to Barbara, who took the girl's hand and muttered her condolences.

"I knew your sister," Barbara said. "We all miss her."

"Well, that's the thing. The men who took Marie are both dead, so I s'pose that's justice of some kind. But it doesn't fix anything because Marie ain't comin' back." She looked to me. "I'm mostly here to say thanks. From me and my folks. Wasn't for you, those two scumbags would still be out there, instead of bein' dead in the morgue."

Barbara and I retreated to my apartment a few minutes later. We made love, slowly and gently at first, which was what I thought I wanted. But as we continued on, our lovemaking transformed itself into something more raw, more primitive, more demanding, until we fell back on the sheets, sweat-soaked and exhausted. Maybe that's exactly what I needed. After a few minutes of staring at the ceiling while I tried to catch my breath, I propped myself on one arm to kiss Barbara's throat, then her mouth. Both tasted of salt.

"It's not about Sneak and Monroe," I said. "They're like rats in the wall of your house. You trap them and you kill them. The right or the wrong of it isn't relevant. But the other part, taking pleasure from inflicting pain, hour after hour, day after day. I've known some mean bastards, but this . . ."

Barbara held my hand to her breast. "You remind me of my cousin, Frankie. He joined the marines the day he graduated high school. That was back about ten years ago, when we were still fightin' in Iraq. Frankie was deployed three times before he left the corps, and he ain't the same person who enlisted. I don't mean to say that he's crazy or dangerous, because he's not. He's got a good job, a good woman, and three kids. But he just isn't the same. Whatever he saw there, whatever he did—and he never talks about it—changed him for good."

Although I didn't believe an hour of combat in the woods above Sardis Lake equal to three deployments in Iraq, I took Barbara seriously. Certainly, I'd never forget Monroe as he appeared in the cabin window, his face and arms streaked with blood, or Cassie Howard's wounded body and the fear in her eyes, or the stench of drying blood, as rotten and corrupt as Mathew Monroe's hell-bound soul. But there was nothing I could do to change any of it, and I suddenly found myself drained. I put my arm beneath

Barbara's shoulders and gently rolled her toward me until her head rested on my chest. A moment later, I fell into an empty, dreamless sleep.

I awakened on the next morning, Sunday, to voices coming from the outer room of my apartment. Skid and Barbara. I stumbled into the bathroom and brushed my teeth, but if my breath didn't smell, everything else did. I needed a shower, bad. Skid wouldn't mind. I'd come upon him in worse condition more than once. I wasn't so sure about Barbara.

"I was about to wake you," Barbara said when I walked into the room. "You promised to visit Cassie Howard this morning and it's closin' in on ten o'clock."

I stared at her for a moment. Every hair was in place and her makeup had been meticulously applied. She smelled good, too. I headed for the coffeemaker and poured myself a mug. "You here to talk about Alma-Beth?" I asked Skid.

"And to see how you're doin'."

After walking away from Monroe, I'd located Cassie in the woods, then carried her to the clearing where I'd parked my truck. I was about to put her in the truck when Skid arrived, leading a small motorcade with an ambulance at its tail. Cassie was taken from my arms, laid on a gurney, and wheeled to the ambulance. Skid then asked me to walk him through the crime scene, while the eight cops who'd accompanied him stayed behind.

Skid wanted to make sure I got my story straight, an unnecessary precaution. The physical evidence told a story that confirmed

Scott Michael

everything I said. Even Monroe cooperated. He was conveniently dead by the time we got to him.

I spent the following several hours waiting by my truck. Then an officer escorted me to the stationhouse in Oxford where I gave a written statement before being dismissed. This was a police matter now and I wasn't a cop.

"I'm good, Skid," I finally told him, which wasn't the truth. "Tell me what's up with Alma-Beth."

Skid repressed a smile. "You know I'm not supposed to talk about the investigation, right?"

"I do know that, but what I'm sayin' is that you need to disregard that directive in the name of our long and deep friendship. Not to mention the party invites. Not to mention the fact that I outweigh you by thirty pounds."

Barbara laughed when I settled onto the couch beside her. "He does have a persuasive way about him," she noted.

Skid rubbed his eyes and yawned. "Ain't slept all night," he said. "You're my last stop." Then he turned to Barbara. "You're gonna have to keep this to yourself, Barbara. That means nobody else. Just you, me, and Rooster."

"Scout's honor."

Skid continued to look at her for a minute, then turned to me. "Right out of the box, Alma-Beth admitted to 'helping her brother out.' No denial, no complaint. Didn't even wait for me to ask. Just up and said it. Then she claimed that Monroe forced her to participate, that he beat her for the slightest thing, that he'd been kickin' her narrow ass ever since he got big enough to throw a meaningful punch. That's why she was thrilled when Monroe was sent to prison. For the first time, she felt free. For the first time, she lived without fear. But then Monroe came out and started in again, just took up where he left off, only he had Sneak with him."

"Lemme guess," I said. "When she told you this, she didn't know that Sneak and Monroe were dead. She offered to testify against them."

"Yes, on both counts. Alma-Beth was taken into custody before I got to you. She had no idea what happened to Sneak and her brother. So what I did was tell her they were on the run. I don't think she believed me altogether, but it was the only story she had."

I smiled to myself as Skid leaned forward and looked from me to Barbara. Like most cops, he knew how to tell a story. Barbara was enthralled, staring at him with her mouth slightly open. "Is that legal?" she wanted to know. "Lyin' like that?"

"Sure is, Barbara. Alma-Beth had her rights read to her. She could have asked for a lawyer. She didn't." Skid paused for second, then returned to his story. "Little by little, she admitted to both elements of the case we plan to make against her. She used her position at the Department of Health to initially target the victims. She used her gender and the fact that they knew her to get into their homes or lure them out of their cars. I even had her describe each incident, what she said, how the victim reacted. Then, once I had every plank nailed down, I told her that her brother and his partner were both dead and her testimony would not be needed and that she would be charged with six counts of kidnapping and six counts of aggravated murder. Remember, we videotaped every word, so there was no room for denial."

"Did she fall apart?" Barbara said.

"Nope. She leaned back in her chair and said, 'I got somethin' else I wanna talk about, only I need to speak to a lawyer first. But you could trust me on this. What I got to say, you definitely need to hear.'"

"Who'd she get?" I asked.

"None other than Landon Lake IV. The man wore a linen suit and a floppy tie, just in case he ran into any TV cameras. He was thrilled, even before he spoke to his client. When he came out, he was walkin' on air. Alma-Beth told him that she could 'prove' that Price Sibley was runnin' meth out of the county. Him and Ink Howard. She wouldn't talk to us, though. She wanted the Feds, and she was demandin' protection until they arrived. Now, Landon Lake ain't the brightest legal mind in Mississippi. I say that because there was a detective from the sheriff's office in the room when Landon made his demands. That's when the phone calls started. Between the chief and the mayor, between the mayor and the governor, between the governor and the FBI regional office in Jackson, between the sheriff and anyone who'd listen."

Skid paused for a moment as church bells rang out from several locations. It was Sunday morning in Mississippi, and the Square would be deserted until early afternoon. Plenty of time to get to the hospital and back. I made a note to ask my downstairs manager to check our stock. I expected a busy day, and I didn't want to run out of anything I could sell.

"You think she's bluffing?" Barbara asked.

Skid shook his head. "I think Alma-Beth's been a step ahead of her brother from the get-go. She saw this day comin' and she took steps to protect herself. As for Price Sibley? If Sibley had done his job, this whole business would've ended a lot sooner than it did. Me, I'm willin' to let Alma-Beth live if she can bring the bastard down. There's no question of immunity here. If Alma-Beth doesn't die on a gurney, she'll spend the rest of her life in a cage."

At the hospital, I ran into a little army of Howards. The Howards, the aunt, uncles, brothers, sister, and cousins, were introduced to me. A point was being made here. The entire family was in my debt. It was all very formal, but two things caught my attention. A number of the introduced Howards sported Henchmen colors, and all present deferred to Abraham Howard.

"I s'pose I should give you some advice," Abraham said as we approached Cassie's door. "'Cept I don't have no idea of what that advice might be." He opened the door. "And thank-you again, for the whole family. You ever need anything, all you got to do is ask."

I nodded, then opened the door and stepped inside. Cassie lay on the bed with her head raised, eyes half open. Much of her face was bandaged, small dressings for the most part. Around her, on cabinet tops, bouquets of flowers spread a fragrance that covered the sharp odor of antiseptic cleaners. I stepped past a tray table to the side of the bed and looked down at her until she came back from wherever the painkillers had taken her. Cassie's pupils were pinpoints.

We stared at each other for a moment, until I again found that reservoir of hope. "You look good in white," I said.

Slowed by the drugs, Cassie took a few seconds before her mouth expanded into a slow-motion grin. "Everyone keeps lookin' at me. Like they never seen me before in their lives." She motioned me closer as she raised her head. "People look at you like that, they'll lie to you, too. You know what I mean. For your own good. But I trust you. Tell me if they're really dead."

"They're dead, Cassie. I saw their bodies. Sneak and Monroe, the both of 'em. Never even got to a hospital." I watched her settle back on the pillow, watched her eyes flutter.

"They're dead and I'm alive," she said. "I expect I'll have to get used to that. But that's what I'm gonna do, Rooster. You hear me? I ain't gonna let those bastards take my life from me. I'm gonna live while they burn in hell. That's why I asked for you, what I wanted to tell somebody who'd understand. I'm gonna live a life while Monroe and Sneak burn in hell."

And what could I say to that? Except, "Amen, sister."

ABOUT THE AUTHOR

Scott Michael is the owner of one of the most renowned hotspots in the South: Rooster's Blues House, a blues bar and restaurant. Located in Oxford Mississippi (named one of the best small towns—and top six college towns—in America). The venue offers the very best live music and caters to families and the college students in the picturesque area.

Scott Michael also owns Velvet Hammer Security, which has provided protection and security services for musical venues, concerts, and bands such as The Red Hot Chili Peppers, Ozzy Osbourne, Nirvana, and the Rolling Stones.

This is Scott's first book in the Rooster's Blues House Mystery series.

2060